THE SILENCE IN THE SALOON

was thick enough to cut. Then the bartender said, painfully, *"MILK?"*

Philip said, "Yes, please. Or a glass of water will do."

Before he knew what was happening, the crowd's silence turned to jeers, and rough horseplay became a dead-earnest fight.

When it ended, he was holding one man high above the floor by his throat, covering the room with his victim's gun.

And the strange fire in his brain told him something his life on Pillar Mountain never had — he was ready to kill. . . .

MAX BRAND

PILLAR MOUNTAIN

WARNER
PAPERBACK
LIBRARY

A Warner Communications Company

WARNER PAPERBACK LIBRARY EDITION
First Printing: January, 1971
Second Printing: March, 1974

This Warner Paperback Library Edition is published by arrangement
with Dodd, Mead & Company, Inc.

Cover illustration by Tony Alonso

Warner Paperback Library is a division of Warner Books, Inc.,
75 Rockefeller Plaza, New York, N.Y. 10019.

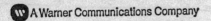 A Warner Communications Company

Printed in the United States of America

CHAPTER I

LOAFER was a big dog who looked like a buffalo wolf; he was gray against one background and pale yellow against another; like a buffalo wolf, he had a great leonine body covered with a loose hide which humped in a wave above his shoulders at every lurch of his gallop. Strangers always said "Wolf!" when they saw him (there were four bullet scars upon him), and no one said "Good dog!" except his master. However, he was too busy most of the time to be bothered by human opinions which, also, seldom came to his ears. On this morning he was hunting on the broad breast of Pillar Mountain not for food but for revenge; his enemy was a lop-eared rabbit.

There never was a time when wolf or wolfish dog could match speed with a Western jack rabbit; but in brains the difference lay on the other side and, since puppyhood, Loafer had been certain that no rabbit could live a week in his domain save by permission. The little darting idiots always could be scared into the waiting teeth. At least, that was his opinion until he encountered Lop-ear; and after that the life of Loafer was poisoned.

Lop-ear was a perfect Achilles among jack rabbits, and he was an Odysseus, also; nothing stirred on the mountains or on the broad desert that he could not outrun, and there was very little that he could not outthink. Above all, he was familiar with Pillar Mountain, and he grew up to a splendid maturity under the nose of Loafer. They sharpened their wits on one another, like scimitar on scimitar, and each grew great because the other was a proper metal. Yet, victor of a thousand contests with the big dog, swelled with the pride of his own fame, Lop-ear on this morning made a serious mistake. He had filled his belly with newly

5

sprouted twigs, flavored with keen spice, rich with juice, tender as watercress; and now he sat in the sun with his head drawn back upon his shoulders, his eyes a mere glimmering black thread of watchfulness, and his ears fallen flat on his back.

They should have been erect like two towers of watchfulness, drinking in all sound, tenfold more watchful because the south wind was cutting straight up the side of the mountain and blowing away the scent of all who hunted down the slope. Also, the eyes of Lop-ear should have been wide open, so that he could have seen the big stalker, approaching like a great yellow ball of thistledown, soundless, drifting with speed and infinite cunning straight into the eye of the wind.

To Lop-ear, it was like rousing from a nightmare and finding that it is not a dream! When the gray-yellow bolt sprang, Lop-ear hugged the ground one dreadful instant; then with a scream he leaped straight under the head of Loafer. A side rip of those flashing teeth sliced the hip of the rabbit, but he went down the first little cañon so fast that the rocks blurred as they flew past. For once in his life he had forgotten that he was Lop-ear, and a king, and he consented to take refuge in the common strength of his race—sheer, blinding speed. So he ran like mad, putting in not one spy-hop in twenty, and quite forgot that the cañon traveled in a precise little semicircle.

Loafer did not forget; he had never forgotten, since the day a mountain lion taught him that it is dangerous to sleep even in the broad light of noon on the threshold of the master's house. Now he cantered across the arc of the semicircle and Lop-ear, after a tremendous burst of sprinting, found himself running down the very jaws of his foe. He dodged with a speed that would have made the most famous halfback faint with envy, but the white steel of Loafer's teeth clipped the air just in front of his nose, and therefore he doubled and headed up a difficult slope of broken rock.

That winded him more than ever, and as Lop-ear flung himself down the mountainside, he knew that he was not half a hop, half a thought beyond the reach of death. He cleared the brook from bank to bank at a single glorious bound, but as he landed the teeth clicked at his tail again, and the mind of Lop-ear went black and dizzy, like blown mist at night. The yawning door of the hut seemed to him, at first, some sort of a haven, but it was reeking with the terrible scent of man, so Lop-ear swerved to the side and almost perished again because he did so. Then, knowing that his wind was gone—for he had burned it up like a fool, rather than a wise king—he did the one thing that remained to him: he dived into a hole that showed under the edge of a jagged rock.

There, in the black depths, he cuddled small and smaller into the moist darkness and prayed to the God who cares for all good rabbits.

Loafer lay down and hung a forepaw as big as the hand of a man into the mouth of the hole. He laughed as he lay, and the wrinkles of laughter made his big hazel eyes small and wicked with delight. For he knew all about that hole. He had known about it ever since he was a little puppy, when he himself had been small enough to escape from the wrathful hand of the master and dodge into this haven. It ran straight down, for a bit, then straightened ahead; and there were two things worth knowing—one was that it filled with water only after the very heaviest rains—the other was that the hole could not be driven deeper, because it ended against solid stone.

So Loafer laughed, and withdrawing his paw, he put his muzzle at the entrance and inhaled the sweet fragrance of steaming rabbit—rabbit steamed in fear, and spiced with the delicately familiar and long-hated scent of Lop-ear himself.

Even children know that good things should be enjoyed slowly, and Loafer was no child. He began first by enlarging the mouth of the hole. Then he inserted his arm to the shoulder, and heard a squeak of terror; the sound went electrically through the body of Loafer; it went sweetly through his soul.

Listening again, he heard frantic scratching. But he knew all about that hole and the consistency of its walls; therefore he laughed again, and when Lop-ear heard the almost soundless laughter, the scratching stopped. Dreadful, waiting silence began.

7

After this, with leisure and with system, Loafer enlarged the hole. The whole upper level was porous sand and gravel which he could rip away with his strong claws, and having done that, how simple it would be to reach in and paw out the rabbit! Now and again he paused to listen, but the silence of despair continued in that death-hole; only from the house he heard the young voice of the master singing. How far, how faint, how utterly dim and unreal are the joys of mankind, thought Loafer, and bent afresh to his task.

With both forepaws he labored and the hole ripped wide; then he lay down and his whole shoulder fitted into the aperture, his elbow came to the bottom of the downward shaft, and his right paw touched Lop-ear.

That paw began to tremble with the thundering heartbeats of the victim. He reached farther. He felt the shrinking shoulder and the soft throat of the king of rabbits, but just as he was about to scoop Lop-ear out of the hole he heard a grinding sound, the big rock settled, and drove a sharp stone into his forearm.

He lurched back, but the hole had collapsed, and his arm was held as by a glove. The edged stone worked into his flesh like a tooth; his whole shoulder was being crushed.

Then Loafer forgot the rabbit, and his mind flashed back to the master as an electric torch picks something from the night. He barked; he whined with pain and fear; and the master stood suddenly above him, leaning with kind, thoughtful face.

"I'll get something for a lever," said the master.

Loafer groaned.

"By heaven," said the master, "it's breaking his leg!"

And he bestrode the jagged rock.

It was as black as iron and almost as heavy. Deeply rooted, massive, it defied his strength. Mightily he heaved, and Loafer saw the feet of the man thrust ankle deep in the yielding gravel. He heard the creak of grinding joints, the snapping of tendons drawn with a merciless power, and then the groan of the master in the full agony of his effort.

The burden which crushed the leg of the dog was lightened. He snatched out his leg. But still the man persisted in his labor as though he did not know the work was done; Loafer limped around and stood before him, looking up into his face, which was mixed red and purple, and running with perspiration. His whole body shook; his breathing was a succession of groans; but the stone began to rise.

That Loafer himself had been saved was one thing; but vaguely the dog understood that something of infinite more importance now was going on. Lop-ear ventured from the hole and fled away unheeded; only from the corner of his eye the dog watched his old enemy flee; but in this mighty work of the raising of the stone, whatever its meaning, he wished to assist. The roots of the rock worked loose with a sucking sound; the black, wet belly of the stone came slowly up to view; it was poised; it swung to the side and fell, crushing a dozen smaller stones to bits in its fall.

Then the master sank down, also. He lay at full length, moaning, his eyes closed, his body shaken with spasms, and Loafer was filled with terror and amazement. This man was the center of the universe. At his bidding, beyond doubt, the wind blew and the sun rose. He killed afar and gave food to his humble companion. In the blast of summer heat, his hut was cool, and in the winter his red magic gave the house warmth to which Loafer was welcomed. Yet now he lay sick and stricken. When Loafer licked his face he neither spoke nor turned away. When Loafer licked his trembling hands, they made no response, and for the first time the caress of the dog was unreturned.

He crowded close to the youth as though winter cold made him seek for warmth, and lifting his great wrinkled head, Loafer called aloud to the old gods of his people.

There was an immediate response; an arm passed around his neck, and while he whined with joy, the master dragged himself to his knees, to his feet. He stood wavering, and yet he began to laugh.

"I've done it!" he said over and over again; "I've done it."

9

Then he went into the hut and slumped heavily on to a bunk. Loafer sat beside him, on guard. His mane bristled when he considered what dreadful deeds he would perform for the sake of his master.

CHAPTER II

OLD Oliver Aytoun came home to the shack after dark and found the hut filled with the steam and fragrance of frying venison. Through the smoke of cookery the boy smiled at him, and he smiled in return.

"Have you had a good day, Philip?"

"A very good day, Uncle Oliver."

They said no more. Oliver Aytoun washed his hands and face in a basin of warm water which Philip prepared for him; by the time he had dried himself supper was laid out on the table. It was a good meal of the venison, in place of honor, excellent corn bread, boiled greens, coffee, and plum jam, made from small blue plums which grew wild on the mountain, unmatchable for perfume and flavor.

They talked very little. Oliver Aytoun had been delayed because he had walked over a tentative new-line for their traps and it had taken him almost to Ransome Peak. Then Philip told how he had spent the morning hauling down saplings by hand from beyond the clearing and piling them behind the house, to make ready for the building of the lean-to.

"This afternoon?"

"I did only one thing," said Philip. "It's a surprise for you."

They smiled at one another again; between them was a beautiful and perfect understanding.

Yet they appeared totally dissimilar, for Oliver Aytoun was a lean man of more than sixty; mountain labor and mountain weather made him appear ten years older in the face and ten years younger in the body. Philip was a mere youth of twenty or so with a great leonine head and a massive throat and shoulders to support it, so that looked at from behind he seemed a formidable man, but viewed in full face his eyes were so large and so blue, his mouth so femininely tender and smiling that he looked less man than child, and rather a simple child, at that.

After the meal, Aytoun sat in the open doorway and watched the shaggy mountain rising up against the stars; Philip washed the tin dishes and the pans, rinsed the dishrag, and hung it on a peg behind the stove to dry. In all that time he only said: "Can you see the lights, Uncle Oliver?"

"I can see them," said Aytoun.

When the work was ended by the sweeping of the floor, Philip sat on the threshold beside the older man and for a long time the silence went on between them, for they were watching the lights. If there was the least water vapor in the air, or a trace of dust, the great valley to the southwest was a dark, deep ocean, but on dry, clear nights such as this, in the great bottom of the bowl they could see the lights of a town glimmering and twinkling busily—like stars, but more yellow, and more alive. To Philip that meant the world of man.

Even on the brightest, clearest day he could not see a trace of the town, though from year to year he had watched the area of the ploughed lands growing in a darker stain each autumn, a larger patch of green each spring. Once the fall ploughing had made only a handful of shadow near the silver streak of the river, but now it extended from foothills to foothills. However, that was a mere spot upon the map, a faint indication, whereas this starry twinkling in the hollow hand of the night stirred the boy with a sense of the flaming souls of men.

He knew nothing but the hut and the mountains. Their only contacts with the world were made by the old man, who twice a year piled their crop of pelts on the backs of the two mules they kept and went down to some crossroads village of which he never had told Philip so much as the name.

Of course he asked many questions, and Oliver Aytoun liked nothing so well as to talk about the great world beyond the mountains and the cities and the ways of men. He was willing, once in a long time, to tell of his own early life. For nearly forty years he had lived here on Pillar Mountain, but before that he had come out of the East full of curiosity and love of adventure. But the strong taste of Western life had been too much for him. He had turned as wild as an Indian and on one unlucky day in a barroom at a mining camp he had killed his man. There was no law, really, to hound him, but Oliver Aytoun did not know that. He fled away into the mountains and reached this spot, and here he had remained.

At first he thought, as he struggled like a new Robinson Crusoe with the wilderness, that as soon as the memory of his crime had died out among men, he would go down among them again. But time made him love the mountains; he felt, too, like a poor flagellant, that there was some divine purpose, some divine punishment in this lonely life in which he found himself. He accepted the emptiness and the pain of it and hoped that he was being purged of sin. And every day, he told Philip, a remorseful time came to him during which he saw his victim lying with his head and shoulders hunched against the wall, young, and strong, and dead.

"I've got to be going," said Philip.

At this, the other turned his head, but did not actually ask a question.

"Down, I mean," said the boy, and pointed towards the lights in the valley.

There was such a quality in his voice that Loafer got up and came to look in his master's face. However, the old man answered: "You'd better wait till you can lift the rock, my lad!" He added: "Or until you can budge it, at least; your father picked it out of the mouth of the spring, you know!"

Then he looked out not on the valley or the stars but on his own thoughts, seeing again the picture of the strong man. He had not spoken six times of Philip's father, but every mention of him was lodged in the boy's mind. First of all he had described how the man came, riding on a great black horse, with a two-year-old boy in the hollow of his arm. This big man wore a beard and mustaches and his hair was prematurely gray; his age might have been anything between twenty-five and thirty-five. He was handsome, he had the true eagle eye, and his ways were quick, his manner a little imperious.

He spent that night at the shack, and the next morning, while they were eating breakfast, the child went outdoors and presently they heard its choked cry. When they ran out, they found that it had fallen down into the spring; they could see it far beneath arm's reach with face strangely not convulsed, looking up at them with great blue eyes.

The stranger seized the black rock which covered the spring and tore it up, then leaped into the bubbling well of water and brought up the child.

The water was as cold as ice; the little boy was weak with the shock and the fright of it; it was patent that he could not be carried forward that day, or perhaps the next. However, his father could not tarry, and promising to be back in the course of a week, he galloped away on his powerful black horse. Other men followed during several days, all asking if the rider of the black horse had gone that way, and all cursing and rushing away towards the valley trail when they heard the answer. It was plain that Philip's father was no law-abiding citizen, and Oliver Aytoun's opinion was that he had not returned for his child because of those same angry pursuers, who must have overtaken him and beaten him down by numbers, in spite of his gigantic strength. There was no way of learning the truth, because Aytoun never had learned the name of his guest; he had given his own family name to Philip.

On those few occasions when Aytoun spoke of the boy's father, he did not try to make him out an ideal figure but frankly admitted that he seemed a rude, uneducated man; nevertheless the unknown had loomed gigantically in the mind of Philip Aytoun, and the great black rock which lay beside the bubbling of the spring had become a sacred symbol.

Once Aytoun had said, pointing to it: "You ought to be a good man, Philip. Your father paid down a heavy price for you!"

13

And if all the pounds of that mighty stone had been bright gold its value would not have been so great as it was now in the mind of the boy.

Always he had felt that he would need to be multiplied many, many times in order to make such a piece of a man as his father had been before him; and still beyond the words of Aytoun, he had the spectacle of the great black rock before him from day to day giving the giant of his imagination actual hands, at the least. Now with his own hands he had raised that stone, no doubt with more pain than yonder rider of the black horse, no doubt with a greater weakness thereafter, but the miracle had been accomplished. If he had been a trifle more religious, he would have felt that God was in his act.

"D'you think," said Philip, "that a man who can handle the rock is strong enough to get along in the world?"

"I think so," said Aytoun.

"I picked up the rock today," said Philip.

Aytoun hurried to the spring. There was just enough starlight for Philip to mark the manner in which the old man remained half bent and still beside the squat shadow of the rock; just beyond him the spring was bubbling, so that old Aytoun seemed to be standing in the rising and falling glimmer of the water.

He came back after a time.

"I hope you will be a good man in the world," said Aytoun.

Philip stood up beside the door.

"I am going to work very hard," said he. "As soon as I have made some money, I'll come back here for you, Uncle Oliver."

To this the old man did not make a reply. Philip waited a long moment, the brightness of joy fading from his face by degrees, for he felt that already something had stepped between them after these many years.

Loafer suddenly began to whine. Because Philip felt great pain in his own heart, he leaned and patted the great head of the dog and spoke very gently to it. He no longer looked down at the lights, but he wished that the morning would come quickly and that he were away, with the sense of guilt left behind him.

He went to bed, and lay with closed eyes, breathing deeply and regularly as though in sleep; for he was afraid that Uncle Oliver might begin to talk to him.

CHAPTER III

THEY were up with the dawn, both of them exceedingly cheerful, for cold air makes the blood dance; and though this was the golden time of the autumn, on that high mountain-shoulder the nights and the mornings were very sharp.

But when they sat down at the table, the constraint fell upon Philip again, so that he ate busily, made a good deal of noise with his fork and knife, patted Loafer, looked out the door, spoke about the mist which was rolling in thin silver up the mountainside with the aspens standing in it like streaks of tarnished gold. Nevertheless, the more he busied himself and the more carelessly self-conscious he tried to appear, the more keenly was he aware of the thoughtful face of Oliver Aytoun.

At last he could stand it no longer; he pushed back his stool and cried out: "But, Uncle Oliver, I am coming back!"

The old man nodded and smiled; his eyes were looking into distance as though he had heard words read aloud out of a story-book.

"You'll want this rifle," he said at last, "and you'd better take this revolver."

"They are your two best guns," exclaimed Philip.

"*Our* two best guns," answered Uncle Oliver.

Philip began to choke. He gathered up the dishes rapidly and began to wash them, scowling so that the tears in his eyes might not be seen. He felt so weak and uncertain that he could not believe that with these same hands he had lifted the black rock the day before.

Aytoun went about the preparation of a pack. He put into it some socks and shirts and flannel underwear and a bit of food. He spent some time examining the cartridge belts, but at last he selected one, and he had everything ready by the time the dishes were finished, and the dish-cloth had been spread out neatly to dry.

At length Aytoun said: "If you ever should have a quarrel, I hope that you won't use a gun, Philip."

"No, no," said Philip, "I won't quarrel, because every-one down there is sure to know a great deal more than I do."

"Perhaps they will," said Oliver Aytoun, and closed his eyes.

"Not that you haven't taught me a lot!" exclaimed Philip. "Dear Uncle Oliver, I shall remember every day of my life—"

"Hush," said the old man. "I wish that I had a horse for you; but a mule will get you along."

"Take one of your mules? I wouldn't dream of it!"

"You must take one."

Philip looked wildly about him. For many years all his dreams had walked down into the valley towards the sparkling lights and he had told himself that they lived a small, poor life here on the mountain, but never had he seen the truth so clearly as on this morning. It was a hovel that they lived in, and like beggars they had carved their existence in the wilderness from the hand of nature. But somehow his eye fastened and held upon the dishrag, be-cause it made him think of fiercely cold winter evenings when the dishwater turned cold and greasy almost at once, and the tins rarely were really clean; one's fingers would slip a bit upon them.

"I'll take nothing more from you," said Philip huskily.

There was no further argument. He stood at last outside the hut, with the pack strapped behind his big shoulders; the rifle he carried slung loosely in his hand; the revolver was worn on his right thigh. His clothes were tough woolens which fade with time, but which rather stiffen than wear thin. The cartridge belt sagged heavily about his hips and yet he scarcely felt its weight for every day he had strode across the difficult mountain heights until the metal of his body was like the supple steel of sword blades.

The mist had made the rocks and the soil black; from a pine tree near the house there was a constant dripping, like the sound of rain.

"I'd better be getting on," said Philip.

"You'd better be getting on," said the old man. "There's Loafer showing you the way!"

In fact, Loafer was scouting down the mountainside, as though he knew in what direction his master would be walking.

"Good-by, Philip," said Aytoun.

Philip took his hand.

"But I'm coming back!" said Philip desperately.

The other nodded.

"When you come to the town, get some cotton underwear," he said. "It'll be a lot warmer, down there in the valley."

Philip marched stiffly away. Loafer, once sure that the journey was to be in that direction, disappeared into the distance. At the edge of a scattering of lodge-pole pines, Philip paused. He wanted to look back, but somehow he dared not risk another glance at the shack, and therefore he stumbled ahead. Aytoun had taught him three prayers; one of these he began to murmur to himself, hardly knowing what he said, but the words made it easier to breathe, and when he came out on the far side of the lodge-pole forest his mind was clear enough for him to see what lay about him.

The mist was much thinner, except in hollows here and there where the sun fell upon it and made it as blinding white as snow, but the golden aspens sparkled everywhere through the veil and the ground could be seen, tanned with withered grass except where the rocks broke through. Taking note of all this, Philip was oddly comforted, and he walked on at a greater pace.

He entered the belt of spruce and big pines where the air was wonderfully sweet and the cold of the night remained. Loafer came back to him, panting, his red-shot eyes gleaming with lust for game, but now for a time he kept just ahead of his master, glancing back over his shoulder, once in a while, as though to read the mind of the boy, and then trotting on. It was very easy for Loafer to change his home, thought Philip. One meal in three days was all he needed to have, and his sharp white teeth were sure to earn food at least that often; but he, a man, with a man's weakness, needed far more.

Once he came to a stop, resolved to go home and say to Aytoun: "I'm not very old; I don't know a great deal; I'll stay with you a while longer, if I may!" But then he thought of the white, fierce winter when the winds come leaping out of the north and he went on again.

By noon he had come, after steady traveling, to easier country. The forest was taller than ever, but it was open, rarely choked with underbrush, and often it gave way to broad clearings where the tanned grass rolled pleasantly and smoothly over the hills.

In one of these clearings he heard the sweet, far-off tinkling of a bell that walked gradually towards him. Philip halted, full of wonder, but at last it was only a brindled cow that walked over the hill with a brown bell tied around her throat. She stopped and looked at him, but then passed on unafraid and drank from the stream that went down the valley.

Philip sat down near the same spot to eat a lunch. He found that his food supply consisted of slices of cold bacon, fried crisp and placed between thick bits of corn-pone, and it seemed to him that there never had been food so delicious as this and nothing so good to drink as the bright water that swerved past his feet.

Loafer lay down to watch with his red eyes for crumbs. Bits that were thrown to him he slashed out of the air with his white fangs, capable of cutting through the flank of an elk to the life in a single stroke. However, he would need better and more food than this. A rabbit raised its foolish head from a tuft of grass a hundred yards away; Philip sent a bullet from his Winchester through that head, and Loafer was off at a gallop to bring in the prize. He brought it back and laid it at the feet of the master. It was a big, fat jack. With terrible desire, the jaws of Loafer slavered, and his belly muscles worked; so Philip gave it to him with a gesture and in an instant the rabbit was gone and Loafer curiously sniffing the bloodstains on the earth.

Philip studied him as he often had studied the dog before, for he saw in the greed and the cruelty and the hunger of Loafer a continual contrast with the goodness, the wisdom, the gentle grace of man, for whom this world and all the mountains and rivers and forests and beasts have been made. All has been prepared for him as by a kind father for a child; for so Oliver Aytoun had said, almost in those words. And Philip, looking up from the big wolfish dog to the hills, to the forest, to the sky, felt his heart run over with wonder and shame and gratitude. He felt that he was a weak and foolish creature, indeed; he prayed that he might become wiser, stronger, better, so that men would be willing to accept him as a brother!

After this, he set about reloading the rifle—for he wished to keep the magazine full; and the first thing he discovered was that one of the pockets was empty and into it had been thrust a little roll of paper.

He took it out and spread in his hand thirteen dollars.

One by one he examined the frayed slips of paper, as though on each there were written some special message for him. It was all the money that Uncle Oliver possessed, and he sprang to his feet and faced the upward slope, determined to return to the shack and give back the money.

That purpose, however, did not endure, for he saw that it was more than money that Aytoun had given to him; if he gave back the money, he could not return the kindness and the love with which they were enveloped.

Such was mankind; wise, gentle, tender of heart!

He wrapped up the remainder of the provisions and was fitting them into the knapsack when he heard the sharp clicking of the hoofs of a horse, and he saw a rider come around the shoulder of a hill, close to the little creek.

This man was pushing with whip and red spurs a little exhausted mustang which acknowledged the spurs and the quirt with a sudden flattening of the ears, but with no increase of speed. Philip watched the cruel progress with amazement. But he decided that he would not judge too quickly, for the world was a most complicated place and the motives and the needs of man might be quite past his understanding.

19

Just as he had come to this thought, the stranger marked him, and with an exclamation dropped the reins and jerked a rifle from the holster beneath his leg. Straight into the barrel of that rifle, Philip found himself gazing.

CHAPTER IV

THE rifle appeared to grow greatly in size as it came nearer; it presented a yawning black cavern to the gaze of Philip. Then, behind the gun he saw a man in a red flannel shirt, the sleeves rolled to the elbows over hairy forearms which were sunburned almost to blackness. He wore blue overalls, tightly belted at the waist. His open shirt exposed a black outcropping of thick hair on the neck and chest. His felt hat was worn slid back so far that both his cheeks and the tip of his nose had been fried to a bright red. He was fat, yet he appeared strong, active, and ready for work.

He said, as he drew closer: "Who in hell might you be?"

"I am Philip," said the boy.

"Philip what?"

"I don't know," said Philip. "I have no other name."

The man of the gun looked earnestly at the youth; then he gradually lowered his rifle.

"Got some chuck there?"

"Yes."

"Gimme," said he, and Philip gave the rest of his provisions.

The stranger stowed a whole section of corn bread and bacon in his fat face and yet he was able to speak around it, though in a painfully choked voice.

"This ain't bad. Where you come from?"

"Yonder."

"That's Pillar Mountain. Nobody lives there."

Philip was silent. He felt that he was having an odd introduction to the world, but no doubt there was much kindness behind the strange manner of the horseman.

"You got a horse nearby?" asked the rider, stuffing another wedge of food into his mouth before it was half empty.

"No," said Philip.

The face of the stranger was so stretched with eating that he could show emotion only with his eyes, and these grew round with impatient anger. He tossed his head over his shoulder and glanced down the valley; then he stared back at the boy.

"What else you got around you?" he asked. "Lemme see that rifle. Butt first, mind you!"

Philip presented it duly, butt first. But he was greatly troubled, because he felt that the weapon was about to be taken from him if it were better than the stranger's own gun, and that it *was* better seemed patent to the first glance. So he presented his rifle, but he kept his hold on the barrel of it, and at the same time he caught the barrel of the rider's gun.

"Leave go, you poor fool!" said the other, with a snarl.

He wrenched mightily at the rifles; it was as though they were fixed in rock, and all at once he ceased his struggle. His eyes grew round again, but not with anger.

"What's wrong with me havin' a look at your gun?" he asked. "I'm not gonna steal it! Leave go of mine then, will you?"

"I don't know," said Philip. "I'm just thinking it over."

"I'll give you a hell of a quick start for your thinking, in another second," said the fat-faced man.

He shifted his hand from the butt of Philip's gun to the butt of a gun which thrust out of the saddle holster.

"Don't do that, please," suggested Philip. He poised his released gun as he spoke, so that it was like a club, held as light as a feather, and the other rolled his eyes up at the impending danger.

"Damnation!" he murmured under his breath, and he removed his hand from the revolver in his holster. "Call off your damn dog!" he added, his voice pitched several notes higher, in what was almost a squeak of fear.

21

Loafer had failed to understand a good deal of what was happening, but the brief struggle for the rifles was self-explanatory. He slipped around to the side of the stranger and a little to his rear, and then he crouched, waiting for no more than a whisper of command before he launched his great white fangs and a hundred odd pounds of muscle at the rider.

Philip drew back half a step and shifted the rifle in his hand so that the butt caught under his forearm, and his finger was on the trigger. In this fashion, it was like a revolver, and it pointed at the breast of the other.

"I don't want to make any trouble," said Philip. "You're welcome to the food, if you're very hungry; but I think you wanted to take my gun, and you haven't any right to that."

"Me?" said the fat man, making a gesture of protest and rolling his glance to the heavens. "Me? A thief? God bless me, me boy, what sort of a gent d'you take me for?"

"I beg your pardon, I'm sure," said Philip.

"Me!" said the brown man, his excitement growing. "That have run cows on ten thousand acres, more or less. Me steal a gun! Well, son, I dunno how you was brung up!"

"I'm ashamed!" said Philip, growing a hotter crimson than before. "I really beg your pardon! If—if you'll sit down here and finish your lunch, I'll rub down your horse for you!"

"I dunno but what I will," said the brown man, and cast another glance down the valley.

Then he dismounted and sat on a rock, munching the food and keeping his rifle across his knees. Still, from time to time, he looked down the hollow, but he bent most of his attention on Philip. The latter in the meantime was hard at work over the mustang. He knew all about taking care of exhausted animals, for sometimes the work on the trails of Pillar Mountain wore the two mules to a shadow, and Aytoun had taught the boy what to do in such a case.

First he would have stripped off the saddle, but the stranger stopped him with a yell of protest.

"I might be wanting to start on, any minute," he declared. "You leave that saddle rest, will you?"

So Philip simply loosened the girths and pushed the saddle back. Then he fell to work, stripping the flabby muscles of the mustang with such an iron grip that the little animal squealed in protest. Nevertheless that enforced circulation soon made the flesh stand out firm and strong again, and the mustang soon was lifting his head and making active efforts to bite his tormentor. When he could not manage this, he merely dashed his heels at the empty air and then turned his attention to the nearest wisps of grass. Then Philip allowed him a single swallow of water and backed him off into a thicker stand of the dun-dried forage.

"He's better now, you see," explained Philip.

"If you dunno men, you know horses, kid," declared the fat man. "That's a trick that I can use on the trail— if I got the hands for it. Lemme see your hands, will you?"

Philip obediently offered them for inspection, and the stranger, like a connoisseur, bent back the long fingers and looked earnestly at the big tendons of the wrist.

"There's something to have," murmured the stranger, looking up from the inspection after a time. "There's something to have. There's something to wring necks with!"

He stood up and began to draw up the cinches of the mustang. Over his shoulder, still looking down the valley, he said: "Thanks for the lunch. If you're ever stuck for a job, you come to me."

"Thank you," said Philip.

"You got no idea who I am?"

He was seated in the saddle, once more, smiling complacently down at the boy.

"No."

"If you had," said the fat man, "you'd be feelin' sick. But I tell you, I'm always easy on a tenderfoot. I'm always easy on a kid. You hear me."

"I do," said Philip, not quite understanding what was meant.

The stranger rode his horse into the stream.

"If you was to see anybody coming along after me," said he, "you might say that I'd sashayed over into the woods, there. You hear?"

23

"I do," said Philip.

The other waved a hand and then started to guide the mustang up through the rapidly flowing little stream, keeping to its bed until it turned out of sight within a few hundred feet. Philip put on his depleted knapsack. He worked slowly at the buckles of it for his mind was whirling; his first taste of humanity left him most ill at ease!

He had not walked on down the valley for five minutes when a little host of riders broke out of a wood and came storming down on him.

"You seen Joe Dorman up this way?" yelled one in the van.

"On a dead-beat pinto?" burst out a second.

Philip shrugged his shoulders. He was very ill at ease.

"I don't know what to say," said he.

A man more elderly than his companions, a hard-faced, keen-eyed man, came to the front.

"I'm the sheriff," he remarked, and turning down the lapel of his coat he revealed a silver-bright star of office. "Now I ask you—have you seen Joe Dorman?"

"I never heard that name," said Philip.

"You lie," said the sheriff coldly. "And you lie like a fool. Everybody knows Joe Dorman. You seen him— where? Where was he going?"

"I don't know," said Philip.

"You idiot!" shouted the sheriff. "You half-wit! Which way was he headed for?"

Philip remained silent. He knew that a sheriff stood very, very high, and his heart was in his throat, but for some reason it was impossible that he should betray the secret of Joe Dorman and his spent mustang.

"Will you talk?" yelled the irate sheriff.

"He's a half-wit, sheriff," said a kinder voice. "He don't know nothing."

"You ought to be able to read his mind if he's a half-wit," said the furious sheriff. "I tell you, he's blockin' the law. You take that fool in to town and lock him up in the jail. I'm gunna make him an example. You hear? A damn hot example is what I'm gunna make out of him!"

He gathered his men with a shout and they all pushed up the valley in a crash of hoof beats. But when they struck a sharper slope just ahead, their horses slowed down to a staggering trot. Every one of them was terribly spent.

"They'll never get him," said Philip aloud. "They're worse done than he!"

He was relieved.

CHAPTER V

WHEN he looked back from the disappearance of the posse, he found the quizzical eye of his guard fixed upon him.

"Well, kid," said he, "what you thinking of?"

"I was only wondering something," said the boy. "I suppose Joe Dorman has done something wrong?"

"You suppose?" grinned the other. "I suppose so, too."

"What has he done, then?"

"What *is* there to do?" said the guard. "He's done everything there is. Gimme your guns, kid. I gotta walk you down to the town. Just hand 'em over right pronto," he added in a stern voice.

For the boy had hesitated a little; but then he remembered the caution which Oliver Aytoun had given him—there must be no trouble when guns were in hand—and how narrowly, perhaps, had he escaped a tragic quarrel with yonder hunted man only a few minutes before!

So he passed over his rifle and then his revolver. The guard looked upon them approvingly.

"You know how to keep a gun, kid," said he. "Who taught you?"

"My uncle," said Philip.

"Where you from?"

"That way yonder."

"But that'll be Pillar Mountain."

"Yes."

"And nobody lives on Pillar Mountain."

"Yes, I lived there."

"Who's your father?"

"I don't know."

The other frowned a little.

"I hope to find out, some day," said Philip cheerfully.

At this, he thought that he detected the ghost of a twisted smile on the face of the other.

"We better start along for town," said the rider not unkindly. "I better introduce myself. I'm Rivers. Mostly they call me Doc, which I ain't one, though. Come along, kid!"

They went on down the valley. Rivers was both curious and kind, which made rather a singular and uncomfortable combination.

"You been to school, ever?" said the gentle Doc Rivers.

"No."

Mr. Rivers whistled.

"That's a hell of a shame," he declared. "Wonderful what schooling does for you. It's mean work and it's slow work, but it helps a good deal. It brings you on. Amazin' what it would do for you, if you was able to read or write."

It came to the mind of Philip that he might undeceive his genial companion. Certainly he could read and write, and no doubt there had been some pain involved in the learning, for he could remember the long evenings of labor when Oliver Aytoun sat as tutor and corrected the tasks.

And yet he was held back, because he felt that it might embarrass Rivers to know that his prisoner had been compelled to read certain hours of each long winter day.

"You talk pretty good, though," commented Rivers. "But then," he explained to himself, "a gent can pick up a lingo."

"I can read and write a little, too," said Philip.

"The hell you can," said the rider. He turned in his saddle and regarded his prisoner.

He went on: "You never heard of Joe Dorman?"

"No."

"I guess you never read newspapers, then?"

"I never have read a newspaper," said Philip.

The eyes of Doc Rivers expanded. He began to rub his chin.

"Think of that, now," he said, more to himself than to his companion. "Never read no newspaper. Got no education. And raised right here in the old United States!"

Presently he asked: "D'you ever have any trouble with your head?"

"What sort of trouble?" asked Philip.

"Sort of a pain when you try to think?"

Philip examined the question frankly and earnestly: "Yes," he admitted, "I do."

Doc Rivers made a clucking sound. His sympathy was manifest.

"It's all right," said he. "It's all right, kid. We got places in this here state for taking care of folks like you. Don't you worry none. I'm gunna take a personal interest in pushing your case through. I know some folks—you wait and see! I'll land you plumb comfortable!"

He was so filled with his own thoughts that for some time, as they journeyed on, he nodded and murmured to himself.

"Now," he said at length, "what can you do for yourself?"

"I don't know," said Philip.

"You don't even know that!" said Rivers sadly. "Might I ask, can you ride a horse?"

"I never tried," said Philip.

"You never tried!" breathed Rivers.

"But I can ride a mule," offered Philip.

"You can ride a mule!" said Rivers, who seemed so overwhelmed that he could merely repeat the words he heard. "And you can stay on the back of a mule?" he asked with a gentle sarcasm.

Philip thought back to the painful days when the youngest of the two mules had been brought up by Aytoun. It was a wiry young gray devil with a small eye as bright as polished glass and a fire behind it, shining redly through. For a whole month he had struggled with

27

the devilish wiles of that creature; a thousand aches and pains shot through him as he recalled the struggles.

"If it's a gentle mule I can ride it," he admitted.

Mr. Rivers grinned. But he banished the smile at once, as though ashamed of it.

"These here guns," he indicated the captured pair and added, "you'll get 'em back, all right, don't you worry. But these here guns, you was taught to clean 'em?"

"Yes," said Philip.

"Did you ever shoot a bullet out of one of 'em?"

"Yes," said Philip.

"Hit your mark?"

Philip thought of a jack rabbit, dodging like lightning among rocks.

"Sometimes I hit," said he.

"And sometimes you don't," grinned Rivers.

"Sometimes I don't," said Philip, and turned his big, frank eyes upon his companion.

"You never used a rope, none?" asked Rivers. "You don't know how to use a rope none?"

"Oh, yes," said Philip, "I can use a rope to tie a mule to a manger."

"You can use a rope—to tie a mule—to a manger," echoed Rivers, in the voice of one in pain. "Sweet—sufferin'—mama!"

Then he added: "Can't do nothin'—can't use a rope—can't ride a hoss—I dunno what's gunna become of you, kid! But the state'll take care of you," he said firmly and righteously. "Oh, yes, the state'll take care of you, or I'll make a scandal out of it. I'll put it in the papers!"

Philip considered; but he hardly knew how the state was to take care of him, or what being put in the papers might mean. He felt, however, that he was face to face with some sort of a catastrophe.

"Can't even shoot!" said Rivers.

"But I can—a little," protested Philip.

"All right," said Doc Rivers. "Here's your own rifle, all nice and clean. There's a stump over yonder, nice and handy. I give you three shots at that!"

Philip accepted the rifle.

"I don't like to try," said he.

"Does it seem prettty far?" asked the kind Rivers.

"It's standing still, you see," explained Philip.

Mr. Rivers opened his eyes very wide. A light of real terror was in them as he croaked: "So it is; it's standing still. Mostly in your part of the world, does the trees run around a good deal?"

"What I mean to say," began Philip.

And then he broke off short, for a quail launched from beneath a bush near by and whirred down the valley with wings grown invisible with rapid motion.

At that, the rifle of Philip leaped to his shoulder. He followed the flight of the bird for half an instant with wavering muzzle, and then fired. The quail veered, a few feathers fluttered in the air, and it was gone into a clump of shrubbery.

"I'm very sorry," said Philip. "It rather surprised me. I mean—jumping up that way right at my feet!"

Doc Rivers hurried on with a preoccupied look, and leaned from his horse to examine the spot where the feathers had drifted to the ground.

"That's a hundred yards if it's a quarter of an inch," he observed to himself.

"I'm sorry," repeated Philip. "But often I hit them, you know!"

Doc Rivers merely responded: "Sweet—sufferin'—mama!"

His thoughts had drifted far off; suddenly he demanded harshly: "Gimme back that gun!"

Philip, hurt at the tone, returned the gun, and watched Rivers examine it with the greatest attention.

"There ain't nothing funny about it," said Doc Rivers. "It ain't nothing but a damned old Winchester. It ain't no different from my own gun."

He puckered his lips, as though his thought had left a sour thought in his mind. "I used to think that I could shoot a bit, myself," he observed.

"No doubt you can," said Philip, anxious to be pleasant. "No doubt you are really a great expert, Mr. Rivers. My Uncle always let me know that I had a great deal to learn."

"Who is your uncle? God?" asked Doc Rivers. "Maybe with a revolver you ain't very good, neither? Maybe you can only roll a small stone along the ground, or a tin can?"

"Yes," said Philip humbly. "That's about the hardest thing that I can do."

"You can do it, can you?"

"Yes."

"Here's your Colt. You got no trigger on it, I see. Does that mean that you fan it, kid?"

"Oh, yes," said Philip. "My uncle said that was the proper way to use a revolver. My uncle—"

"Oh, damn your uncle," said Doc Rivers. "Lemme see you roll that little ol' stone, will you?"

Philip looked askance at his companion. He felt that, although he did not wish to quarrel with any soul in this wide world, and though Doc Rivers had been the height of kindness up to this point, yet a slighting remark concerning the good, the wise, the kind, the gentle man who lived on Pillar Mountain was not to be tolerated.

However, he determined to do as he was bid and make no more disturbance about it.

The stone indicated was a rounded white pebble a couple of inches in diameter. He looked carefully at it, then he whipped the gun suddenly into play from the hip and the stone leaped wildly like a frantic living thing, striving to escape. Five shots made it leap five times, but the sixth shot missed the ground behind it.

"I'm sorry," said Philip, apologizing again. "But," he explained, "my uncle never was satisfied with the way I used a revolver. I haven't the patience to practice long enough; and ammunition costs such a great deal of money, you know!"

Doc Rivers, in silence, was dismounting from his horse. He picked up the small white stone, wrapped it in a spare bandanna, and placed it carefully in his pocket.

"Is it a rare specimen?" asked Philip politely.

"Is it a rare specimen?" echoed Rivers. "Sufferin'—sweet—mama—I'll tell a man it is!"

CHAPTER VI

PHILIP began to grow excited. The trail was joined by another; presently they were riding along a road which was rutted by wheels and which wound with a pleasant carelessness back and forth among the woods. He felt that they were bound to come upon men soon and his heart quickened with anticipation, for these other encounters hardly could be typical of what he was to expect of society. He had met, first of all, a fugitive criminal; and hot on the trail of that wicked man he had found a sheriff, fierce in the pursuit, and surrounded by savage manhunters. As for Doc Rivers, he was pleasant and kind enough, but since the episode of the revolver and the little white stone, he had fallen strangely silent, only turning a quick and searching side-glance at his companion from time to time.

Now, before them, they heard the rapid sound of a horse trotting up the road, and presently a mustang came in view with its rider sitting sideways, his left knee hooked over the horn of the saddle. He gave a hunchbacked appearance in the distance, smoking a cigarette, his head bobbing up and down with the jar of the trot, but when he came nearer, saw them, and straightened Philip made out a strongly built young man with a rather handsome, lazy face.

"Hello, Lew," said Rivers.

And: "Hello, Doc. Whacha doin' up here?"

"Been Dormaning."

"Is he loose again?"

"Ain't you heard?"

"Nothin' lately."

"He got Bud Chalmers, at last."

"The hell you tell me."

31

"The hell I don't."

"Is this part of Dorman's gang?"

"Him? He ain't part of nobody but himself," Rivers explained Philip.

Lew appeared curious, but Rivers merely added: "I'd introduce you, but I ain't got time to write a book. Anyway, his name is Philip. This is Lew Thompson."

"Philip what?" asked Lew Thompson, shifting his cigarette across his mouth on the tip of his tongue.

"Philip nothin'," answered Doc.

"How do you do," said Philip out of a book. "I'm charmed to meet you, Mr. Thompson."

"Hello," said Thompson, the cigarette bobbing on his lips. "Where did you get it, Doc?"

"Loose up yonder."

"It ain't branded?" continued Thompson in the same curious, impersonal manner.

His attitude seemed to Philip rather rude; he did not like to be talked about as though he were a rock or a tree, but at the same time he understood so few of the remarks that he hardly knew how to take offense.

"He ain't branded," agreed Doc.

"And he's too young to be a maverick?"

"I guess you read him right, Buddie."

"Listen."

"I'm hearin'."

"You two come sashaying up to me shanty. Lil'll have a snack for you."

"I don't mind if I do," agreed Doc Rivers.

They turned back with the stranger

"What happened to his hoss?" asked Thompson.

"He ain't never rode nothin' but a mule," asserted Doc Rivers, and he turned a blank eye upon Lew, and Lew turned a still blanker glance upon Philip. There was a taste of innuendo in the air, as it seemed to Philip, but he said nothing, and decided that he would certainly follow the advice of his uncle and never look for trouble until it stood bodily before his eyes.

From the main trail they branched on to a thin bridle path, so faintly worn that the horses were continually weaving to avoid brush or the stretched arms of trees.

"We're losin' a lot a time," said Doc Rivers.

"You hook on," said Thompson. "Maybe I'll need you."

"What for?"

"Lil is what for."

"You been out?"

"Kind of."

This conversation was astonishing to Philip. He guessed that it must be a species of shorthand, much significance being attached to short phrases, and he was rather depressed when he thought how much time he must needs spend in mastering this vernacular before he could converse freely with his fellows.

Now they broke out of the deeper forest and went through an area of ugly stumps, and beyond this to cleared ground, in the center of which stood a small log cabin.

Philip now hung in mid-stride, because on the threshold of the hut, the interior of the cabin blank and dark behind her, sat a stalwart, handsome girl nursing a baby at her breast. She put the child away when she saw the three approaching and stood up.

Now Philip had seen the glory of storms in the wild country above timberline, and he knew the golden moment of the year when the first frost streaks the mountain forests with gold or crimson or purple or staring yellow, and he had lived among wild animals, and watched the rivers go mad and glorious after the thaw of May, but never had he seen a sight so beautiful as this first woman, and never had he seen anything that so filled him with awe. Out of his reading, phrases and lines of poetry leaped across his mind; he could have fallen upon his knees—beauty, motherhood combined!

"Look at the kid," chuckled Doc Rivers. "He's scared of Lil."

"That ain't so funny," remarked the husband.

Then he took off his hat and waved it.

"Hello, honey!" he called to her with a cheerful voice.

The brown beauty at the door of the cabin said nothing! She merely looked steadfastly upon her spouse.

"Brought home ol' Doc Rivers," said Thompson gaily, "and I thought—"

Musical and brief the voice of the girl responded: "Where you been?"

"Me?" asked Thompson, with most gentle tone of surprise. "Where I been?"

"Lewis Thompson, where you been? What you been doin'? Who you been rampin' around with these two days? You been drinkin' whisky!"

"I ain't," said Lew Thompson, without conviction. "I ain't been doin' no such thing. Ain't you gunna be reasonable, Lil?"

"Lew Thompson, are you gunna come home lyin' and sneakin', you no-good, ornery, low-down varmint, you!"

"O God," moaned Lew Thompson to Rivers, "she's gunna open up. Doncha leave me, Doc. Oh, man, doncha leave me noways, will you?"

Philip rested a hand against the sweating shoulder of Doc's horse; he needed something to sustain him. For he had come to the verge of heaven, to the opening of the very gates of Paradise, and this was the discord to which he must listen!

Lew Thompson went up to the girl with one hand extended.

"I wanna tell you," he said, "about a business deal I been talkin' over that'll—"

"Don't you come up to me like I was a hoss," said the fierce girl. "I ain't gunna eat out of your hand."

Thompson thrust the offending hand into his pocket.

"Lil, for God's sake, doncha go disgracin' me in front of folks!"

"Is Doc Rivers folks?" said the terrible virago. "There ain't nobody this side of the Pass that's half so low-down and wuthless as him; but he's good enough for you to go spendin' your money on him, he is! I got enough of this. I don't have to stand it; I ain't gunna stand it!"

"We better go," said Doc Rivers to Philip.

He might have spoken to a stone and been heard more clearly. These dreadful words which he had just listened to withered the whole joy of existence from the mind of the boy. Paradise? No, it was the deeps of hell into which he peered, and saw it seething with red fire and crossed by jagged arms of smoke. He could not draw his frightened eyes away.

"I don't want nothin' but a coupla minutes quiet talk with you, Lil," said Thompson in persuasive manner. "I gotta scheme up my sleeve that oughta change everything for—"

"So've I," said the girl. "I got a change up my sleeve, too. It's a change of address. The only reason that I been waitin' this long for you to come back was to tell you what I thought about you, and let you know where to send my mail, you low skunk, you Lew Thompson."

"Aw, honey," said Thompson, and stepped desperately close.

That instant the hand of the girl which had been held behind her swept into view, bearing a stout homemade broom. It looked more like a quarterstaff than a mere broom, and with this she cut fairly at the head of Lew Thompson. He raised an arm to protect himself, and yelled with pain as the arm took the blow.

"You she-devil!" shouted Thompson, and smote her on the root of the jaw.

Philip caught his breath, and blackness spun before his eyes. Somewhere he had read of it in books. There were wild and terrible romances which spoke of such things as men beating women. He looked forth again.

She was staggered, but not down. Broad, massive, clothed in hard muscle, it was a Homeric jaw upon which Thompson had struck, and it withstood the blow. She reeled, and crashed with an audible grunt against the wall of the cabin. Then, more horrible than all else, it was seen that Thompson was rushing in upon her, his fists clenched, his face fierce.

"I'm gunna give you a bringin' up and a draggin' down," cried Thompson. "I'm gunna be a pa and a ma to you, you chunk of female bronco, you—"

The distance was great, but the need was dreadful, and with one bound Philip crossed the intervening space. He caught Thompson's shoulder and drew him around.

"You mustn't," breathed Philip.

"Why, you damn young fool!" said Thompson, and raised his burly fist to strike a real blow.

He was forestalled. Hastily, with not half his force, Philip struck—as a bear might strike back-hand at a cub. But like the crash of a bear's forepaw was the effect of that blow. The wind was jammed out of Thompson's body in one gasping, whistling rush and he fell on his side, one leg drawn up beneath him, one leg kicking violently as he struggled for breath and knocked himself about in a circle like a dying hen.

"Good heavens!" cried Philip. "I hope I haven't—"

A loud yell beat into his mind. He saw the girl coming at him like a tigress.

"I'll teach you, you murderer!" said she. "I'll break your head for you, you sneaking traitor, you—"

The blow missed the ear of Philip and crashed upon his shoulders, and the weight of it broke the stout staff of the broom as though it had been a straw. He did not wait for another, with the shortened truncheon of the staff. He merely fled, shouting to Loafer in time to stop the big dog as it flew at the throat of the girl.

On the edge of the trees, Philip looked back and saw the young mother on her knees beside her winded husband, calling pitifully to him to open his eyes, and assuring him that she loved him more than diamonds or mountains of gold.

Philip went slowly on, rubbing the bitter pain in his shoulder. And as he walked, he blinked at the dreadful images which had been thrust before him in the last few moments.

Behind him came a sound of loud laughter, and there was Doc Rivers, reeling in his saddle with his mirth. Loafer followed last of all, casting keen glances over his shoulder, as though he longed to be back in the fray.

CHAPTER VII

"You gotta take time," said Rivers. "You can't learn in a minute! That was a fine swat that Lew got in on her, wasn't it?"

His eyes shone with pleasure and admiration, but Philip looked on his companion as on a madman.

"A little nearer to the point," argued Doc Rivers, "and he'd have put her down; and a happy day for poor Lew if he'd done it. She's a tiger. Doggone me if she ain't a tiger! I says, the day that Lew married her: 'There goes a hero!' says I. She heard me say it, too, and I get a cold sweat when I think of what she'll do to me some day. I'd rather play with a forest fire than fool with her. Say, where did you learn to box?"

"Box?" sad Philip gently.

"Yes, box," replied the admiring Doc. "We used to think that Thompson could fight a little until a wild Canuck came down here like a twelve-mule team and ran over him. But that wasn't nothing like this. Spaff! I never seen such a punch! A left shift to the wind, it looked like to me. Lew will have to wear a mustard plaster for a month to draw his insides back to their right locations. He'll need to get all resurveyed. I thought I seen your fist come out through his back. How much do you weigh, kid?"

"I don't know," said Philip, who understood only one word in every three from this speech. "I never was weighed."

"You never was what? Well, you got the makings of something. I ain't gunna take you to the jail. I'm gunna set you up and manage you. A good heavyweight gets something for his trouble."

Philip paused as they reached the main trail; and Loafer, who had reached his side, paused also, and looked up into his master's face.

"I wasn't dreaming it?" suggested Philip rather wistfully. "He actually struck her?"

"He actually didn't do nothin' but," chuckled Rivers. "It was his good ol' right, too! You know women?"

"I?" murmured Philip.

He closed his eyes for an instant, and far away he saw a bright procession of fairy forms, and gentle ladies on milk-white palfreys, and lovely Una with her hand upon the lion's head.

"No," said Philip, "I don't suppose I do—actually—"

"They take practice," declared Doc Rivers, "but always you gotta come over them with a high hand. My old man was always in hell. Outside, he was as tough as they come. He had hide as tough as the skin of a rhinoceros. You could of busted a Bowie knife on my old man's hide. But when he come home, he wanted to rest and take it easy. He was always talkin' about his aches and pains and waitin' for some sympathy. Well, I seen him wait for twenty-five years, and he never got none. I never seen him get but one smile out of the old woman, and that was when he was stretched out inside of boards. Then she sat down and folded her hands: 'He's been a hard job, but he's finished at last,' says she. That's woman, kid!"

"I don't understand," said Philip.

"Ain't I talkin' the language?"

"Have you been talking about your own father—and —your own mother?"

Doc Rivers turned a little in the saddle and looked down on the boy.

"I sort of get your drift," he said. "You're kind of Sunday School. That's the spoilin' of you! Women," said Doc Rivers, "is lightning on skates. Women is steel cases with a lead core. Women is a long trail with a blizzard blowin'."

He fell into gloomy thought which continued for a long time. "Back East they got a new invention," said Rivers at last. "It would be a help to you."

"Yes?" queried the boy politely.

"They got wagons with gas engines in 'em that run without hosses. Automobiles they call 'em. You could use one; otherwise, you're gunna be walkin' through a pile of mud before you're much older!"

The road was so dry that the dust was blowing, and therefore Philip saw no meaning whatever in this remark, and a moment later he had another thing to take his attention, for the trail, which recently had grown deeper and more worn, now joined another road which had still more the aspect of a main thoroughfare and where the two intersected there was a shambling, sunburned group of buildings. A long watertrough in four big sections, green-dripping along the sides, the surface of the water freckled with dust, stood before the largest of the structures.

"There's Miller's place," said Rivers. "I guess we can afford to pull up and likker there, kid. What you think?"

They dismounted in front of Miller's, therefore. Certainly it did not resemble a palace out of the Arabian Nights' Entertainments, but it was far the most imposing work of man that the boy had as yet seen, and he paused a moment in the white-hot dust of the street to regard the shambling façade with reverence, thinking how many backs must have been bent to raise this monster, how many handstrokes must have been used to fasten the timbers. No wonder the paint was burned and peeled from most of it. A veritable ocean of color and oil would have been needed to re-do the surface.

"Come along, kid," said his companion. "I'm getting so dry that I'm kind of blind. You might have to lead me by the hand, unless I can smell my way to the booze!"

The floor of the veranda creaked loudly beneath their boots. Then they pushed through a swinging door and Philip found himself in a long, low, narrow room where already half a dozen men were leaning at a high wooden counter, turning glasses between thumbs and forefingers.

It would have been possible, indeed, to locate that room because of its fragrance, which was partly that of many fuming Bull Durham cigarettes and a sharp, sour scent of beer, and a pungency of stronger liquors, though none of those perfumes could have been identified by Philip. However, he liked the dim coolness, and the strands of wet sawdust sprinkled on the floor, and the comfortable chairs that lined the wall. Outside the sun was raging; the burn was still between his shoulder blades. But this was a moist, misty Paradise of coolness.

Truly, wonderful were the ways of man, and good and beautiful was this shining world of man's devices!

The six dusty forms before the bar turned slowly towards them with a general, throaty: "How-d'ye." Behind the wooden counter a tall, sad-faced man leaned towards them, notable for a jacket which once had been white but now was streaked with stains of varying shades of amber and of brown, sometimes edged with black dust.

"Well, boys?" said he in a mournful voice.

"Red-eye—and a double one," said the eager Rivers. "What you drinking, kid?"

"Milk, if you please," said Philip.

Then he was aware of a dreadful silence which walked through the room, casting cold on either hand.

CHAPTER VIII

PHILIP looked to his companion for an explanation, but Doc Rivers was clutching the bar tightly with both hands. A tremor, or what seemed a tremor, shuddered through him. Beyond him appeared half a dozen blank faces of men who were slowly craning back or forward in order to have a clear view of the last speaker. As for the bartender, a light of terror and wonder appeared in his eyes, and he was the first to break the silence with a hoarse voice.

"Milk," said the bartender.

"Sufferin'—sweet—mama!" said Doc Rivers.

A deep and sympathetic voice added, from farther down the bar, "It's these here damn cooped-up autumn days. They burn the heart out of you. They burn the head out of you. You better lay the kid out and wrap up his head in wet towels. He's gunna be took right bad in a few minutes."

"I'm very sorry," said Philip. "If you haven't any milk, a glass of water will do very well for me, thank you."

Another silence followed, but it was shorter. The bartender slowly and carefully moistened his white lips.

"My God," said he, "this here is a bad case. Bill, you've done some doctoring in your day, ain't you?"

"Hold on!" cried Doc Rivers, as though returning to himself. "Hold on, boys. Lemme ask the kid a few questions. Son, have you ever tasted beer?"

"No," said Philip, "I haven't."

Doc Rivers waited for this important information to be heard upon all hands, in the meantime turning a triumphant eye about the barroom and challenging every face.

Then he added: "I ask you a simple question, kid. You try to recollect. Did you ever see a glass of whisky?"

He underlined these words with little pauses before and after every one. But Philip answered at once: "Oh, no. But my uncle once had a glass of whisky."

Even Doc Rivers, who seemed braced and prepared for some such reply, who had led on the others towards the shock of it, seemed fairly unstrung, and as for the rest, they simply were staggered. One man, heavy of body and red and round of face, sank into a chair with a crash and remained there. The others wandered slowly in the direction of Philip and came to a focus upon him.

"Is it real?" said one slender and sun-dried man. "It ain't a dream, boys," he added in rather pathetic tones. "It ain't something that you're puttin' over on me?"

He reached out and touched Philip's shoulder with the tip of a forefinger, and then he started back a little, almost as though he had been burned. Loafer began to rumble a danger signal, and the crowd scattered a little.

"You better fork over that glass of water," said Doc Rivers, and when it was presented to Philip and the latter had drunk it, he added: "You might go out onto the veranda and rest yourself a minute. I won't be long."

To the veranda Philip went. He would have preferred to remain among these strangely silent men in the cool of the barroom, but he felt that the suggestion was more or less of a command. So he went out on to the veranda, shadowed, to be sure, but drenched with the heat which was reflected from the street. Before the watering trough, one hip sagging, and mouth still adrip, Doc Rivers' mustang was submitting to the flare of the sun, just as the other horses of earlier arrivals were doing, here and there.

Sadness fell steeply, like midnight at midday, upon the soul of Philip, for he felt now that between him and others of his race there existed great voids and gulfs of difference which he might spend half a life-time attempting to cross and yet never arrive at the goal. Behind beer and whisky there lay, apparently, some important mystery. He would attempt to learn what it was, in due time.

A pleasant breeze was rising, and fanning against the swinging doors of the barroom, it kicked them open a trifle and allowed flashes of conversation to float out to him.

"He could hit the white of your eye at a thousand yards, that's all that he could do."

"Come off the mountain with a damn wolf that he called a dog."

"Never knew nothin', never seen nothin', never heard nothin'. He was raised in a glass case!"

He felt, with no real assurance, that some of these remarks, at least, were intended for him, for it was always the voice of Doc Rivers, and then he heard a burst of loud laughter, a stamping of feet, and Rivers protesting in shrill tones.

The swinging doors were thrust open.

"Kid, you come on in!" commanded someone.

Philip rose and faced a burly man with a neck as knotted with strength as the trunk of a tree. Two small, overbright eyes, now sparkled at him, now were lost in gloom, as the heavy brows of the stranger twitched up and down.

"You come on in. I'm gunna teach you some tricks!" laughed the stranger.

Philip passed through the doorway, obediently. He hardly liked the appearance of this man, and certainly he did not like an ugly quality which lurked behind his voice.

"Me an' Archie, we're gunna take you in hand," said the other. "What in hell could a dried-up runt like Doc Rivers do for you? Me an' Archie, we'll make you a regular college graduate, in no damn time whatever. I'm Chisholm. I'm Bert, and there's Archie. Maybe you've heard of us?"

He leered, and Philip blinked once or twice to clear his eyes, to clear his mind.

"I really haven't," said he.

Someone in the barroom chuckled, and Bert Chisholm swerved with a roar of anger.

"Who started a horselaugh?" he asked fiercely.

All at once, there was silence. Doc Rivers was pale and stiff, gripping his glass hard. The tall bartender had begun to bite his lips anxiously.

"Here's your place," said Bert Chisholm. "Right over here in the middle."

He took the arm of Philip with a mighty hand and placed him in the center of the bar.

"Here's Archie on one side of you. Here's me on the other. I guess you ain't got pretty good company, eh?"

He leered at Philip again.

"I'm a man-maker, or I'm a man-breaker," said Bert Chisholm. "Ain't I, Archie?"

"I don't appear to see nobody that says you ain't," said Archie. "But maybe I ain't hearing good, today. I thought I heard somebody laugh, a minute ago, and I been waitin' for the coyote to howl agin!"

Philip looked anxiously to Doc Rivers for a clue as to what he should do, or what was expected of him, but Rivers had a face of stone.

"Now," said Bert, "you see this here glass? This is whisky, kid. And you're gunna drink it."

"Certainly," said Philip meekly, and took the glass.

He was certain that scorn and derision appeared on the face of both the giants who surrounded him. However, he took the glass and tasted it. He set it down and coughed. Fire had been introduced to his throat.

"I can't drink it," choked Philip. "I don't like it, you know."

"He don't like it," said Archie Chisholm.

43

"He don't like it!" repeated Bert. "He don't like it. It ain't milk, is it?"

"No," said Philip. "It's not milk."

"But when I say it's milk, it *is* milk."

"I don't understand you," said Philip. "I'm sorry sir."

"He's sorry, sir," said Archie, and began to laugh in a vast flood of noise.

"He calls me 'sir', now. He's gunna call me God A'mighty, in another minute," said Bert Chisholm. "And this was your idea of a dangerous man, was it? This was your idea of a fightin' man, Rivers?"

Rivers, attempting to speak, made only a faint bubbling sound; and his face was a dreadful thing to see, so splotched was it with white and with purple.

"Drink it up—drink it down!" bellowed Archie. "He shoots out the whites of a gent's eyes, does he? I'm gunna see. I think he's a yaller dog!"

Philip sighed. He felt rather sick and cold. And then he raised the unwelcome glass of fire again.

"Stop it, and put it down," barked Doc Rivers.

He obeyed with a start.

Then, after a terrible hush, two burly heads turned towards Rivers.

"It ain't possible that I heard somebody speak?" suggested Bert Chisholm. "It wasn't a skinny fool by name of Rivers, was it?"

"If there ain't any shame in the kid, there's shame in me," said Rivers. "I'll die before I see you make him take water!"

"Whisky, son. Whisky—not water. But maybe water, too. You're gunna stop us, are you?"

"I'm gunna do my best," said Rivers.

He was trembling violently, his back to the bar. His Adam's apple rose and fell as he swallowed with difficulty.

"You—hell!" said Bert Chisholm, and his big hand shot forth.

It was only his left hand, but it was enough. It grazed the head of Rivers and shot him sidelong to the floor. At the same instant the other bystanders leaped for the wall, and Philip saw Bert standing over Rivers, a gun naked in his hand.

"You pull that gun," screamed Chisholm, "and I'm gunna kill you as sure as God made little apples. I'm gunna drill you. I'm gonna blow you to hell!"

Doc Rivers, blood on his face, lay still; he no longer fumbled at the gun which was belted at his hip, but he raised one hand and covered his eyes as it to shut out some dreadful sight, and Philip could guess that the terrible picture had something to do with himself.

"Now," said Archie Chisholm, "we're gunna get back to that little drink of whisky, brother?"

CHAPTER IX

YOUNG Philip, the drink raised in his hand, paused and looked at it—paused as on a mountaintop and looked at life and at himself. He did not need more experience of men and their ways to teach him that he would despise himself and be despised by others if he submitted to this bullying treatment; more particularly after Rivers had volunteered to at least step into the breach for a moment.

And what was he to Rivers?

He thought, on the other hand, of Pillar Mountain; and it chanced that looking through the dusty window he could see one lofty shoulder of it raised against the sky, so that Uncle Oliver Aytoun and his words came strongly home in his mind. He was to have no trouble with men with guns. And this was his very first day in the world as others lived in it!

Bert Chisholm was saying, with a sneer in his rumbling voice, "Now doggone me if it ain't just like out of a book. Here's the tenderfoot at the bar, and here's a couple of mean, rough cowpunchers invitin' him to take his drink, and aimin' to wring his neck if he don't. Now, how does it usually end up in the story-books, boys?"

45

"We get our jaws bashed in," grinned the other brother, "or else the tenderfoot, he's a killer in disguise, and he punctures the two of us without hardly looking—one in front and one behind him. That's the way in the fool stories."

"So it is," assented Bert. "Now, kid, are you out o' a book? Or are you off of Pillar Mountain?"

Philip looked about him. If there had been any help, he would have asked for it, shamelessly. But there was no help. The others in the room, as appeared by their disgusted faces, did not like this proceeding, but they were not prepared to stand up in behalf of a stranger. The only appeal could be to the two Chisholms themselves!

But when he looked at them a peculiar darkness lurched across the eyes of Philip, such as never had obscured his mind before, and with that darkness there was a burning of his blood and a fierce heat which, all in an instant, ran like quicksilver from his heart to his brain, and back again, and all his body began to tingle.

"I don't want to make trouble," said Philip, in a husky, almost breathless voice.

"He don't want to make trouble!" mocked Bert. "You ain't gunna make no trouble, kid. Don't you go thinking that you will!"

"Bear up a little," said Archie. "Look at him shake!"

"I suppose that I ought to fight," suggested Philip, in the same voice, so unfamiliar to his own ears.

"I suppose that you had ought to," answered the sneering Bert.

He waited another moment, and then added.

"I'll give you while I count ten—and I'll count to myself!"

It had become impossible for Philip to think. He strove desperately, as though the ghost of Oliver Aytoun had been standing before him, but no words came to his lips. That odd dimness was gone and in its place he saw everything with a tremendous brightness, as though intolerable lights had been focused on every face. Thousands of details thrust into his mind quite against his volition. He observed senselessly that Bert wore a check shirt, and that it was rubbed and soiled with grease in the hollow of the right shoulder. There was a small wart in the cleft of Bert's chin, and from the wart grew a long hair, which curled twice round. But Archie was different; he was a comparatively tidy fellow, and in this crisis, as though to defend the brutal attitude of his brother, in which he himself was supporting Bert, he blurted out: "You fix yourself up as one of Joe Dorman's hired men, and what in hell d'you expect from us, kid?"

It seemed to Philip that the count of ten had been vastly prolonged.

Then it was over; the eyebrows of Bert Chisholm rose and made his eyes like the little, red-stained, round, fierce eyes of a boar. At the same instant, accepting the signal, Archie Chisholm knocked Philip down.

There are men who say, and they are men wise in the West, that it was the manner of his fall that made the story of Philip's other days worth writing about. If he had been hurled straight down to the floor, perhaps he would have lain there. Yonder was an example, for instance— Doc Rivers sitting bunched on his heels, but not quite daring to rise in face of the desperadoes. But it chanced that the mighty blow of Archie Chisholm launched the boy full into the chest of his brother.

With arms outflung to break his fall, Philip pitched forward, and as he struck Bert, he clasped him to his breast and turned, presenting the body of Bert to Archie's gun.

That gun remained hovering in the air, like a bird, uncertain where it shall land upon the solid earth, and in the face of Archie was blank bewilderment. For he knew his brother as a twin should, and since his earliest days of memory he had regarded Bert more as an explosive than as a fighting man—more as a rending, roaring, irresistible charge of powder than as so much mere human bone and muscle—but now he saw Bert's arms crushed helplessly against his sides. The back of his neck in that instant had turned fiery red and begun to bulge, and his head toppled back with the long, horrible gasp of a breathless man.

"You—" said Philip "— I beg you to leave this room,

or I'll kill you. I want to kill you. I'll give you till I count ten to leave this room—and I'll count to myself!"

With his left hand he took Bert Chisholm by the throat and held up those two hundred pounds with that one hand as a shield, and Bert hung limp, motionless, with his dreadful face hanging back and to one side. With his right hand, Philip drew Bert's nearest revolver and held it at his hip. It had a familiar feel. There was neither trigger nor sight, and the hammer worked softly under the pressure of his thumb.

Archie hesitated. All the days of his life Bert had done his thinking for him. Bert was an invincible and terrible God. But the God was now a helpless, hanging weight, senseless, speechless, with horrible sounds gurgling in his throat.

"I dunno what—" began Archie.

Then, having hesitated, he was lost. He began to back up towards the door. He flashed a glance towards the others in the room, and if he had read in one eye contempt or disgust he would have fought the thing out to the death, then and there, even if he had to drive his bullets first through the body of his brother. But not a glance met his. On the contrary, there was only one point of interest, and agape, with bulging eyes, the bartender and the rest of his patrons stared at it.

So Archie, lacking the necessary spur which would have kept him from shame forever, took another stride back and was through the swinging door. Then Philip cast his throttled man upon the floor. Heavily fell Bert Chisholm, as weighty as some Homeric hero in armor of bronze, and the boards crashed beneath him and a cloud of dust went up like a great puff of smoke from the lips of a smoker.

The intolerable brightness left the brain of Philip and in place of the fire that was in him cool streams of weakness trickled back through brain and body.

"I didn't want to," said Philip aloud. "I didn't want to—and—and I didn't use a gun—"

He hurled the weapon which he had taken from Bert Chisholm through the window, smashing the glass to a thousand bits, and letting the picture of Pillar Mountain stand undimmed before his eyes. Then he dropped his elbows on the bar and his face in his hands.

People were murmuring and whispering, like voices in a sick-room, and at last a bubbling, gasping cry broke on the ears of Philip. A hand struck his shoulder; the voice of Doc Rivers said harshly: "Get out of this with me!"

And he followed his companion through the swinging doors.

There stood Archie Chisholm, his face still blank, the revolver hanging from his hand, exactly as he had stood there from the moment that he left the barroom. He did not appear to see them as they went past, but he lurched forward through the doors.

"Run for it!" cried Rivers softly, and throwing himself into the saddle, he offered a stirrup leather to Philip.

"I don't think I'll run," answered Philip.

He walked quietly down the middle of the road. Twice he turned and looked back.

And twice his throat seemed drier than the dust of the street with a thirst that could be satisfied yonder in the saloon where there were many men, and two, at least, men ready for a fight.

Yet each time he forced himself to swing away, for the doors of the saloon did not yawn open, and there was no spectacle of men mounting swiftly for pursuit.

Rivers kept at his side, twitching and turning nervously, apparently very eager to be gone at a full gallop, but the same sense of loyalty which had bound him to Philip in the barroom bound him still and kept him back with the boy.

Now the road turned, and when the rest of the town was shut behind an elbow curve, and when the evergreens threw the sweetness of their breath in his face, Philip was able to breathe more easily. When he came under the shadow of the first grove, he asked permission to rest a while, and Rivers without a word drew rein.

There, elbow on knee, knuckles grinding into his chin, Philip tried to work out this thing which had happened to him, but made little headway. The more he tried to clear the matter up, the more cloudy it became and he was only sure of one thing—that when the crisis came yonder in the barroom his own soul had made way in his body for the spirit of another. That had been his first instant of life; before that he was a dim, unborn thing; no light ever had entered his eyes until the white-hot flood had poured out from him upon the world. There had been no joy for him, either. To follow a trail to an ending, to look at the stern beauty of the mountains in winter or the gold of the autumn, to listen to the gentle voice of Oliver Aytoun, to fall into happy dreams—nothing was more than a phantasm compared to that blinding ecstacy which had fallen upon him.

He told himself that he thanked God his hand had been held, but no matter what words and judgments he thrust into his mind, he knew that his heart was wild with a new hunger which had not been satisfied that day and which never would leave him until it had been fed!

CHAPTER X

A PINECONE dropped past his ear. Above him he heard the shrill barking of an angry squirrel, and he looked up but only saw the brown branches, the host of gray-green needles, and a deep immensity of sky beyond. His humor softened.

"What have I done?" he said to Rivers.

"All you done was to choke Bert Chisholm and make his brother Archie take water," said Rivers. "Neither of them things is possible. That's all you done in the last section of your day."

"Why do I have such trouble?" asked Philip sadly. "Wherever I meet men I want to be friendly. I want to learn from them. I want to be kind and good. But they fight with me immediately. They steal my food; they beat me, even the women; they threaten me with drinks that choke my throat; they take my guns away—"

Rivers started violently.

"Guns?" he said. "I forgot, damn if I didn't. Here you are, kid. I don't hanker after these guns. I don't want 'em. As a matter of fact, I wouldn't have 'em. Here you are, kid. You take back your guns, will you?"

He fairly thrust them into Philip's hands, so that the latter was forced to receive them, as it were; but he held them back towards his guard.

"I can't take them," he said. "Because they've been confiscated by the law. The sheriff wouldn't like to have you give them back to me until I've been cleared—"

"Oh, damn the sheriff!" said the other.

Philip glanced over his shoulder; he was frightened.

"But the sheriff is the law!" he exclaimed.

"He's the little finger of it and the thumb too, around these parts," admitted Doc Rivers. "All the same, I tell you that the sheriff don't want your guns."

"How can you tell?" asked the guileless Philip.

"How can I tell? I can guess—just!" murmured Doc Rivers. He began to massage with his finger tips the large lumps where the iron knuckles of Chisholm had struck the side of his head. "I can guess that he don't want your guns. Like me, he wouldn't have 'em for a gift."

"I don't understand," said Philip.

"You don't have to," said Rivers earnestly. "There's only one thing important for you to understand right now —and I'll tell you what it is: You understand that I'm your friend. You got that buttoned inside of your head?"

Philip was so roused by this speech that he rose from the bank on which he had been sitting and laid his hand on the shoulder of Rivers.

"I saw it proved this afternoon," he said, in a voice of emotion. "I never shall forget! You stepped in and risked yourself to save me. I never shall forget, Mr. Rivers!"

"Doc, to most folks, including you, old son," said Rivers, "and concerning what happened back yonder, I'm just as pleased to forget my part of it, if it's the same to you."

"Certainly," said Philip. "I never shall mention it again!"

"Thanks," said Rivers. "Now we better blow along if we want to get home before the night comes."

"The jail is in the town, I suppose?" said Philip.

"Jail?" said the other.

He closed his eyes, and his face was a study of pain.

"Jail?" he repeated. "There ain't any jail for you, as far as I'm concerned. No, kid. You forget. I'm your friend. Now, you write that down in red ink and never let it rub out!"

He patted the massive shoulder of Philip anxiously, as he said this, and Philip opened his big blue eyes and smiled affectionately at his companion.

"You are very kind," said Philip. "I never shall dream of doubting you!"

So great was the friendship of Rivers, that after a time he insisted that Philip should take his turn on the horse, and he seemed genuinely distressed when the boy assured him that he preferred to remain on foot.

Their way led through a narrow cañon, presently, with the walls shooting straight up on either hand. In the center a brook twisted back and forth raising gentle and sad echoes up and down the little valley.

All was damp and cool. Vines hung from the rocks; the brush seemed sprinkled with spray. And constantly the broken trail turned here and there among the boulders or the great trees.

"Kid," broke out Rivers, after they had gone for some time in silence, "how come that you ain't scared of death?"

"Of what?" asked Philip, ready enough to be alarmed.

"Of what, he asks me!" echoed Doc Rivers. "Sweet—sufferin'—mama!"

Then he exploded: "Of the Chisholms, kid! Ain't they enough to make a nightmare in the middle of the day, I ask you? I tell you, old son, that they'd eat you raw, without no salt and without no paprika!"

"The Chisholms!" replied the boy. "They looked very dangerous, didn't they?"

"Didn't they only that!" sighed Rivers.

"But as a matter of fact," said Philip brightly, "they turned out to be very easily handled. They were like old wolves; not half so formidable as the noise they made and the picture of their snarling. You know the one called Bert—really, he simply crunched in my arms like shingles, or something. Oh, no, they're not at all dangerous!"

Rivers laid his hand on the bump which decorated his head.

"Of course," exclaimed Philip, blushing when he saw what he had said, "they got in a lucky blow at you—"

"Lucky?" said Rivers. "Lucky?"

He was silent again, only shaking his head from time to time, while they climbed to the head of the ravine and came out upon gently rolling ground.

The sun was westering fast; the eastern mountains were turning pale gold; all the cañon mouths, stretching into the wider valley, were brushed across with delicate mists.

"Yonder's where we bunk tonight," said Rivers.

"Ah?" said Philip, and following the designated direction, he made out through a break among the trees a distant glimpse of a farmhouse with a tangle of smaller buildings and many fences around it.

"Does a friend of yours live there?" asked Philip.

"Friend?" repeated the other, his eye wandering blankly. "Friend?"

"I mean, some acquaintance? Or is it a wayside tavern?"

"That," said Rivers with instant heartiness, "is what it sure ain't. There's nothing wayside and there's nothing tavern about it, and that you can take from me. But as for the friend part—" he hesitated.

"It's my mother's place," he finished shortly.

"Your mother!" echoed the boy.

They had passed into the bottom of a little swale of ground, and there Philip paused and instinctively took off his battered old felt hat. So he looked up with a smile and saw nothing before him but the rich blue of the sky, with two or three happy white clouds blowing softly across it.

"Your mother!" said Philip again. "Ah, well—how I wish that I had one!"

"You do?" asked Rivers, with much curiosity. "Why, might I ask?"

"Why?" cried Philip. "But of course you're joking! A mother? When I think of gentleness, goodness, sweetness,

53

I think of that word. And some day," he went on softly, to himself, as it were, "some day I may find her! My own mother!"

This tremendous and beautiful thought so filled him that his eyes shone with tears, and these he brushed away, unashamed of showing them, and smiling happily at his friend.

"If you want to find her, I hope you do," answered Rivers briskly. "I hope she pans out pretty well, too. You never can tell. But for my part, I'd rather take a header in a wildcat mine than bank on a mother turnin' out so fine!"

"I don't know what you mean," said Philip stiffly.

"Aw, you'll find out," replied Rivers with a shrug of his shoulders.

"But the hand that cared for you when you were sick," said Philip, turning the pages of some book in his mind, "and the voice that—"

"I know what you mean, all right," broke in Doc Rivers, "but you save those ideas for somebody else. Ma has been too busy to do any caring for the sick. But as a grand cow-woman," he went on, raising his voice with a real enthusiasm, "she stands off by herself. Wait till you see her. And if you don't see enough, you'll hear enough. I'll promise you that!"

He chuckled as he spoke.

Philip found himself condemned to a long fit of musing. For he began to guess that there was much of interest to him that was not of interest to Doc Rivers, and no matter with how kindly an eye he looked upon his companion, or with what determination he tried to see only the good, he could not help feeling that Doc Rivers was, at the best, not exactly a poetic soul. About his very face there was something dry, withered, practical. One never could imagine him failing in a pinch to have very nearly what he wanted; but Philip could not see him storming the cloud-lost heights of any great ideal.

He was sorry to guess at such things, and he promised himself that he would suspend all judgment until Rivers had a chance to speak more clearly for himself both in words and in actions.

In the meantime, they were voyaging steadily across the hills, the mustang at a trot, and Philip at an easy, swinging run. Rivers, keeping the horse just behind, watched the boy go down hill and up dale, never slackening in his pace, while the strangely luminous dusk of the mountains closed in about them, and just ahead, the yellow lights of the ranch buildings began to glimmer cheerfully.

When they came to the barn behind the house, Philip was breathing easily. More easily, indeed, than the big wolf-dog which had dogged his heels.

And he heard Rivers mutter, as the latter dismounted, "All steel—and no wear out!"

CHAPTER XI

"We'll be just on time for supper," said Doc Rivers. "We'll wash over here."

They came from the barn to the smooth-beaten ground behind the house, and there they found a pump, with a wooden stand beneath it, a bucket, and several basins of granite wear, rusted thin in many spots. There was still enough light for them to wash by, and they hurried through the ceremony and went on towards the house.

There were many lights inside, and there was a stir of many voices, and the fragrance of cookery steamed through the air and reached the nostrils and the very innermost spirit of Philip, for he had gone many and many a mile since lunch time.

They stamped across the creaking boards of the rear porch, a screen door screeched under the hand of Rivers, and then Philip found himself blinking, his heart bumping and thumping, as he stood in the presence of the first dinner table he ever had seen.

That table was so big that there were two lamps, one for each end, suspended by chains from the ceiling, and under the double glow Philip saw more than a dozen faces.

All were men, saving two at the head of the table. And there, presiding, was a woman with a square, brown face, and small, bright eyes, and stubby, strong hands.

She pointed with her knife.

"Take that dog out of the house!"

Loafer crowded back against the legs of Philip and snarled in silent defiance.

"Why, doggone me if it ain't a wolf!" said the lady of the square brown face.

And she leaned forward, more interested than before.

"I'll take him away," said Philip, greatly disconcerted by the sudden battery of faces turned upon him and his dog.

His mind was spinning, too; it was not thus that gentlemen and ladies conversed together at the board in the books which he had read!

"Aw, wait a minute!" growled Doc Rivers. "Ma, this here is a special friend of mine—"

"The dog?" asked Mrs. Rivers, without a smile.

"Have a heart," said Mr. Rivers, with a rapid and murmuring voice. "I'm gunna explain things when I get a chance. Hey, kid, you can take care of the dog in here, can't you?"

"Oh, yes," said Philip. "He always sits behind me. If he were outdoors, and happened to meet another dog," he hesitated.

"We'd be minus a dog, ya mean?" said the lady of the house. "All right, you two. Pull up a couple of chairs and break in down there. Hey, Chang, rustle some more chuck. Skinny's back again."

They drew up two chairs, obediently, Philip hardly daring to look about him, so numerous were the strangers. He was cold with excitement, and with fear.

"But if that dog does anything wrong," said Mrs. Rivers, "I'll skin him, young man!"

She turned from the subject of the dog and canted her knife athwart her body towards a girl seated at her left.

"You ain't seen Maizie yet, Doc."

"Hello, Maizie," said Doc.

"Hello, Skinny. How's every little thing?"

"Oh, not bad."

"That's great. You been Dormaning, I hear. How many did you catch?"

"Nothing," said Doc, frowning at his plate.

"Where's the sheriff?"

"How do I know? Still wandering, I suppose."

"But you got lame and took pity on your hoss. Was that it?"

The girl chuckled, and there was loud laughter from the men. Philip, under cover of that burst of mirth, which he did not understand, looked about him at lean, weather-hardened faces, and mouths that gaped widely with the laughter, and forelocks uncontrollable by brush or comb.

He looked past them at the matron, whose habitual frown had not unbent for this poor sally of wit. He looked hastily from her to the girl, and there his eyes stopped suddenly. It was like pulling up a wagon with all the brakes set down hill.

The ladies of his dreams were pale and delicate, large-eyed, languid, toying with harps and velvet clad, and their golden hair, intertwisted with ropes of pearl, flashed like rich metal beside snowy throats and bosoms.

But Maizie, yonder, though she was as brown as a berry, though her hair was sun-faded in its outer puffs, though her eye was as bright and straight as the eye of a man, somehow stepped instantly into a corner of his inner world. She was wonderfully pretty, bright and gay.

Those eyes of hers crossed his glance, and Philip looked hastily down at his ham and eggs.

"Where you been Dormaning, Skinny?" called that rich and carelessly musical voice.

"Oh, up the valley."

"That's kind of general," said Maizie.

"Why you pickin' on me?" asked Doc gloomily.

"If I get famous, it won't be for you, Maizie. Been taking your share of scalps, lately?"

"I try to keep busy," said Maizie. "I've been working on Charlie, here, but I don't seem to get on."

She laid her hand on the arm of the stalwart who sat beside her. Instantly his face was painted crimson, and roars of appreciative laughter rushed from every throat.

57

Philip listened, amazed. No, they were not from the world of his dream. They were far, far from that! Only the girl, somehow, was fitting in—in some remote corner, some garden spot.

"But Charlie's my darling," said Maizie, "until I can get somebody else. Aren't you, Charlie? Jus' for a day or two?"

Philip, looking up under cover of the mirth, found that the straight, keen eyes of the girl were full upon his face, inquiring and probing and testing with a sort of practiced skill. In haste, he looked down again, but attention was bound to fall upon him.

That rather husky, rich voice called again: "Skinny!"

"Aw, leave me be, will you?" growled Doc Rivers. "Call off the dogs, Ma, will you?"

"Skinny, if you're rude to me, Charlie will fight you. Won't you, Charlie? Skinny, I just think you're terrible rude not to introduce your friend. Why keep the good things all to yourself, Skinny?"

"Him?" snapped Doc Rivers. "Name of Phil."

"Hello, Phil," called the girl. "Tickled to death to meet you. Ain't we, boys?"

"Are you?" said Philip, sitting very erect, and bowing a little to them all, while his great blue eyes turned in a frightened manner from face to face. "Are you really?" said Philip.

Silence was flicked across the room, like the shadow of a flying lariat. He was aware that everyone was staring quizzically at him. Even Mrs. Rivers was giving him some attention.

"Of course I am," said Maizie, tilting forward and smiling gently upon him.

There was something absorbing in her gaze and something which enveloped Philip as with many magnetic hands. He grew rather breathless.

"You all are very kind," said Philip. "Of course, it's delightful to me to be here."

The silence continued. Glances began to be interchanged.

"Hey, Skinny!" called Mrs. Rivers. "Where did you get it?"

"We still don't know your last name, Phil," said the girl.

Philip colored a little more deeply.

"I have no other name," said he. "My only name is Philip. I—I—"

He paused. Curious, unsympathetic eyes were fastened upon him.

So he proceeded with difficulty on his explanation.

"I really am hoping to find a father and my mother, you see," said he.

"Oh!" said the girl.

But hers was the only voice which spoke. All knives and forks had been laid down.

"You haven't come to cigarettes yet, boys," sang out Maizie. "I hope you have luck, Phil!"

The hint from Maizie started the eating again, but a battery of penetrating side-glances continually darted at Philip. He felt that he had done something very wrong, very odd; he could not for his life guess what.

At the farther end of the table, Maizie looked at Mrs. Rivers, and the latter lady was seen to tap a significant finger against her forehead.

Then: "Hey, Dick, don't you dare light that butt! You wait till you're outside," cried Mrs. Rivers. "I never seen such young fools. Always soakin' themselves in nicotine. No wonder they can't see a cow bogged down or tell a calf from a hayrick. First thing in the morning—last thing at night—tobacco. They're all soaked in it!"

"Maybe not all," said Maizie. "How about you, Phil? Your fingers look pretty clean. You a cigarette fiend like the rest?"

"I never have smoked," said Philip, shaking his head.

"What do *you* do, the last thing at night?" asked Maizie gently.

"I say a prayer before I go to sleep," said Philip.

Damned up waters will at last break through. An enormous tide of laughter rushed and boomed and reëchoed through the room. And Philip sat up white and still and looked straight before him. A sudden dimness had crossed his eyes, and something like hot quicksilver was working through his heart.

Then, as the laughter eased a little, Doc Rivers said loudly: "I forgot to tell you about Phil when I introduced him. He's out lookin' for work, y'understand? His last job was just a little affair up the valley this afternoon, where the two Chisholms jumped him. All he done was choke Bert and throw him on the floor, plumb silly, and back Archie through the door and make him take water before everybody. So Phil is feeling real kind of impatient and he'd like to get something to do? No? The way you was laughing, I thought maybe that you could! I thought maybe that you could! I thought maybe that you was hankerin' to! But I guess you was sized up wrong. Maybe you wouldn't be interested? No, I see that you ain't!"

CHAPTER XII

THE challenging speech of Doc Rivers seemed to Philip to contain so much savagery that he would have burst out with an explanation and showed how simple the fight with the two Chisholms had been, but he had no chance to do so, for Doc turned to him sharply and said: "And don't you, like a damn fool, try to talk yourself down."

A puncher whose buck teeth made him appear continually to smile, now turned gravely to Rivers: "We ain't been hearing crooked?" he suggested. "You really seen that happen? I mean, it was *both* of the Chisholms, that was hunting together?"

"It was both of them," Doc assured him. "And here's the proof that I was around at that party."

He pointed to the lump which stood out on the side of his head, and though this was proof of a most oblique nature, yet it was not questioned in the slightest degree: Philip became a marked man, and the admiration and wonder of the table was poured out upon him.

It worried instead of pleasing him, for the wild and sagacious faces of these men made him feel like a child in their presence, and he was afraid that he had been highly overvalued by them all. Like one who has made a false reputation, he wanted to be away from that house as soon as possible, and he was glad, above all, when the meal came to an end.

In the midst of the screeching of chairs pushed back from the table at the end of the meal, and the scraping and clumping of high-heeled boots, Mrs. Rivers confronted young Philip.

"And *you're* another of these gunfighters, are you?" asked that formidable woman.

"No, no," Philip assured her. "I never fought with a gun in my life!"

She returned with uncompromising force: "Well, don't you start the bad habit around this here ranch. That's all!"

And she swung past him with the stride of a man, and a man's swing of the shoulders. Philip felt that there were smiles about him, but no one would meet his eye, and there was a covert quality about this mirth that made it more than scornful, he felt. They would laugh aloud, when they were well out of sight.

He was glad when Doc Rivers took him away from the crowd and, at the kitchen door, got a plate of food for Loafer. That hungry monster wolfed it down in an instant, and then Doc took his companion around the side of the house and to the front veranda.

"We can sit out here, pretty safe," he said. "What a lot of long-horned fools they all sounded like! Don't you pay no attention to 'em, kid. They're plumb ignorant. It's the lack of education that makes a gent act like a fool when he spots anything new. You're new. So they smiled. But you keep your spurs off of your heels till you start to ride 'em. They dunno you kid. They dunno, or they wouldn't act that way. Smoke?"

They sat on the veranda, their chairs tipped back, looking out through the tall trees which formed the rude natural garden of the house. There was not much wind, but enough to sift the dry needles with a whisper from time to time, and enough to make the trees sway gently

61

from side to side in the upper branches. The moon was up, and the moon glow filled the upper sky with palest gray blue. Since sunset, a chill had been dropping down, and now the air was wonderfully pure and sweet, but without the biting edge with which Philip was familiar in the upper mountains.

"That Maizie, she's a devil," said Doc Rivers. "She's an outstandin' bronco, and him that busts her and teaches her manners and gentles her down will be doin' a man-sized job, I tell you. But what she says don't you mind. She's gotta talk so much. If she didn't talk, she'd choke, y'understand? She's got a sweeter way with her, she's pretty and bright, but her and Ma are cut out of the same kind of rawhide. You never could think they was the same, but they're drawed together a good deal. Twins, they are, Twins!"

And Doc Rivers grunted and then swore softly in the dimness.

Philip settled back more comfortably in his chair. The air was delicious, the beauty of the trees filled his eyes, the scent of the cigarette was a delicate aroma in his nostrils; and so he surrendered to the situation and let Doc talk. But all the time another voice was at work in his memory, stirring quiet pools and still lakes never before touched.

It was Maizie.

He had revolted against the comparison between her and Mrs. Rivers, that blunt driver and maker of men, but he felt that there must be some justification for the comparison. At least, in both he sensed a purpose as strong and as steady as steel. But there were other qualities in her which, he assured himself, never could have been found in Mrs. Rivers at any time in her life. He struggled with this problem of Maizie. She was unlike the delicate women of his books and his thoughts as spider web is different from wire. But there was an electric charge running through that wire. He tingled with it still; it shot through him and made him breathless. In one instant he was vastly intrigued and vastly afraid.

Doc Rivers finished his cigarette, then announced that the cold was too much for him, and that they had better go to bed. So he guided Philip through the house, and up the carpeted, worn stairway, and so to a small attic room where there were two cots.

"I don't rate nothing more'n this," he said gloomily. "You'd think, to hear Ma talk, that I was still a little kid in short pants. She ain't got any understanding of a man!"

"Hasn't she?" asked Philip in amazement. "I thought that she must understand almost everything in the world!"

"You thought so? Well—I dunno. There's a lot of folks that agrees with you."

Doc Rivers at once began to undress, but the room was stuffy with the heat which it had absorbed through the roof all during the hours of sunshine, and it made Philip think with longing of the coolness of the outdoors. Moreover, he had not finished the retasting and summarizing of the events of the day, which had piled so thickly upon him that to untangle them was like untangling a delicate problem.

He went down the stairs and out into the front yard—like a forest with its masses of great trees—and he had barely left the veranda steps when he heard the loud, clear voice of Mrs. Rivers saying: "I dunno. I tell you what I think. You'll never have no luck out of him. Because there ain't any luck in him. If you got a foundered hoss, sell him if you can, shoot him if you can't. Because he'll never do you no good. You cross him off your books. That's all that I can say!"

Philip turned to retreat, but as he did so, Mrs. Rivers and Maizie came clearly into view in the moonlight that poured down among the pines. He felt that he should step forward to announce himself, but he was afraid to do so, because it might look, he thought, as though he had been following them and spying upon them, and their talk seemed to have been of the most private character. Where he stood, the shadow fell steep and thick, and he was certain that he would not be seen. Having hesitated one instant, nothing could have induced him to go forward to confront them.

Maizie, as one in the greatest trouble, closed both her hands together and then pressed them against her breast; she looked up, and the moon gave a sudden transparency to her complexion so that she melted easily into all of Philip's dreams of lovely women.

"There has to be some way out," said Maizie.

The retort of Mrs. Rivers was, as usual, brisk, brief, and to the point.

"You're gunna hang onto this here job until you make a fool of yourself. Maizie, quit it. It's man's work!"

"And we have no man to do it," said Maizie in the quiet of despair.

At that, a mad impulse came to Philip. He wanted to dash forward and say in a ringing voice: "Perhaps God has sent me to you! Let me try to work for you. I may not be strong enough, but I shall try!"

However, he was instantly shuddering with embarrassment at the very thought of surrendering to such a bold impulse.

"What can you do?" asked Mrs. Rivers bluntly. "You can't take your job to the sheriff. Well, that rules the law out of it, I guess."

"It does," said Maizie. "I'd have to trust to a friend."

Said the virago: "It'd be a pretty good friend that would stick himself up agin the whole Purchase crew. Oh, Maizie, when you see you're beat, throw down your cards. Don't bet on 'em. Don't chase good money after lost money. Be a sport and take your licking."

"I could do that," said the girl. "I could do that as well as the next one, but I'm not going to quit while Jolly's life is at stake."

"Why doesn't the fool cut and run for it?" asked Mrs. Rivers.

"Because he thinks that after he leaves, the Purchase clan will come down on us."

"Would his being there keep them from coming?" asked Mrs. Rivers tersely.

"I know that it ain't logical," admitted Maizie. "But there's some things that you can't be logical about."

"I don't know what they are," responded the older woman bluntly. "But tell me what you hope? Now you just tell me why you come over here, will you?"

"Because I wanted to get advice from you, dear Aunt Agnes!"

"Dear Aunt Agnes your foot," said Mrs. Rivers. "You come over here because you think that maybe Doc could help you out of the pinch."

"Skinny?" cried the girl in certain, scornful tones.

"You see that's a joke, don't you?" chuckled Mrs. Rivers. "And it *is* a joke. But you didn't know that for sure until you looked at him at my supper table tonight and saw for yourself how thin he'd flatten out if the Purchass gang landed on top of him. He'd be so thin, honey, that you could use him for gold leaf—except that he ain't made of that metal!"

She began to laugh at this thought of her own, and her laughter reminded Philip horribly of the braying of a mule.

Maizie laughed a little, too.

"You're too hard on Skinny," she said. "But after all, you're right. He wouldn't do for the job. And I *did* have him sort of in mind when I rode over."

Mrs. Rivers put her arm around the shoulders of the girl.

"I love you, honey," said her harsh voice, "because you're honest to me, though you're a lyin' little devil to the rest of the world."

"Tell me," said Maizie suddenly, "what about the new one?"

"Who?" asked Mrs. Rivers. "That Philip? That high-headed young fool?"

CHAPTER XIII

In one instant the heart of Philip had leaped into his mouth; in the next it had sunk again like lead, until it remained as a cold lump in his throat. He had been picked up—and cast away instantly as worthless junk.

He hoped that the girl would come at least one step to his defense and he was not mistaken.

"I don't know," she said thoughtfully. "I don't know. Did you hear what Skinny said?"

"About him licking the two Chisholms? I heard it. I tell you, my honey lamb, that nobody ever licked two of the Chisholms on one day. Nobody!"

"Skinny said so, and I believe him!"

Mrs. Rivers shook her head; then she argued the matter with some subtlety with herself.

"If he was good enough to lick the pair of them— which ain't hardly possible—then he's just what I told you —a high-headed young fool!"

Phillip was worried by the expression. He could understand fool, well enough, and he would have been the first to agree that he was most ignorant of the world and of its ways; but he didn't understand what "high-headed" could mean. It was explained almost at once, for the girl asked: "Did you ever see a more humble sort of a boy than Philip? I watched him. He was pink all over when Skinny told what he had done."

Mrs. Rivers snorted.

"And I don't see," said the girl, "why you call him high-headed. He could hardly raise his head out of his plate during all of suppertime."

She laughed, a little scornfully, and that one touch of scorn from her hurt the boy more than all the bludgeoning which he had received from the lips of Mrs. Rivers.

The latter began to explain with her usual terseness:

"What's a high-headed horse?" she demanded.

"A fool that can't work," said the girl readily enough.

"That don't mean it can't move?"

"No. They often have plenty of foot."

"Well, they have too much spirit, I'd say."

"Maybe they have."

"That's this new boy."

"But he hardly could look up."

"You listen, my girl. You got to give him the spur to start him. After that, he won't work. He won't cut out cows for you. He'll run away and smash you into a tree. He'll break your neck."

"I don't see how you make that out!" murmured Maizie, thinking with a dark brow.

"Well, I'll tell you. How big are the Chisholms?"

"Oh, I know them. They're brutes, of course."

"Does he look fit to handle even one of 'em?"

"No, no. Of course not. But looks—"

"They don't tell all that's in a man?"

"No."

"You bet they don't," exclaimed Mrs. Rivers, and slapped Maizie heavily and loudly on the shoulder, so that the girl began to rub the stinging spot.

"You bet they don't," repeated the older woman. "Now, if he's got enough in him to handle one of the Chisholms, I call it wonderful. I'd call him a man."

"So would I. You think just the way that I do."

"But look here—is he very big?"

"He has a pair of shoulders!"

"Sure he has. So have the Chisholms. I tell you, if he could beat the pair of them, then he's more'n a man. He's a devil."

"All right," said Maizie, shrugging her shoulders. "All right. *I* think he could be driven with silk threads."

"Most men are fools," said Mrs. Rivers. "*All* girls are. Now listen here: I know men. I paid for my knowing. I paid forty-five thousand dollars for it. And I've been working like an idiot day and night ever since I put my man in a grave trying to make back what he lost for me. I know men; I've paid for the knowing. I tell you this: steer clear of that kid with his baby eyes. He'll wreck you."

"I don't think he will—I don't think he's too hard to be handled!"

"You sassy young flirt!" exclaimed Mrs. Rivers. "D'you know more than me?"

"No, no, Aunt Agnes!"

"Well, then, take my word for it. He's dangerous. He's too dangerous for you to be handling him. You keep away from him. That's all I'll say."

"But suppose that he could save my poor Jolly?"

"He might save him; he'd break him before he got home like a bad egg. That's what Jolly is. He's a bad egg."

"Aunt Agnes, I won't let you say that to me!"

"Now you got your blood up. Your family's sacred, is

it? Well, I'm sorry for you! Good night, Maizie. You make me tired. I gunna go to bed! Come along."

"I'll stay out here a while."

"What you gunna do? Wait for one of the punchers? You gunna hold the hand of one of the boys?"

"Aunt Agnes, you make me out a—"

"No, I don't. But I know. I was young once, though I never had your face, thank God. What I picked up was bad enough, after all!"

She turned her back on her companion and then stamped away for the house, the gravel grinding loudly under her heels. Maizie looked after her with a short little, soundless laugh. Then she disappeared among the trees.

A cold muzzle touched the hand of Philip, and he looked down at the great head of Loafer. The dog slipped out ahead of him, as though urging him to take up the trail of the foe but Philip merely smiled at him sadly and beckoned him back. There was a great misery in his heart. It chiefly concerned Jolly, for he feared that Maizie was married and that this was the name of her husband. And yet he would not face the reason that made him fear she was wedded.

He turned away through the woods, wandering blindly, trying to think, but never managing to. Pictures took the place of thoughts. He kept seeing Maizie in the moonlight; he kept hearing her voice. He was soothed and excited.

Out of that darkness of the mind, he suddenly came upon a sound of muffled sorrow; someone was sobbing. He passed through a single row of poplars, silver-bright and polished in the moonshine, and there he saw a girl seated on a log with her head buried in her arms. He knew it was Maizie by the paleness of her hair, and by the roundness of the back of her neck; and he was filled with foolish delight and with foolish fear.

Even then he would have turned back—or thought he would—but Loafer slipped ahead and sniffed at her dress, and growled. So she looked up, and then she sprang to her feet.

"Hello, hello!" said Maizie. "I must of fallen asleep. That's a silly thing, eh? You saved me from pneumonia, maybe! Look," she added, "I was crying in my sleep, too!"

She dashed away the tears with a fine gesture.

"You bet I'd never cry when I was awake," said Maizie. "Ask the world, and they'll tell you!"

Philip could not speak. He thought it was the bravest and the very finest thing that ever he had found—outside of a book. Well, books grew less important, after a time!

"I'm going in," said the girl. "Thanks for wakin' me up. Or should I thank your dog?"

She tossed that over her shoulder and went on towards the house. All that she was pleased Philip. He wanted to stop her at once, but it was a delight to see the way she walked, softly and with a swing—unlike women, surely unlike men as music is unlike the harsh chorusing of a storm in the mountains.

At length he strode beside her.

"Would you stop for a little moment?" asked Philip.

"Sure I will, if you got anything to say," said the girl. "What is it, Phil?"

"I want to say," said Philip, and stuck there, looking down at her. "I want to say," he began again.

"That we were a rough crew at the table, eh? We *are* rough. You gotta get a thick skin around us, Phil!"

He waved that suggestion amiably away.

"I didn't mean that. I meant you——"

At this, he felt he had gone too far, and blushed; but either the moonlight covered his hot color, or else she was too earnest to notice such a small thing.

"Something's bothering you," said the girl. "All right. I'll listen. All the boys tell me their troubles," she went on. "What's bothering you, old son?"

"You are," said the grave Philip.

"I?" said the girl, and lifted her eyebrows. He saw that he had blundered and wished mightily that he could have said something else, but he seemed in too deep to be saved. She, however, was wonderfully kind.

"Have I stepped on your toes?" she asked him gently. "I'd be sorry about that. Because I like you, Phil."

"Do you?" cried Philip. "Do you really like me?"

"Of course I do," said the girl. "Why not?"

"How wonderful," said Philip, "and how strange."

"Not a bit. Because you look like a straight-goer, to me. I hate the boys that interfere. I like to see 'em run straight."

"I don't understand," said Philip.

"It's just English," said she, "or it ought to be."

"Will you be patient, then, and let me try to explain?" he asked her. "I have not talked with many people; I don't know a great deal."

"You go ahead," she encouraged him. "Patient is my name. Maizie Patient or Patient Maizie is what they call me, or what they ought to call me. Go on, old hoss."

"If you will try to understand, I must begin at the first."

"You go right ahead."

"It began at the table, this evening," said Philip. "It gave me so much happiness to look at you!"

CHAPTER XIV

AT this, she drew back from him a step and frowned.

"Hello, hello!" said Maizie. "What's coming now?"

"I beg your pardon," appealed Philip. "I don't know how to talk to you!"

"Don't?" she asked, in what appeared to him to be a most suspicious voice. "I dunno. You seem to me to get right on. What comes next?"

"Afterwards," said he, "I could not go to sleep. The room was warm."

"Skinny's room is a kennel," she agreed.

"I came out to walk. I thought I was coming to enjoy the cool sweet air. But I'm afraid that I was only walking out to think about you."

"Am I a kind of a puzzle, maybe?" asked Maizie.

"You're so beautiful," said Philip.

"I'm which?" she gasped. "All right, all right!"

"Have I said something wrong again?" he asked.

"Do you always start right in leading trumps?" inquired Maizie.

"I don't know what you mean," replied Philip.

"There goes the joker," remarked Maizie. "Aces wild, I suppose."

"Shall I stop?"

"Not a bit," said Maizie. "I enjoy it a lot. It's different."

"Thank you," said Philip. "I was thinking of your beauty, and of your lovely voice."

"Well, well, well!" broke in Maizie.

"I beg your pardon?"

"You go so fast we'll be in town before we have a chance to enjoy the ride. But go right ahead, Phil. Where did you learn to work?"

"I was raised on Pillar Mountain; my uncle taught me everything," said he.

"I'd like to meet the gay old boy," nodded she.

"He's really a sad and quiet man," said Philip.

"Sure he is; sure he is!" murmured she. "I wouldn't doubt you for a minute, Philip. So am I on Mondays. You were doing a lot of thinking—you left off there—shall we sit down here on this rock?"

"I'm afraid you'd catch cold," said Philip earnestly.

"You're which?" echoed she.

"Did you understand me?" he asked.

"I did," she replied, "but they wouldn't believe this in church. Go on, Phil. I don't know where you're going, but I love your footwork."

He sighed, and then he shook his head. Nearly everything was quite beyond him. It was like listening to a foreign language.

"While I was thoughtful, and not seeing things before me very clearly, all at once I heard two voices—and you and Mrs. Rivers—"

"What! Were you there?"

"I want to explain," cried Philip. "At first I was about to step forward; I don't want to be an eavesdropper. But somehow, I hadn't the courage to step forward. I'm afraid I'm very timid before women!"

"You are? I'd never say so. I think you're a hero," said the girl.

71

"I don't understand you," replied Philip.

"I knew you wouldn't," replied she. "But go ahead. You stood there and listened to the whole talk?"

"Can you forgive me?"

"You got roasted and salted down by Mrs. Rivers, didn't you?"

"Of course she doesn't know me," remarked Philip. "But I'm not thinking of what she said about me. I was thinking, on the contrary, of your own difficulties."

"You talk just like a book, Phil," said she.

"I'm sorry," he protested.

"I like it," said she. "It's a good book, I think. I like the way that it starts."

"I could not help hearing," he went on, hot of face, and gripping his hands, but determined to go through to the end, "I could not help hearing that you were in great trouble, and that you were intensely worried about a Mr. Jolly who is, I presume, very ill——"

Maizie began to laugh. And Philip stopped to listen. He was rather angry. He was sure it was very rude of her, and yet he was delighted with that low, rather husky laughter. It floated into his very soul.

"Jolly's my kid brother," said she. "I mean——he's older, but he's just a crazy kid. Go on!"

"I'm glad he's your brother!" said Philip with ardor.

"You are? Why?"

"Because I thought he might be your——I——I mean I thought——"

"Go on, Phil. Don't stop for the little things. What are you driving at?"

Then he managed to say briefly: "You seemed to be in great trouble; and only a moment ago I found you crying——"

"In my sleep!" she protested.

"Yes, yes. I beg your pardon. I didn't mean to question what you——I——"

"You found me crying. What's the next step?"

"I hoped that if I offered my service to you, you might be persuaded to use me, if you think that I could help!"

At this, she interlaced her fingers and stared up at him for a long time, until the moonlit face and the great shadows of the eyes began to trouble the very heart of Philip.

"You got me beat," said the girl.

"I hope not," murmured he.

"You're all by yourself," she went on. "I'd need a magic carpet to keep up with you. Phil, are you offering yourself to ride along and help me in my trouble?"

"Nothing," said Philip, "would make me so happy as to think that I was making you happy—I mean to say—"

"You say it beautifully," she answered. "But wait a minute—I don't want to be a wolf."

"A wolf?"

"Or a golddigger."

He was bewildered.

"You know the Purchass crew, do you?"

"I never have heard of them."

"Did you say that you lived in the mountains, Phil?"

"Oh, yes."

"And you never heard of the Purchass tribe?"

"No."

"You never even heard of the Colonel, I suppose?" she asked ironically.

"I don't know what colonel you mean," said he.

"But there's only one!"

"Colonel Purchass?"

"Let it go, then! Let it go! But I'll try to tell you about the Purchass people. Let's begin at the Chisholms. You know them?"

"I've only met them once," said Philip.

"You've only—well," murmured the girl, "you *are* all by yourself. But what did you think of them?"

"I'm afraid that I didn't like them very well."

"You didn't like them? Nobody ever liked them. Not even in Sunday school. They're too bad even to pray for. Weren't they a pair of devils?"

"They frightened me very much," admitted Philip.

At this, she stared again; and finally she began to nod.

"It looks like we can do business," she said. "But all the money will be on your side. All we can put in will be good will and the naming of the ropes."

73

"I try to follow you," explained Philip in despair, "but I don't seem able to."

"I'll cut it short, Phil. The Chisholms bother you. But they're just a pair that belong to the Purchass tribe."

"Belong to them?" he echoed.

"That's it. Body and Soul. Slaves. Worse. They go to old man Purchass and ask can they be allowed to draw breath."

"It seems very strange," said Philip.

"Strange? It's worse. It's a nightmare. Well, Phil, the Purchass crew is after Jolly; and that's why I came over here. I didn't think there'd be any help here. But I just had to come. I couldn't sit home any longer. I was getting dizzy, I was so scared!"

"Yes!" said Philip, his heart beginning to swell.

And all at once she threw out her hands to him, and she pressed them against his breast.

"I love dear Jolly!" she said. "Because he never was any good—he was always so crazy—everybody loves dear old Jolly!"

Philip trembled violently.

"He is your brother," he said huskily, "and I'm sure that I would like him very much."

"They're after Jolly! They're after Jolly!" she repeated in a frenzy, though she kept her voice low by dint of clenching her teeth, "and I'm not going to let them get him!"

"I want to help you!" said he.

"Dear Phil, I love you for saying that!"

He trembled more violently than ever; and a blur of darkness swam across the moon; his heart was a small triphammer, striking rapidly and regularly in the center of his forehead.

"I'm only one, though," he suggested.

"One good man—one great man can do anything," she said. "The Colonel might beat them. But he costs too much. We couldn't hire him. He costs too much."

"There's the law of the country!" urged Philip.

"The law wants Jolly almost as bad as the Purchass people want him!"

74

Then she explained hastily: "It's too long to tell. I can tell you the whole story tomorrow. But if I talk it out now, it'll make me despair again. I want to go to bed and dream about you, Phil. I want to dream about you riding over with me—"

"I'll have to walk," said Philip. "I have no horse. I hope that won't spoil everything!"

"You—," she began, and then, as had happened before during the odd interview, she seemed to be stopped by some extraneous force.

"Nobody!" she repeated with conviction, "Nobody near you—all out by yourself!"

Then she added: "Will you wait till the morning to hear the whole story?"

"I'll do anything that you wish," said he.

They walked down the winding, half-made walk through the trees and towards the house. One light sparkled from the front of it, shining dimly through the moonlight.

"You're terribly silent, Phil. You're not beginning to change your mind about this?" she asked suddenly, her hand pressing his arm.

"Ah, no. I was thinking of something else!"

"Of what?" she insisted.

"Of you," said the boy, "and of how glorious and how noble and how good you are!"

"Wait a minute!" said she.

He stopped and she made him face her, saying: "Look me in the eyes!"

And he obeyed her until presently she exclaimed: "Good heavens!"

"Is something wrong?" asked Philip nervously.

Instead of replying, she turned and hurried on towards the house. Only at the veranda steps she paused sharply.

"May I say good night?" he asked her.

At this, her faintly mocking chuckle returned to her.

"It all depends," said she, "but it's a pretty large night. I suppose you may."

He leaned and raising her hand, he pressed it to his lips.

"Good night," said Philip.

"Good heavens," said the girl again, and she went slowly up the steps, looking back at him as though she were very much afraid.

He wondered what he had done that was wrong, and he stood with one foot on the lowest step, looking after her, with one hand pressed against his heart, for there was a great pain of sorrow aching in it.

CHAPTER XV

PHILIP, on his knees until his bones were aching, said all three of Oliver Aytoun's prayers over and over again. He hardly knew the words that were passing through his lips, but the whisper seemed to drain the anguish from his breast, and at last he had peace.

He did not undress. He lay down, wrapped the blanket around him, and watched the moonlight pressing softly through the skylight, gleaming on the varnished back of the chair, and on the tangle of clothes which Doc Rivers had flung upon the floor. Then he would close his eyes and recapture the moments of the evening second by second.

All the day, which had seemed so crowded with gigantic images, now drew far away, as though long years and oceans lay between it and the evening which had followed. Nothing really mattered except the music of Maizie's voice and the trees, as they had stood beneath the moon, and how she had looked in profile, delicately made. And how when her chin was raised. And how when she turned her head and smiled. And how, going up the steps, when she looked back to him, afraid.

Afraid of him!

One moment he could have laughed aloud, joyously, at that. And the next moment he was wretched. He felt that he could not dare to face her the next day. He had talked like a fool.

At last, after long hours, he drowsed. Finally his

shoulder was shaken, and he wakened to find that the dawn was there, and Doc Rivers leaning above him.

"Wake up, kid. Wake up. I been calling you for half an hour and all you been saying is: 'I want to help!' You want to help what?"

Philip sat up and rubbed his eyes.

"I'd better get a plunge into some water. Is there a creek near the house?" he asked.

"Wait a minute. You didn't undress. You look white. You been sick?"

"No," said Philip. "I don't think so."

"You have, though. How's your stomach?"

"It's quite all right, thank you."

"Got a headache, then?"

"No, I never have them."

"Rheumatism, by jiminy! That's from sitting out yonder on the veranda in the evening air. You're soft, kid, in spite of your muscle!"

"I haven't any rheumatism," Philip assured him.

The other scratched his tousled head.

"Ah," he said, very serious, now. "You've got a bit of a bad heart! That's it! D'you feel faint?"

"No, no," murmured Philip. "I'm really all right."

His host stood away, frowning, thoughtful.

"What you do after I went to bed?"

"I just took a little walk."

The voice of Doc changed suddenly.

"You took a little walk, did you? Where?"

"Why—just among the trees, you know."

"Meet anybody—just among the trees?"

"Why—ah—" drawled Philip in confusion.

"You met—why—ah, did you? Hell, is that it?"

And he dropped the subject abruptly, to Philip's great relief.

A bathtub he refused; but in the creek he found the pool and spent fifteen minutes driving himself through the water until his brain was clear, his eyes sharp, and his heart freed from the soft, persistent aching which annoyed him.

After he had shaved and dressed, he came back to meet Doc and they went in to breakfast, together. The punchers had had their breakfast, for there was work on a distant part of the range. Only the girl, Mrs. Rivers, and the two men sat down together.

To Mrs. Rivers, Philip was able to speak. To the girl, he was only able to murmur meaningless sounds. And then he sat down with his eyes riveted upon his plate.

Conversation, for some moments, lagged. Then Doc Rivers began it.

"Maizie!" he said.

"What you want?"

"You toad!" said he.

"You're another," she replied with ready courtesy.

"You tree-toad!"

"You long-billed butcher bird," said she.

"You chicken hawk!" said he. "Look what you went and done!"

Maizie was silent. At last she said: "Don't go and be a fool, Doc."

"No? I'm gunna, though. I'm gunna talk, me proud beauty!"

"I hate you, Skinny," said she.

"As if you didn't have enough!" said he.

Philip began to sit stiff and straight, his jaw set hard.

"Oh, quit your jawing, will you, you two?" asked Mrs. Rivers.

"It's Maizie," said Doc. "As if she ain't had her hands full. She's gotta have the world with a fence around it. She makes me sick!"

"Don't bother me," said the girl, and Philip noticed with compassion that she was growing flushed.

"She always did make me sick," reiterated Doc Rivers.

"Leave her be, Skinny," said his blunt mother. "You'll be getting in trouble, in a minute."

"Men ain't enough. She wants veal and lamb," declared Doc bitterly.

"Mr. Rivers!" exclaimed Philip suddenly. "May I ask you to step outside with me a moment?"

"I told you so," said Mrs. Rivers to her son, and yawned largely, without making any futile attempt to mask her weariness with the world and with that conversation in particular.

Doc made no reply, but he pointed excitedly at Philip, while continuing his attack upon Maizie.

"Look what you went and done!" he said.

"Skinny," said the girl, angrily, "you're wrong—you—you—I simply hate you, Skinny—"

"You baby thief!" cried Doc Rivers.

"You're simply contemptible!" said the girl. "I won't sit another minute at the table with you—"

And she started to her feet.

Philip rose also. Dreadful rage mastered him; his breast was heaving; his hand he laid upon the bony shoulder of Doc.

"Mr. Rivers," he repeated, "I have something to say to you—outside—"

Still Doc with extraordinary indifference merely shrugged, snapping:

"There you are! You see for yourself! Now sneak out, and let him murder me!"

"I hope he does!" cried the girl, now brightest red, and trembling visibly. "I hope he has!"

She fled to the door.

"What's more," shouted Doc, "he will! He's gunna do it now!"

At the door she turned, hesitant.

"Phil," she said suddenly, "don't be an idiot! Leave him alone!"

And she hurried away.

Philip sat down suddenly in his chair. The madness was struck from his heart and his brain.

"I beg your pardon," he said in the faintest of voices. "I seem to have— I beg your pardon, Mrs. Rivers. I beg your pardon, also, Mr. Rivers—I—the fact is—"

"Aw, go on and eat your breakfast," said Mrs. Rivers.

He could not take that advice. He sat miserably, perspiration dripping down his face. Mrs. Rivers and her son looked steadily at one another.

"Aw, say something, Ma, will you?" said he.

She nodded, and turned her gaze on Philip.

"Don't take no notice of them two," she advised. "They're always clawing at each other's throats. Don't bother about 'em. I never do!"

Philip passd a hand across his brow.

He looked with haunted, wounded eyes at Doc Rivers, and the latter suddenly reached out and clapped him on the shoulder.

"You're all right, kid," he said, "but there's a lot of things that you don't understand."

"Ah, yes," said Philip from his heart of hearts. "How true that is!"

Suddenly Maizie was back in the room.

"You oughta be ashamed, Skinny," she said sweetly. "I'm sorry I spoke that way, Phil. You forgive me?"

And she smiled upon him.

"Look at her," groaned Doc. "Right in the broad daylight. There ain't no shame about a tiger!"

Philip, standing as one stricken, felt the wild pain shoot again through his heart, and with his right hand pressed against it, he strove to drive that pain away.

"Ah, yes," said Philip. "I forgive you!"

CHAPTER XVI

To Philip it seemed impossible that the stern Mrs. Rivers ever should notice him, but he was surprised when she came up to him on her way out of the house, after breakfast. She was ready to mount and ride; no man, it was said, covered more leagues of range during the year than Mrs. Rivers. So, riding whip in hand, she approached Philip and said briskly: "Maizie tells me that you're riding over with her to her house. Now you go slow, young fellow, and maybe you'll have luck."

With this rather enigmatic expression, she walked away; and Philip was flattered, for she had noticed him, and at least not unfavorably.

He did not have a great chance to ponder upon this happy state of affairs, for presently the sheriff and his returning posse swept up to the house. He had failed to keep the trail of the fugitive of the morning before and he was tired and angry, and all of his men with him. Doc Rivers buttonholed him, so to speak, at once, and strove to put oil on very troubled waters. It was a difficult task, for the sheriff was of opinion that it would be an excellent thing to let young Philip go to jail and meditate there on the evils of this world until something was learned about a possible past connection between him and Joe Dorman. The sheriff was greatly excited. And when Doc protested at length, Philip heard the man of the law say: "You never get something out of nothing. He cleaned up the Chisholms, didn't he? Where did he learn that sort of business, I ask you?"

"Look here, Jeremiah," said Doc Rivers, "if he was that wild he could handle me, couldn't he?"

"He could, son."

"And he didn't. I mean, he stayed right in my hands, and he's here now, pantin' with eagerness to throw himself on the broad breast of the law, you chicken thief! Go and take him, if you want him. He ain't even carryin' a gun."

The sheriff hesitated, and then he scratched his head.

"You're an ornery devil, Doc," he admitted, "but I guess you're right. Only tell the kid that I'm watching him. I got a lot of doubts about him. That's all!"

So the sheriff disappeared, and Doc Rivers came back to his friend.

"The old man has his eyes on you, Phil," said he. "If you blink an eye at anybody, he'll be after you. So watch those two hands of yours. You understand?"

Philip looked aimlessly down at his hands. Yet, in a way, he understood, and said so.

"And now," went on Doc Rivers, "we gotta talk about something else. You start with Maizie. Is that the plan?"

"It is," admitted Philip.

"And who goes as your guardian?"

"Why," said Philip, "I don't understand that!"

"I'd rather," said Doc Rivers, "expose a doggone baby to the hot sun than you to that tiger. Hold on—don't get hot! No, kid, if you go to the house of Maizie Delmar, I go along with you two."

"That," said Philip, "would be delightful."

"I'm gunna go break the good news to Maizie," said Doc Rivers. "This'll make her talk French."

Maizie he found sitting on a corral fence smoking a cigarette and looking over a number of saddle horses.

"Look at that gray," said she.

"I see it," answered Doc.

"You say that the kid ain't ever rode a thing but a mule?"

"That's what he told me."

"D'you think he could sit on that gray?"

"I dunno. It looks peaceful. Got any mean tricks?"

"Hoists up behind a few times in the morning, just to get warm, but that's nothing."

"Nothing to you, honey," said Doc. "Nothing to a string of rawhide and tanned leather like you, but it might bust the kid's neck."

She turned her head languidly and looked him up and down.

"Run along, Skinny," said she. "You bother me."

"I'm gunna bother you more," he answered. "You're takin' the kid away, I hear?"

"I am, and what's it to you?" she said without turning her head.

"Nothing, except that you're taking me, too."

"A mouse with the elephant, eh?"

"What d'you mean by that?"

"Look in your third reader and you'll find out. If you can read that far! No, Skinny, I won't take you. You gotta pay admission to come in to this circus."

"I'm gunna come along," said Skinny. "The kid is under my wing."

"Hum!" said the girl. "I think the gray ought to do. If it's up to his weight. You stay home, Skinny."

"Look here," said Doc. "If you had a son, would you send him into a place where there was yellow fever ragin'—and let him go alone?"

"I'm yellow fever, am I?" asked the girl.

"I was just makin' a comparison," said Doc. "I don't mean to say that you're like yellow fever. I wouldn't be that unfair to the fever."

"You had a right good touch of me yourself," said Maizie, yawning at this idle chatter.

"I never been the same man since," he replied.

"You never was a man, Skinny; don't kid yourself," answered the girl. "But you stay home."

"Not unless you can ride him away faster than I can follow."

Here she confronted him, slipping down from the fence rail.

"You mean that?"

"Listen, Maizie, do I ever talk to you unless I have to?"

"You're trying to spoil this for me!" she exclaimed.

"He was born simple," explained Skinny. "He never had no education. And you're gunna step out and scalp him, now! You ask me why I'm gunna go along? To give him chloroform and put him out of pain, when the right time comes."

She bit her lip, eyeing him with bright disdain.

"Saddle up three hosses, then," said she. "That's mine; that pinto mare. You make me tired, Skinny!"

So it was that Maizie surrendered, but dark were the glances she cast at Doc Rivers when the three at last rode forth. Philip, his eyes starting, his face pale, clutched the gray horse hard with his knees, but that mustang went along smoothly enough until it came to a white stone lying near the trail. There are some horses that feel they must have an excuse, however small, before they begin to make trouble, and the gray was one of them. As he reached the stone he leaped wildly into the air, landed on stiff legs, and then spun like a top. Philip was hurled through a prickly bush and got up with ten thousand stinging little cuts imprinted on his face and hands and body. But he caught the gray and mounted again.

"Catch the fool mustang by the head," called Maizie. "Don't let him buck again, Doc!"

"He'd better have it out," suggested Philip. "That was always the way with the roan mule. He had to get his bucking done before he'd do his day's work!"

So saying, since he lacked a whip, he struck the gray with a stick which he held and the mustang promptly obliged with an intricate bit of fence-rowing, followed by some lofty sun-fishing. Twice or thrice Philip was more on the air than on the horse, but he managed with a little luck to keep in his place. After all, it was not as bad as the roan mule; and when the gray settled down as suddenly as it had begun, he whacked it again. There was only a switching of the tail and a tossing of the head, while the gray broke into a canter.

The girl and Doc closed in together and pursued.

"You said that he couldn't ride!" she said fiercely. "What stuff have you been telling me, Skinny?"

"What stuff has he been telling me?" retorted Doc Rivers. "He's deep. That's all. He's deep!"

But thereafter they worked briskly ahead on the trail and Philip began to enjoy that morning's ride more than anything he had ever done in his life. The morning chill was still in the air; all the forests were hung with gold, or with withering tan, and deep in the heart of the woods something of the night mist remained, like the breathing of dragons from a fairy tale.

They cut across the broad heart of the valley, and the road carried them, now, past big fields, sometimes dark with summer fallow and sometimes golden with unharvested grain, or bright gray-yellow with the stubble. Philip saw houses covered to the eaves, as it were, in wrappings of vines, often with half the leaves fallen, so that they looked like broken veils. All those houses were substantially built, with dormer windows and with gables of an old fashion, for prosperity had been long in the valley, and there had been time for the fence posts to begin to blacken and break, and the rusted wire hung in great sags, or tangled into knots. The surface of the wooden culverts was worn to long, soft splinters which gave up a deadened sound as the hoofs of the horses trampled across them.

All of this was pleasant to the eye of Philip. Even the wreckage of the Bad Lands would have pleased him, in fact, for Maizie was with them! She rode with a little smile, her head tilted up. It was the proud head of youth, it was the mysterious smile of a beautiful girl. Philip was in the land of pure enchantment.

"Skinny," she said at last, "you'd better tell Phil about Jolly."

"Had I better? I had better not," replied Doc Rivers. "You can tell the pretty story yourself. Then maybe you can work up to a happy ending, but doggone me if I can see him living happy ever after!"

"All right," said the girl. "I'll tell the story. I want you to know, Phil, that everyone always has loved Jolly. Because he was always straight and fair in everything, and honest, and upstanding. Oh, Phil, there never was really a better-hearted boy than dear old Jolly and—"

"Aw quit it, will you?" broke in Doc Rivers.

"Quit what?"

"Hold on a minute, and I'll tell you the truth about Jolly Delmar."

CHAPTER XVII

Doc Rivers sighed, after having delivered this announcement. He whistled to Loafer, running ahead of them, and the great dog turned and snarled with white-flashing teeth.

"Pleasant, ain't he?" grinned Doc Rivers. "Well, about old Jolly. He looks something like Maizie."

"Ah!" said Philip.

"Kind of good looking, like her," said Doc Rivers. "Better looking, maybe. I mean, his nose ain't pushed up so much at the end. And his mouth don't look so big."

"Are you gunna tell this story about me or about Jolly?" asked the girl sharply.

"I gotta sort of mix the two of you together," said Doc Rivers, with a malevolent smile. "You sort of illustrate each other; there ain't another pair like you!"

She stirred uneasily in the saddle.

"Just leave my face out of it, will you, Skinny?"

"I can't without leaving out his. All right, kid. We'll leave Jolly with a nose and a mouth, because his sister don't want him to have anything more. Well, Jolly had a happy kind of a way about him. Like Maizie. The difference is that Maizie puts on her good nature and takes it off again like a hat. She puts it on when she wants to get out o' the sun; she takes it off when there ain't anything to gain by being happy. You can see the wrinkle coming there beside her mouth—"

"I see a dimple," said Philip earnestly.

"You're a little cockeyed," remarked Doc. "But to go on with Jolly: he was remarkably good-natured and cheerful. Folks could get along with him, and pretty often they couldn't get along without him. Especially the girls. He was terrible popular with the girls, kid. They come to him so fast that he had to keep changing them every week, so that there would be enough Jolly to go all around the circle. Just the same with Maizie, here, and the boys."

"Will you leave me out?" asked Maizie angrily.

"I can't," said Doc. "I gotta use you for an example, so's the kid can see Jolly before he lays eyes on him. Of course everybody has been in love with Maizie," continued Doc Rivers. "I was, once. Everybody's been. She don't mind, do you, Maizie?"

Maizie merely sighed, and she turned a saddened pair of eyes towards Philip.

"Will you believe him, Phil?" she asked.

"Oh, no," said Philip. "Of course I won't believe him, if you—"

"If she tells you not to?" broke in Doc. "Don't be a fool in the broad daylight, kid. Now listen about Jolly. He grew up as big as most men and as strong. He could ride as well, shoot as straight, hit as hard, run as fast, as most folks. There was only one thing that he didn't take to. That was work. He didn't somehow fancy it."

"Like you, Skinny," put in the girl.

"Ay," said Skinny shamelessly, "just like me. I like to sit in the sun, but Jolly likes to sit in the lamplight. A dance program fitted Jolly's hand better than a rope, and a waxed floor was smoother going than a new-broke

86

mustang. But at that kind of a thing he was never likely to give up. He went to all the dances in fifty mile of the valley. All around this here range for the last ten years there ain't been any conversation among the girls except what Jolly has said, what Jolly has done; 'Jolly wrote his name right here on my program; ain't Jolly the sweetest thing!' Same way with Maizie. Who's makin' love to Maizie now?"

"Poor old Skinny," said Maizie. "That's his way of making fun, Phil. He can't tell a joke from an axe handle. You gotta get used to him. But he never does no harm around here, except with strangers that take him seriously."

"Well," went on Doc, unperturbed, "somehow you can't get rich holding a girl's hand and telling her that you been looking for her everywhere, and at last you've come home. Jolly has worked up callouses holding hands, but it didn't do. Poor Jolly. Then he decided that maybe there was a short cut, and he tried cards, but the cards wouldn't work for him. He got so's he could run up a pack pretty well, but he always met somebody that could stack better than him, and so he'd go bust and have to come home for a fresh start!"

"Doc," cried the girl, "you really are a coward to say that behind Jolly's back. He never played a dishonest card in his life, and you know it!"

"And every time he went home," continued Rivers, "doggone me if they didn't lead out a fatted calf and skin it for him. There was nothing too much that they could do for him, and they wouldn't sit down and tell him that he was a damn fool, because they might hurt poor Jolly's feelings, and how much better it was for Jolly to go right straight to hell than to have him see that though he was traveling fast, he was going down hill, every lick of the way! So Jolly kept getting broker and broker, and it's been about five years since anybody but his old man would lend him any money. Jolly was pretty expensive for his pa. Old man Delmar had to sell the southeast quarter section, and Jolly took another whole year to run through that—"

"It isn't true," cried Maizie, "but poor dear Jolly wanted to work out a scheme for—"

"For milking tourists and suckers, and it didn't work. So Jolly had to try something else, and he began to sell gold mines on the desert where there was plenty of sand, but no gold. But even that didn't bring in any money, and old man Delmar, he sold off the northeast quarter section, too."

"There isn't a word of truth in that," exclaimed the girl. "You know perfectly well it was that scoundrel Ralph Mills that got Jolly into that game!"

"And," went on Rivers, "things run along like this until about a month ago, when young Jim Purchass, he found that his girl was forgetting him because Jolly had smiled at her and let her kiss his hand."

"You contemptible creature, Skinny," cried the girl. "Poor old Jolly! If he only knew—"

Philip looked from one of them to the other.

It was much too complicated for him; he only managed to follow the main drift of the narrative and gather that there were two sides to the character of this interesting brother of Maizie.

"Jim Purchass," went on the speaker, "finally asked Jolly to go out for a walk with him. And they rode out together. Jolly says that they got real friendly, and that they soon were exchanging guns and trying snapshots at jack rabbits and what not. But in the middle of the fun, Jim tried a fancy double-roll and shot himself through the heart. And the unlucky thing was that the gun that he shot himself with was Jolly's old forty-four.

"Jolly come in and told the story, and laid down the body of Jim on the steps of the post office, in town, but he didn't dare to take him to the Purchass house, because that Purchass tribe shoot first and ask afterwards.

"However, there was questions asked by other than the Purchass folks, and the sheriff particular wanted to have his say to Jolly. But Jolly thought it would be better to talk later on and get in some mileage first. Because if he stood his trial, mind you, he'd simply be sitting pretty for the Purchass folks to take a few shots at him. And their shots don't miss! You begin to see through the little puzzle, kid? If he stays to square himself by the law, some Purchass murders him. If he don't stay to clear himself by the law, the Purchass gang and the sheriff together give him a run for his money."

"I begin to understand," said the boy slowly. "I see what a terrible thing it is! And where is Jolly now?"

"Hanging around his pa's house, most of the time, not daring to come too close, because then the Purchass gang, which it's always watching that house, would be apt to spot him, and turn up his toes for him."

He turned to the girl with a gesture.

"Now what, Maizie? You gotta tell the rest of this story. I've come to the end of my chunk of it."

The girl said eagerly: "They watch our house like hawks. There's no law to keep them away from us. There's no real law at all in this country, except what the Purchass people lay down."

"Or the Colonel," suggested Doc.

"The Colonel's too important to bother much robbing the poor people of this neck of the woods," said the girl. "No, the Purchass outfit are the kings here. The sheriff wants to do what he can, but what can he do? Everybody is afraid of the Purchass outfit with their Dormans and their Chisholms, and what-not."

"Is Mr. Dorman one of them?" asked Philip.

"He's nothing but," said the girl. "But anyway, they always have some of their worst men hanging around our place, asking for trouble. If we dared to try to drive them away, they'd shoot down dad in cold blood!"

"I wonder why they haven't done it before," added Doc Rivers.

"Because our house is the trap where they keep hoping that they'll trap poor Jolly, because they know that he'll always keep trying to come back to us."

"Sure—whenever he gets broke."

"Oh, Doc," cried the girl, "you know that isn't true. He keeps coming back because he loves us, as we love him."

"Ay, ay," admitted Rivers, apparently touched at last with shame. "It's true. Go on, Maizie. What's next?"

"Well, of course Jolly knows that the place is watched, and before he tries to come in to us, he always sends us a signal from one of the hills behind the house—a flash by day with a bit of mirror, or a fire by night. And we got a signal from him not long ago, saying that he expected to come back tomorrow night or tonight."

"Go on, Maizie."

"Well, yesterday morning, instead of one or two of the Purchass outfit, we found four of them hanging around in the woods, and so we pretty well know that they've mastered our code—they know what Jolly sends to us. And they're laying their trap!"

"Why don't you signal back to Jolly that they've got the code?"

"Because we don't know how; we only know that he's walking down into the trap, and our hands are tied unless—"

Here she paused, and slowly she turned her head until her big eyes rested sadly, hopefully, on the face of Philip.

CHAPTER XVIII

ONE could see that fortune had turned her back on the Delmars. The first sight that Philip had of the place was of the broken back of a barn, lifting above the surrounding trees, and when they drew closer they were surrounded by broken fences and even the cattle in the fields looked thin, humpbacked, cheerless, as though they had not enough heart left to keep at their grazing in the fields.

The house itself seemed snug and comfortable enough; it was larger than the ordinary place, and the wide verandas that circled it seemed to be holding out empty arms for guests who long since had stopped coming. As they came up through the trees, Maizie suddenly called out softly and pointed. In the distance they had the merest glimpse of a horseman disappearing in the woods.

"That's one of them," said Maizie. "That's one of the Purchass men."

Philip, full of his purpose, was about to swing the gray in pursuit, but Doc Rivers called him back.

"You'd just be running into a snag," he assured the boy. "He'd hear you coming, and stand behind a tree and drop you. Or else he'd lead you on where three or four more of 'em would be waiting to clean you up. No, kid, you stay with me and don't you go nowhere without me!"

Philip reluctantly obeyed.

They came up to the house, circled past it, and left their horses in a barn, and came up to the place, again, by the back way. A tall man of sixty, lean, narrow shouldered, long-armed, came shambling out on the porch and dropped his hands on his hips.

"Hello, Doc," said he. "Have you come over to be a doggone hero?"

"This kid wants trouble," answered Doc, "and I've come over to hold his coat. This here is Philip, Mr. Delmar."

"I'm mighty glad to see you, young man," said Mr. Delmar. "But I dunno that I quite figure what sort of trouble you look for here?"

"I thought—I mean I hoped—" began Philip.

"He's come to help!" said the girl to her father, with fire in her eye. "And if anybody can help us, Phil can. He's just come to help out of the goodness of his heart."

Mr. Delmar made no return to this speech, except to say: "Lunch'll be ready in about five minutes. You boys can wash up, and then we'll set down and feed. George has some chicken hash comin' up and the smell of it has been plumb tantalizin' me for an hour."

He allowed the two men to go to the pump; he followed Maizie into the house.

"He's a grand old man," Doc Rivers assured his companion, as they pumped water alternately for one another, and snorted as they dashed water over their faces. "Take ten days' ride any direction and you won't meet up with a better man than him. You hear me say it!"

It had a redoubled weight, coming from such a habitual cynic and disbeliever as Doc Rivers, and Philip felt his heart warming. After all, Maizie's father could not help but be an extraordinary man! However, it was certain that

91

Mr. Delmar was a homely fellow, and Philip could not help saying:

"Mrs. Delmar must be a great beauty."

"To make up for the old man, you mean? Mrs. Delmar's dead. She was a lady; her hands wouldn't callous."

With this brief and unsatisfactory answer, he led Philip towards the house, and they entered it with Loafer, as usual, at their heels.

They found the other two about to sit down.

"Where's Harry?" asked Delmar, calling towards the kitchen door, and a negro answered in a high and husky voice: "Ah dunno, Mis' Delmar. I jus' see him sashayin' ovah the hill, a while back."

"Who's Harry?" asked Maizie, instantly suspicious.

"Harry's the new hand," said Delmar.

"What new hand?"

"He come lookin' for a job this mornin' and I took him on."

"Dad!" said the girl.

"Aw, he's straight," said her father. "Judge Lincoln sent him out from town with a note for me. Here's the note: 'Dear Delmar, If you need a good man, take Harry Sheldon. I've seen him work cattle and I know you could use him. He's more than he seems, and he seems a good cowpuncher.'"

"What does he mean by that?" asked the girl sharply. "What does he mean by saying that he's more than he seems?"

"Wait'll you see him," answered her father. "He's got more hair than would do two gents; he's a dark and dangerous lookin' gent, Maizie, but he's plumb wonderful with a hoss, and he can make a rope work for him!"

"It's a fine time to get a stranger here!" said the girl.

"Honey," answered Mr. Delmar, "if this gent ain't for us, he can't do no harm against us. There's one thing he don't know, and that's one end of a gun for another. There he comes now."

Someone was heard singing in a soft bass voice in the yard behind the house, and presently there appeared in the doorway a small man with a long, pale face, framed in very black hair that almost touched his shoulders.

"I seen a dun cow bogged by the tank over the hill," he explained quietly, "and I just went down and tailed her out."

He went to his place at the table and acknowledged the introduction to Philip with a nod and another nod for Doc Rivers and Maizie. Then he bent his serious attention to his food and ate in utter silence.

"Maizie tells me that she hears you shoot pretty good," said Delmar suddenly.

Philip raised his head, and suddenly it seemed as though the question must have come from Harry Sheldon, who was sitting just opposite, for the eyes of the new cow-puncher had turned to black velvet and there was a question behind them. Never had Philip faced such eyes before in man or woman. He looked fixedly at the puncher, and when the latter glanced hastily down to his plate, then Philip was able to answer he hardly knew what. It was as if he had received a shock that left him a little dizzy. He could not explain. He only knew that there was something about little Harry Sheldon that worried him.

After lunch, Delmar took him for a walk up and down in front of the house.

Maizie had told him that Philip has come as a volunteer to help in the fight against the Purchass forces, and Delmar wished, in the first place, to thank their new-found friend. Then he added with a chuckle: "I dunno how far you're a volunteer, and how far you were dragged along by Maizie. She's like that. Her ma was the same before her. Her brother's the same, too. But if I was you, young man, I'd start on the high trail and never stop going for a month."

Philip declared that he could not do that.

"Why not?" asked the rancher. "Shamed to go after coming here? Lemme tell you that it's a lot better to be ashamed and living than proud and dead. Don't you answer me. Just you think it over, and if you don't appear for supper, I'll tell the folks that I sent you to town on an errand. And don't you ever come back from that errand!"

93

"I don't understand," said Philip, "how any man could leave you in danger. But I understood, Mr. D lmar, that there is a law which takes care of people in trouble!"

"There's a law," said Delmar at once. "B t the law could take more from us than we could take f om it. The Purchase clan has us in its pockets. All that e can do is to grin and bear it. But you think over at I been telling you."

They had been walking up and down a hey talked, with Loafer, as usual, lurking at the heels his master, looking very much more as though he we trailing an enemy than following the only thing he love n the world. Now Delmar broke off to say simply: "W s the matter with your dog, Phil?"

Loafer had left the heels of Philip and s led softly for the corner of the house. He stalked cro ned low, his belly almost dragging on the ground, a old Delmar whispered: "He's spotted something clos Philip. Let's foller him up!"

Follow him they did, stepping as lightl s they could, when around the corner in front of them e little Harry Sheldon, in the act of lighting a cigar . Loafer rose from his crouch with a blood-curdling rl and leaped straight at the throat of the little man.

He struck Sheldon fairly on the breas t the loud cry of Philip was in his ears and he did drive his teeth home. Sheldon was rolled head over hee n the dust, and lay on his face, the wolf-dog standing h one forepaw on the back of the fallen man and or aised, while he looked to his master eagerly for instr ons.

Philip called him away, and with a of a switch sent him scampering off into the woods.

"He won't come back for a whole y," said Philip.

Then he hurried on to help brush th dust from Sheldon's clothes as the latter stood up.

The little man was greatly shaken. H did not wait to dust his clothes thoroughly but wer with an almost staggering step to the veranda, and th e he sank down, his back against a pillar, and his ey closed. He was white, and looked a very sick man, in eed.

"I seen the flash of his teeth; I thought my throat was tore to the backbone," said Sheldon, when Philip sat down beside him and offered commiserations.

Then he added: "It ain't nothin'. Only," he exclaimed, opening his eyes, which flashed with a terrible light, "if I ever have a chance at him, I'll shoot him in two, sure as hell."

"I wouldn't do that," said Philip slowly, and rising. "I really wouldn't do that."

"Of course not," answered Sheldon, smiling instantly. "Of course I wouldn't. I just lost my temper for a minute."

He stood up, presently, and went away, but still it seemed to Philip that the little man walked with a trailing, uneasy step.

"Son," said Delmar, "you never oughto keep a dog like that. He'll murder a man one day for you."

"I can't understand," sighed Philip. "He never acted that way before. Was Mr. Sheldon spying on us?"

"Him?" cried the rancher, startled. "I never thought of that!"

CHAPTER XIX

PHILIP, however, changed his mind at once. "Of course he wasn't spying," he suggested. "Otherwise, he would have been afraid to walk straight out at us like that—lighting a cigarette."

"I dunno—I dunno," murmured the rancher. "But he can't handle a gun. The Purchass folks wouldn't have a man around them if he couldn't handle a gun. But we'll just keep an eye on him, son. Now about what I was saying. Will you cut loose from this? You're too young to be burned up with the rest of us!"

"I'll go," said Philip, "when your daughter tells me to."

Mr. Delmar stood for a moment rigid, his eyes closed.

"Maizie's gunna have things to answer for when the last day comes," said he at last. "Here she comes now, to start trouble!"

It was trouble indeed that she wished to start. She drew them into conclave with Doc Rivers, and they discussed possible ways and means of saving the situation. They could not read the mind of the Purchass crew, but they could guess what Jolly Delmar was doing. He was waiting among the ravines and hills at the base of Mount Ransome, until at a proper time he would attempt to come in to the house. That proper time, doubtless, would be in the middle of the night. Doc Rivers said what they all thought: that the most feasible plan was for them to scout through those foothills and there attempt to find Jolly. Then they could accompany him towards the house as a guard; or best of all, they could simply warn him that it was practically impossible for him to get to the house at that time, or until the guard had been relaxed. But, as Maizie pointed out, how were they to make such an attempt when they were sure to be under the constant observation of the men who lurked about the house? Doc Rivers unexpectedly suggested a plan. He and young Philip would ride from the place and on the trail back towards his own house. This could hardly be regarded as a suspicious move, and once fairly screened among the trees, they would turn and swing back in broad semicircles, Philip riding to one side and Doc to another. In this manner they could get to the foothills without a large chance of being seen, and when they were in the vicinity from which young Delmar was in the habit of sending in his signals, they could scout around and strive to find him.

This attempt would, however, be made in what was now apt to be the enemy's country. Old Delmar declared that he was certain that the Purchass people had discovered the system of light signals which Jolly used. That was why they knew he was about to attempt a return. That was why they were almost certain to be searching through the hills in an attempt to find Jolly and capture him or kill him, whatever their purpose might be.

However, if either of the two emissaries could find Jolly, they were to give him the warning and urge him to go away for another period. Rivers would be accepted by Jolly as a faithful friend. Philip was equipped with a note from Delmar, which simply said: "This is your friend Philip Pillar" (since a last name had to be coined and Philip could suggest no other). "He brings you a message straight from me. Believe every word that he tells you."

So Doc Rivers' plan was accepted. The horses were saddled again, and the two mounted. Maizie stood close to Philip as he swung awkwardly into the saddle, and she rested her hand against the iron shoulder of the mustang.

"Doc wants to help," she said. "But he won't succeed. It's on you that everything depends, Phil. Poor Jolly's life—and the happiness of all of us!"

"Leave him be!" called Doc Rivers harshly, though he hardly could have understood what was said. "You got him in the fire. D'you have to throw fuel on it now?"

Riding on towards the road they passed the little blacksmith shop where wagon and harness repairs were effected without the necessity of a trip to town; the shop was filled with curling blue-white smoke, and, with tatters of smoke clinging to him, little Harry Sheldon came out of the door to take a breath of fresh air, and watched the two go by. Once more it seemed to Philip that the eyes of the little man grew larger and turned to dead black velvet. It was like seeing a ghost, and though this was the hot, bright midday, a shiver ran through him. He felt at once an inexplicable repulsion, and an inexplicable impulse to approach the man.

"Have you noticed anything odd about Mr. Sheldon?" he asked.

"He's little and he's ornery looking," said Doc Rivers. "I dunno that I've noticed anything else. And you don't call punchers 'mister' except you're introducing one of 'em to a girl. You call 'em by one name, first or last. It don't matter much. Me—I'm Doc to you. Savvy?"

Philip nodded. He hardly heard, for his mind was still far behind him, clinging to the memory of those velvet black eyes, like the eyes of a great cat, half-blinded by the sun.

They journeyed straight down the homeward trail for a mile. There they drew rein, and as being the older and the conceiver of the enterprise, Doc Rivers gave his final instructions.

Philip was to take the right-hand way, cut around the house at a distance of not less than two miles, and then follow up a winding cañon road which he was sure to discover. This would bring him into the foothills, and on one of three of these hills there was a great chance that they would find Jolly. The latter had already been described. He was tall, straight, rode very gracefully and erect, and was a very blond youth. He was also mounted, when he was last at the house, on a strong but ugly black gelding nearly sixteen hands in height and with quarters strong enough to drag a plough.

"Now listen to me," said Doc, "and don't you think that I'm kidding you. You take your spin through those hills, and come up to every sky line like there was a dragon lyin' behind it. Keep ready to drop off your hoss; have your rifle in your hand, and your finger on the trigger, and if you shoot, shoot to kill."

At the mere thought, Doc himself grew pale and grasped the butt of his rifle, where it thrust up from the holster that ran down the saddle beneath his right knee.

"Because," he explained, "when in doubt, you're always safe in shooting at a Purchass. There ain't a one of them and there never was a one that didn't need hanging. And most of them end up that way, or else they turn up their toes in a barroom, somewhere, with a slug of lead through the head. But play everything safe. No matter what you do, you ain't gunna get yourself famous out of today's work!"

After this he paused a moment and then extended his lean hand, which Philip grasped cordially.

"I like you, kid," said Rivers. "I never liked any gent much better, and I wish to God that you hadn't dragged the two of us into this mess. Here's luck to you. So long, and take care of yourself! You're too good a man to get yourself butchered for Jolly Delmar, or for any ten like him!"

With that, they parted, Philip with a full heart, for the kindness of Rivers showed plainly through his rough manners, and this last speech was an open avowal.

He had left Pillar Mountain feeling, from the conversation of Oliver Aytoun, that the world was thronged with brave and good men and no villains; but he felt that this opinion could be strongly qualified, now. Each man might have his virtues, but those virtues were apt to be poisoned with great vices. The old tales were right, and the world was half white and half black. Just now, he was entering the darker domain. The very shadows beneath the trees seemed to him to be cast by the power of the Purchasses!

And yet he had to admit to himself that he was happy. The strange eyes of Harry Sheldon had made him oddly nervous; there was nothing in the adventure that lay before him which seemed to Philip comparable in danger with the strange sense of fear which he had taken from the new cowpuncher on the Delmar place.

He scouted through a mighty woodland, broken only occasionally by brief stretches of grassland where fire had eaten through the heart of the forest and left a wilderness of standing stumps, now given over to grass, but slowly being reclaimed from the edges by the still-standing veterans of the woods. He pushed the gray along briskly, for he had several miles to cover, and the going was rough, without a trail to guide him.

So he came, at length, to the desired locality. It was well after midafternoon; the shadows were beginning to stretch out. Indeed, except for an hour or two in the middle of the day, there is always a suggestion, a foreshadowing or a lingering hint of the night in the hollows, the gorges, the sharp-edged valleys among the mountains. It is truly the land of twilight.

Into the heart of that region he did not have to penetrate, but only among certain hills—such as would have been termed lofty mountains in Scotland, let us say—and searching among these he would find his man if he could.

He obeyed the instructions of Doc Rivers carefully, not so much through fear as because he wished to win from this work not glory, perhaps, but a single smile from Maizie Delmar. He came up towards each sky line with consummate caution, and before each descent, he scanned every covert within eye range and studied it cautiously.

99

A dozen times during that search, his rifle leaped to the shoulder—but in every case it was not the glint of steel that he had seen but the silver flash of poplar leaves, turning like winking metal in the wind.

Over the ups and downs of the first hill he had gone, therefore, and near the top of the second he paused and stared down to the west. The house of Delmar was clearly to be seen, half lost in trees, to be sure, and looking small with distance, but not at all beyond the range of signals that could be studied through a glass.

From this hill, no doubt, Jolly Delmar was apt to send down his signals by fire in the night; and Philip thought of the strained, anxious face of Maizie as she stared up towards that height in the evening of the day, never knowing what words would be sent down to her, or if the dark outline of the hill would remain blank.

After this thoughtful pause, Philip went on to the ridge; but the first thing that he saw, as he looked down from the height, was a pair of men lying sprawled in a shallow nest of rocks, with rifles beside them, and gunbelts laid out on the ground within easy reaching distance.

He did not need glasses to understand that these were the Chisholm brothers; he did not need an interpreter to guess that they were not lying there merely to rest. For from their observation post they clearly commanded the whole rough and ragged valley which ran between this valley and the next—the natural chute which led down from the upper mountains to the house of Delmar.

CHAPTER XX

He knew that he could shoot both those men through the back as they lay there; he also knew that nothing could induce him to perform such an act of brutality. Therefore it only remained to him to avoid the pair if he could.

Reach the third hill past them he could not unless he made a lengthy detour.

He hesitated for some time, uncertain as to whether he should go down to the lower ground and turn up from that side to the third of the hills, or take the higher way round, working across the ragged face of the mountain.

He determined to make the second move, shaking his head in doubt and uncertainty. For it seemed to Philip a half-dastardly thing to permit those two to remain in their post of watch while poor Doc Rivers rode, perhaps, straight under their rifles!

However, having made up his mind, he dismounted, that his horse, having less weight to carry, might be less liable to make noise, and so he retraced his way with the greatest caution, weaving down the hillside and gradually edging to the left and the mountainside.

A dozen times he paused and glanced behind him, but there was no sound or sight to show of surveillance, and so he came to the bottom of the hollow.

He worked from this straight up the next slope to the east, and soon he was weaving among the trees which angled sharply on the mountainside, until he came to a fairly level shoulder, or weather-trenched indentation. There he paused. He had made this entire trip on foot, his horse stumbling behind him, and Loafer scouting skilfully in front. But at this point the wolf-dog halted, bracing back on his legs, his head thrown stiffly to the right. There was danger, to Loafer's manner of thinking, in the vicinity, and Philip threw his rifle across the fork of his left arm, ready to strike back if he should see occasion.

The only answer, for a moment, was a distant, dreary howling, as the wind swept through some far-off chasm of the mountains; but then, just behind him, a sharp voice broke on his ear:

"You, there, now stick up your hands and do it damn pronto."

Philip hesitated. There was a great deal of crisp meaning in the tones of the speaker, and yet there was Maizie in the background of his mind; Maizie expected no meek surrender.

"You fool," said the other in anger, "drop that gun and stick up your hands or I'll send you to hell. D'you think I'm bluffing? Act quick, before that dog starts for me!"

Loafer had whirled towards the voice and now was stealing forward towards the danger.

With all his heart Philip prayed for some inspiration which might teach him how to extricate himself from this menace, but he received no thought from heaven. Slowly he lowered his rifle, and then dropped it to the ground, breaking the force of its fall by catching it with his toe.

"Loafer!" he called.

The dog flashed back before him, and stood there, braced, his magnificent mane rising, very ready to lay down his life for his master. But Philip simply raised his hands above his head and waited, half expecting that a bullet would tear through his back.

"That'll do, I guess," said the stranger. "Now just unbuckle your gun belt, will you?"

It was done. The hands were raised once more as the gun belt thudded heavily on the rocks.

"So!" said the stranger. "Face around here and lemme have another look at you, old son!"

Philip turned, and found himself looking at a handsome fellow of thirty or a little less, extraordinarily pale for a Western mountaineer.

He kept his rifle not at the shoulder, but at the ready, like a man who has the greatest confidence in himself.

"You're one of the sneaks they've hired, are you?" asked the stranger.

"Who?" asked Philip.

"My God," groaned the other, "you ain't gunna try to lie out of it, are you? I've watched some of the rest sliding around through the rocks like snakes hunting for bird's nests. But I'll be damned if ever I saw a poorer excuse at trailin' than you! Who are you?"

"I am Philip," said the boy.

"That's all, eh?"

"Yes."

"Philip Purchass?"

That query opened the eyes of Philip suddenly.

"Purchass?" he asked sharply. "Are the Purchass clan your enemies?"

"That surprises you, I reckon," sneered the stranger. Philip smiled.

"I think I know you," he said. "You're Jolly Delmar."

"It's a grand guess," sneered the other.

"You are he?"

"I am, kid. Now what?"

"I have a note for you," broke in Philip, and handed Jolly the letter which old Delmar had written. Jolly glanced through it with a curious frown, and when he had finished, he did not seem particularly pleased. He merely crumpled the paper and dropped it into his coat pocket.

"How do I know it ain't a frame?" he asked.

"A frame?" said Philip. "I don't understand!"

Jolly regarded him with a deliberate stare. "You dunno what a frame is? Where was you raised?"

"On Pillar Mountain."

"Yonder? The hell you were! And what dragged you into this mix-up of mine? My father ain't got the money to hire extra hands."

"Your sister—" began Philip, when Jolly broke in with a groan of disgust.

"You're one of her men, are you?" he inquired with a grunt. "Well, Maizie's taking them young! Only," he added sharply, "I want to know what made you sashay up here among the rocks? What made you guess that I'd be here? None of the others showed that much sense!"

"I didn't know you were here," admitted Philip. "But my way was blocked down yonder. I saw the two Chisholm brothers lying on a ledge under the top of the hill, and I judged I couldn't go that way unless I killed the two of them."

"And what kept you from that?"

"Of course one can't shoot a man from behind," said Philip, opening his blue eyes.

Jolly Delmar sighed.

"You better sit down here. Go get your guns first. Then tell me what's what."

So Philip picked up his fallen guns and sat down beside Jolly. The latter had chosen a skillful position. Above his head the rocky brow of the mountain arched out and shut him away from observation from that direction. Before him was a semicircle of brush and rocks which concealed perfectly him and his horse. And from this point of vantage, Philip looked through crevices and interstices of the shrubbery across a vast sweep of mountains and ravines, all pouring down into the broader valley. And in the center of the valley, surrounded by the farmlands, he could see the town, now. A brownish mist of dust half obscured it, and heat waves, from time to time, danced it quite out of sight, but at moments he had a view of it, dim with distance and the dusty air. He felt, in that moment, as though Fate were taking direct hand in his life, shutting him away from the little city with a sort of personal malice. Here he was back among the heights again, and enlisted in a service which well might see the end of him before many days.

He told briefly the message which had been committed to him. Jolly's signal of the other night had been spotted, apparently, by the Purchass men. At least, they were showing themselves in force around the farmhouse, and certainly the presence of the Chisholms was proof that they were watching the signal hills. Jolly was strongly advised to keep away. An attempt to reach the house would be suicide at the present time.

Jolly listened to this with half-closed eyes and a faint smile. Plainly, he enjoyed the situation.

"Dad wants me to keep away. The Purchass crew want me to come in. I hate to please them, but I got to get to the house. I got to get there!"

The smile left his lips. He stared earnestly before him, and Philip was respectfully silent. He was fascinated, to begin with, by the extraordinarily close resemblance between this man and Maizie Delmar; except that he felt in Maizie a greater self-control, a quieter strength. There was a reckless carelessness about this fellow, like the carelessness of a gambler who lays his bets without system, defying chance.

"I got to get in," he repeated at last. "And the Purchass boys expect me tonight?"

"You signaled that."

104

"If I wait till tomorrow, they might be off guard a little."

Philip remembered the man he had seen disappearing in the woods near the Delmar home; he remembered the burly backs of the two Chisholms as he had seen them lying beneath him on the mountainside, and he shook his head.

"You don't think so?"

"I don't think so."

"I'll work out a plan," murmured Jolly, and began to walk rapidly up and down, pausing from time to time as some sort of a thought struck him. Philip, in the meantime, straining his eyes west and south, saw the roof of the Delmar house in the distance, barely distinguishable above a tuft of trees.

"Suppose that you signal from here," he suggested.

"The folks never could see the fire unless they stood on the roof, and they won't be there."

"The Purchass men won't know that," suggested Philip.

"What d'you mean by that?"

"They'll think that your father *is* watching from the roof. You send a signal that you'll come in tomorrow night. Can you do that?"

"By simply letting the fire burn, that's all."

"The Purchass people will see that. They'll prepare themselves for tomorrow night."

"And then?"

"Then you slip through tonight. There might be half a chance."

CHAPTER XXI

THEY considered that plan with the greatest care. There was much to be said against it. Philip himself thought it madness for Jolly to attempt to break through the enemy

105

when the latter were in such numbers, but Jolly was determined. Some particular pressure urged him on, and he told Philip that within two days at the latest he must be in the house of his father.

On that point he grew excited.

"I've been the black sheep, kid," he told Philip. "I'm the one that has wasted the money. Well, I'm going to pay up. I'm going to pay up the last penny, old son. I'm going to make Dad's head swim. Maizie is gunna faint. And as for the gang of knockers and yellow dogs that have barked at me all these years—I'll make them eat dirt!"

So said Jolly in a tone between passion and enthusiastic resolve. Philip, hearing, believed that there must be some great and mysterious thing in progress; what it was, he could not tell, but it was an accomplishment now in the hands of Jolly that would reëstablish him beyond all the tongues of cavil or rancor.

They waited until the dusk had thickened; in the meantime, laying their plans with care. Two things would be apt to happen. In the first place, when the Purchass agents saw the signal flame they would be apt to make a movement towards it in the hope of bagging their man at once. Failing of this, in the second place they would probably pay less attention on the rest of this night and far more on the next evening. In the meantime, as soon as the fire was lighted, they were to push down the slope of the mountain, leading their horses. In the valley bottom beneath, they were to attempt an expedient which had come into the mind of Philip as he sat in the blue of the evening and looked down at the rising shadows and the three hilltops like three islands breaking from the soft, thin surface of the evening colors.

The horse of Jolly had been bred and raised on the farm of his father, and he was a sure "return horse." That is to say, loosed anywhere within a reasonable radius, he would drive directly towards the house and come to it in the straightest possible line. A word from Jolly had given the mustang that character, and that word had given Philip his thought: which was that they should come opposite the gap between the second and third of the hills and there loose the black, after lashing some sort of dummy on him, which might look like a rider. The horse would drive straight on towards the ranchhouse and if there were danger on either side, guns would soon begin to pop. If no guns were heard, then they could follow straight on at the heels of the gelding; but if they heard an alarm, they would sheer away to the side and take the next gully that pointed towards the house, hoping that the alarm in the central ravine, in the meantime, would have drawn all the rest of the watchers in that direction.

Jolly considered this plan with care. He pronounced it too complicated; but the idea of the dummy rider delighted him hugely and he determined that the thing must be attempted. Therefore they spent some time during the afternoon in stuffing Jolly's coat, and then in tying Philip's hat securely upon its head. Through the quantity of twigs and dead grass which filled out the coat, they thrust the upper section of a forked branch; the two lower divisions, like legs, straddled the saddle and could be lashed firmly beneath the belly of the gelding. In this manner it would keep upright, no matter how many bullets were poured into it. And Jolly declared that such a stratagem, childishly simple as it was, would be worth dying for, so much scorn and mirth would be poured out on the heads of the Purchass men if they spotted the flying image and tried to down it.

After the dummy was equipped, they brought together a quantity of wet moss and mixed this with dead grass. This fuel they heaped conveniently at the side and under a good pile of brushwood, which was for the signal flame, and when the dusk was thick, Philip started down the mountain with both the horses, and the other lingered behind to light the grass and moss. This would smoulder for some time, and before it burst into a flame, they both hoped to be in the hollow of the gorge beneath, ready to attempt the second step of their scheme.

Philip was more than halfway down the slope before Jolly regained him, panting.

"It's going well—everything's going well—you've brought me luck, kid!" murmured Jolly. "Nothing can stop me! I feel in my bones that we're going to get back to the house. And it'll be owing to you, if I make it. And if I make it—I'll bust things wide open! I'll bust them wide open!"

He laughed joyously.

"I'll be the making of you, too, Phil. I'll set you up. What do you want? A ranch? You'll have it! A damn fine bunch of saddle hosses? You'll have those, too! A good stock of high bred cows? You'll have the best, and I'll pay for it all. I never was a believer in doing things in a small way. A friend is a damn sight better than gold, and you're proving yourself a friend, old fellow! There's Skinny, too. God knows whatever made him come out and risk his neck for me. Of course he didn't find me. Couldn't expect Skinny to do anything well. But anyway—we gotta remember that he tried. Well, I'll set up Skinny, too. I'll make a man of him!"

He bubbled on in this light-hearted manner, his voice stopping with a muffled gasp of alarm, now and again, when the shod hoof of a horse grated noisily on a rock, or started a small avalanche rolling before them. But they came safely to the bottom of the slope, going out along a little gully which was filled with enormous trees whose lofty heads made it utter midnight beneath. They had to fumble their way, Jolly going first and Philip following him, until they saw the trees thin before them.

On the verge of the grove, with the blue of the twilight thick before them, Philip saw his leader halt; then he was caught by the hand of Jolly, and heard the soft whisper of the other: "Stand fast. Catch the nose of your hoss that it don't get a chance to neigh. There's someone coming up the valley!"

A moment later Philip heard the click of hoofs passing over rocks, and next the murmur of voices which momently grew more distinct. One of those voices raised into a sudden sharp cry.

"There goes the signal. He's up there now, the rat. Come along, Jack. We'll head in here and go up the mountain. Chuck the reins and leave the hosses! We can make better time on foot!"

"I got a thousand-dollar hoss, here," answered Jack. "It ain't likely that I'll chuck it for a chance like this. He'll be gone before we get there."

"The hell he will. He don't even know that we're around here. He'll use the fire for his camp, too! He's a careless fool. To hell with the hosses. The old man'll make us rich if we can bring Jolly into camp!"

This seemed to persuade the other. Philip distinctly heard the creak of stirrup leathers as two men dismounted. Then the jingling of spurs as they hurried away.

The footsteps died out, and then the two in covert came forth.

They found a pair of tall animals, already beginning to graze, trailing their reins.

"This is nothing but luck," said Jolly, laughing again, but this time through his teeth. "There ain't nothing but luck for us, tonight. Kid, here's my hoss to take the place of the black. Come along, Jerico!" For that was the name of the gelding.

It was decided that since both the horses they had found were of the first quality, they would borrow them for the night and leave the down-headed gray in their place. So the saddles were swiftly shifted, and then they went on down the valley to gain their desired post at the mouth of the valley between the two hills.

As they went, they could see the beacon which they had kindled beginning to leap to its full height, sending a brighter and a brighter eye glancing across the deepening night.

"There's a thousand of them!" guessed Jolly. "They've turned out for me, tonight. But damn them, you and me can beat them all!"

He added again, for his spirits had risen so high that he could not keep his tongue still: "They know that I'm worth the game. They know that I'm worth hiring a whole army to catch! All the better fun beating them. I wouldn't miss this dodge for nothing!"

They reached the mouth of the desired gorge without seeing or hearing another man or horse. It was the same narrow valley over which the Chisholm brothers had been keeping such careful guard that same day, and here they advanced the black gelding and set him going with a cut of a whip. Away he went, scattering rocks noisily, but presently fell back from a run to a mild canter and so rocked on down the narrow valley.

He had not gone two hundred yards before the trouble began. The two who watched and waited, tense on their horses, heard a voice cry out a challenge, and then a gun barked, sending broken echoes up and down the gorge. Other guns joined in. And Philip and his companion hurried in to turn the flank of the hill and try the next valley, hoping that this alarm might have drawn in the other guards set against Jolly's return.

It was a twisting course which they had to ride in the darkness, with the horses guiding themselves, and picking out a way among sharp-edged boulders or trees that loomed suddenly before them. They were well into the narrow pass as they heard the noise of the guns in the other gorge die out, and Jolly called anxiously: "What is it, kid? Have they killed the hoss or lost it?"

Philip dared not venture a guess, and they began to urge the horses a little more freely. So, twisting around an elbow turn Philip, in the lead for the moment, crashed straight into three riders coming in the opposite direction.

"Purchass?" called one of the three eagerly.

"Purchass," answered Philip, his heart in his throat.

"Purchass be damned," came the rough answer. "You don't sound like one of the boys. Chuck, throw a light on this gent, will you? There's something loose, here!"

Philip sat his saddle like one entranced, with his impatient horse beginning to gather rein against his hand. He saw one of the three strike a match; in another moment the cupped light would fall on his face. Already, at the first flash of the match, he had seen the gleam of rifles in the hands of the first two.

CHAPTER XXII

HE did what the cornered rat does. With no real hope left, he flung himself straight forward into the path of danger. The reins he abandoned, trusting solely to the grip of his knees which sank through the hard leather of the saddle flaps as though it had been cloth. And driving his heels into the tender flanks of the horse, he made it spring forward like a frightened cat.

He who sat nearest in front fired. It should have been a kill in any other time, but the match light had just flared from blue to yellow, and the whole party was dimly washed across with strange shadows. So there was merely a jet of flame almost in Philip's face; and a bullet passed his cheek as his horse darted in. He caught the rifleman with his right arm; in the confusion of his mind, he could think of no other way of checking the fire. But with all his might he met the shock as his horse tore on, and the rider was torn from his saddle and lay writhing and cursing in Philip's arms.

The last of the party, he who had lighted the match, had dropped it and snatched a gun. With that revolver, he now opened fire. The first bullet struck Philip's burden with a shock which Philip himself felt distinctly. There was a wild scream of pain and despair; and with the rush of the horse to help him, Philip raised that groaning body and drove it fairly against horseman number three.

As effectually as though a thunderbolt had struck him, that warrior was knocked from his saddle; a yell of rage and surprise mingled with the shriek of the first victim— and there lay the open trail before him.

He grappled the reins and drew back his frightened mount but Jolly shot instantly past him.

111

"They're all down; ride like hell!" he called as he went by.

And, looking back, Philip could make out three riderless horses milling, and yonder the shadow of a man arising from the ground and pouring out tremendous curses. The other two lay still and groaned.

That was enough. The pass lay smoother before him, now, and he gave his horse the rein and let it fly in pursuit of Jolly. The next moment they were in an open wood, Jolly a scant distance ahead, and the dim trunks shooting past with startling velocity. And presently Delmar drew up, jogging his horse easily.

"Easy to the edge of the woods," he said to Philip. "And then from the edge we'll bolt for the barn. They can't hit us going the pace we'll be traveling, and in this light. They can't hit us except by damned luck, and luck they ain't gunna have. No luck for nobody except us, old son! No luck for nobody except us!"

He seemed in a pure frenzy of joy, and drawing his horse to the side of that which Philip was riding, he grasped the arm of the boy and worked his fingers into the great, rubbery muscles.

"I see why they sent you. My God, I thought it was a chunk of lightning going ahead of me. I thought it was a cannon ball knocking a lane through those fellows. And I see how you done it. I *feel* how you done it!"

He gave another squeeze to the thick arm of Philip.

"I'll never forget, Phil," he vowed. "I'll remember you in the middle of hell. You planned this thing, and you pushed it through. A kid like you has made old Purchass and all his cutthroats a lot of fools. But I tell you, kid, this here is a golden night for you! More gold than there is in the sun!"

He broke off his strange and exultant speech, laughing again in a savage delight.

But Philip hardly heard the words. What Jolly said was all very well, but what was important was the word that Maizie might speak at the end of the trail, if he lived that long. And with his eyes half closed, smiling, tense, Philip waited for that rich moment.

112

They drifted on through the woods at ease. Every inch of this ground was known to Jolly, now, and he guided them perfectly. So they came to the verge of the woods, and it was like passing from dark to dawn, so much brighter was the starlit landscape outside the shadows.

To the left, and a quarter of a mile away—no more— they saw two lights from the Delmar house, and nearer at hand was the looming shadow of the barns.

"Fast, kid, ride fast and hard!" said Jolly. "Aim for the right corner of the barn. Keep low in the saddle. I think we're gunna collect a few bullets on our way!"

Then he started like an arrow and drove his horse, grunting with pain as the spurs went home, frantically across the open. Philip followed, at a much milder pace, with his horse coming up against the bit of its own volition. But they had better luck than even Jolly had expected, for there was not a single bullet fired at them as they crashed around the corner of the barn and brought their sweating horses to a stop at the front of the building.

The shrill voice of old Delmar called from a shadow, somewhere: "Who's that? Answer up sharp, now. I got the pair of you well covered!"

"Dad!" laughed Jolly. "It's me!"

There was a joyous cry in answer, and Philip, taking the horses, led them into the barn, and then busied himself in feeding and watering them. Presently a lantern approached, with the shadows of a man's legs sweeping vastly across the side of the barn. Loafer, as though in fear, crowded back against his master and snarled, with bristling mane.

It was only Harry Sheldon, but as he came closer, Philip had to call out: "Keep back, Shelton! Loafer is going wild again. I'm sorry."

"That dog is a fool!" exclaimed Sheldon angrily. "Can't you teach him better sense than that?"

"I never saw him act this way before," admitted Philip, troubled. "There's something about you that he doesn't like."

"What?" snapped Sheldon. "What's there about me that he don't like!"

113

He raised his lantern so that the light, falling in a wider circle, might strike on the dog. So doing, he showed Loafer with eyes of devilish green crouched before his master. But he also showed his own face, and Philip stared at it entranced. For the little man seemed deathly white under the glare of the lantern. There was an odd smile upon his lips, and his eyes were as Philip had seen them before—blank and dead, like black velvet.

"What's there about me that he don't like?" persisted Sheldon. "I tell you, the dog's a fool!"

He apparently had come to help in putting up the horses, but now he turned on his heels, and the shadow of his body fell in a thick dark shaft over Philip and the dog.

At the open sliding door, Sheldon turned again.

"I gotta say just this, kid. If you want that dog to live, you gotta teach him better manners. I ain't gunna put up with it. You hear me talk?"

Then he disappeared, and Philip wondered why it was that he did not feel a hotter anger choking in his throat. Indeed, he felt no anger at all, but only a cold sense of dread.

A voice began to call from the house. He heard his own name. And as he hurried out from the barn, old Delmar came to meet him, reaching out both hands through the starlit night.

"Jolly's told us something of what you've done, my boy," said he. "Maizie was a wise woman to find you and bring you here. God bless you, my son. I think you've put an end to all of our troubles. Come in with me! We have some things to say to you!"

Philip followed dumbly, but at the door a cold perspiration was on his forehead.

"I don't want to be thanked," he muttered. "It was only a game, Mr. Delmar. You—I—"

The door was jerked open; he was thrust from the veranda into the dining room where Jolly was already seated at the table, with George, the old negro cook, hanging over him in delight.

Maizie, too, was sitting by her brother, poring over

him more like a mother, as it seemed to Philip, than a sister.

"I got him. He didn't want to come," crowed old Delmar. "But I got him. He don't want to be thanked. He says it was a game!"

Jolly threw back his head and laughed.

"Sure it was a game—ninepins—for him. One of them for the ball and the rest for the pins, and he rolled a ten strike!"

CHAPTER XXIII

THE joy and the kindness of the father and the son were pleasant enough to Philip, but what he had waited for in expectation that made him cold had been the greeting of Maizie, and Maizie simply gave him no attention whatever. Only now and again, in the riotous supper that followed, did Philip find that her eyes were upon him, not in mockery, not in careless mirth like the others, but seriously, gravely reading his face, as though it were filled with interesting and new things. Yet, in a way, that earnest regard meant more to Philip than all the praise and the noise of the other two.

There was only one fly in the ointment, and that was Sheldon. He remained only a short time at the table, and then left. All the time he remained seated there he kept his eyes upon his plate, but as he went out from the room he looked down at Philip, and the latter, glancing up by chance as Loafer growled ominously, saw a pale sneer of mockery and triumph on the lips of the little man.

It seemed to Philip such an important thing that he was about to speak to one of the others of it, after Sheldon had left the room, but he changed his mind. What he objected to could hardly be fitted into words; there was not a scrap of actual evidence which he could bring to support his feeling that danger to Jolly and the rest was not over and would not be over so long as Sheldon remained in the house.

When Sheldon left, Jolly went to the kitchen door and closed it. Then he gathered his family about him with a mysterious gesture. They drew their chairs close together while Jolly, resting one hand on the table, leaned above them with something of the gay seriousness of a seller of patent medicines.

"Speaking of money, Dad," said Jolly, "how do we stand?"

Mr. Delmar glanced at Philip and hesitated; so that Philip, taking the hint at once, turned a bright pink and stood up.

"Look here," said Jolly. "The kid is one of us. He brought me home! You sit down, Phil. Go ahead, Dad."

Delmar rubbed his lean knuckles across his chin.

"Well, son," he answered, "I'm broke."

"How long have you been broke?" asked Jolly.

"About eight years."

"You mean that you've been borrowing every year from the bank?"

"That's it."

"You, Maizie," went on the son of the family. "How many new dresses do you have a year?"

"I have enough," said Maizie stoutly.

Jolly smiled upon her. He laid his hand on her head and tilted her face up so that their eyes met fairly.

"Dear old Maizie," said Jolly, and paused a moment, loving her.

"You've been like a poor beggar!" said Jolly. "I know about it. A couple of dresses a year and every dress made over ten times—you sitting up till the morning to do the work! Oh, I know about it!"

He removed his hand and stood straighter.

"I've been the sink into which everything has been running. Is that right?"

"No, no, lad!" said the father. "Don't say that to us."

"I do say it!"

He turned to Philip with his happy smile.

116

"You're going to get a picture of the sort of a worthless gent that you picked up in the hills and brought home, kid. Everything has gone smash here, because of me."

Philip was silent, listening with all his heart. Since he left Pillar Mountain, filled with hope and vast expectation, he had been forced to admit that the world was by no means the ideal place which fairy tales and romances describe. He had met with brutality, avarice, cunning, treachery, hardness of spirit and heart; but now he felt that he was looking for the first time upon men as they should be. Whatever faults could be laid against the Delmars, at least their attitude to one another was what God himself could have wished to find in the hearts of a family.

"I've been a waster and a lazy hound," went on Jolly. "I know it. But I've never known it so well as I know it tonight. A stranger came out and found me and took me home. Damn it, Phil, that was a fine thing! But even more wonderful to me was old Doc turning out as he did and coming on the trail."

"I wish he was back," said Delmar, shaking his head.

"He'll come back," answered Maizie. "He's delayed, but he ain't apt to get into trouble. Doc can smell danger miles away."

"If they've harmed him," declared Jolly, "I'll tear them in two!"

Delmar looked at his violent son with widening eyes, as though fully seeing him for the first time. But Philip saw that Maizie had looked down a little. No matter how greatly she loved her brother, it was plain that she saw him clearly.

"Let Doc go for a minute," said old Delmar. "Now go on, Jolly."

"Well," said Jolly, "I was ready to run for it, you understand, after my last rub with the Purchass outfit. I *was* running, and only luck, you might say, would have put the thing in my way. No, it was more than luck. I got to give myself that credit. But I'm askin' you to remember the chunk of ore that old Treggar brought down out of the mountains five years ago."

"Yes, yes!" exclaimed the father. "Good God!" he added, as he began to understand what Jolly meant.

117

"But it's true! It's true!" cried Jolly. "I tell you, Maizie, I'm going to dress you up in diamonds and pearls and—"

"Sell me to the highest bidder?" grinned Maizie.

"I'm going to make you roll in gold, dear Dad," said the son, in an ecstacy of love and gratitude. "And I'm going to fix Phil forever. I'm going to turn everything over to you, Dad. You'll have the running of it; I wouldn't trust myself!"

"Go on! Go on!" cried Maizie. "I want to know what happened. You're drivin' us crazy, Jolly!"

"It's nothing to the way you'll be before I finish," Jolly assured her. "If I—"

A heavy foot fell on the rear veranda.

"Who's that?" asked Jolly. "My God, could what I've been saying have been overheard?"

The door that opened on to the veranda from the dining room was cast open, and on the threshold stood Doc Rivers. He leaned against the jamb.

"Well, damn my good for nothin' eyes! You ain't been able to get back! Doggone me if I believe it!" he roared. "I hardly could get back myself!"

He flung himself into a chair, and they could see that great hollows were beneath his eyes, and his face was drawn sharply.

"The mountains is full of men. They're growin' out of the rocks. Fightin' men. They got enough to win the battle of Bull Run. I done the running!" said Doc Rivers.

"Good old Doc!" chuckled Jolly.

"I *am* old," said Rivers. "I'm a doggone old and wore out man, after today. Maizie, where's your manners? Ain't you gunna give me anything to eat?"

"What would you like?" asked Maizie.

"A dry crust'll do me fine," said Rivers. "I could eat grass. I ain't had a morsel for close onto ten days, I reckon. What've you got?"

"The finest thing you ever heard of."

"You ain't killed the old turkey, Maizie?" cried Rivers.

"Better than that!"

"There ain't anything better than that," said Rivers. "Only—tell me one thing. Did he get you, Jolly? Did the kid do it?"

"He did nothing but," nodded Jolly.

"He's pretty near half a man," remarked Rivers. "Now what's the joke about all this?"

"Listen to Jolly," said the girl. "He's better than turkey and roast sweet potatoes."

"He ain't equal to a lamb chop cut thin, to me," declared Rivers. "What *you* got to say for yourself, foolish?"

"Nothing much," answered Jolly. "Just sit quiet a minute. I'm telling the yarn. I was reminding the folks about old Treggar that brought in the ore five year back."

"Him that was gunna buy up Rockefeller and Morgan and hire the Astors to hold his hosses? Him that killed himself with red-eye before the next morning come? What about Treggar?"

"Damn Treggar——"

"He's damned, I guess; by this time he must be damned to a cinder."

"Will you shut up, Doc? Will you let me tell this here story?"

"Go on," said Rivers. "But you got no style, Jolly. You can dance, Jolly, but you can't talk worth a damn."

Jolly glared at his old friend.

"All right," he said, "I'll cut this here short. The thing of it is that I was always thinking about Treggar and his find. I knew that the mountains had been prospected from top to heel, of course. But I always had the thing in mind, and one day I got to thinking of a place where— well, to cut the thing short, I went up to that place on my last trip out, when I was running from the whole gang of the Purchasses. And, folks, I found it!"

There was a sound like the breathing of wind through thick foliage. Everyone leaned forward, intense and eager. Philip himself felt his blood leap in one great pulse, and Jolly waited, scanning their faces.

Suddenly he said: "I dunno what it'll go to the ton. You people can guess better!"

And he took from his pocket a stone that filled half his hand and tossed it on to the table.

It broke a plate to bits, in its fall, and cracked the water pitcher up the side, but no one paid the slightest attention to these accidents. Delmar himself caught up the rock. It was jet black, but as he turned it, ten thousand bright facets caught the light.

"Ah, Lord love me!" said Delmar. He held the rock in a shaking hand and raised it to the light.

"It'll go—I dunno—thousands and thousands of dollars to the ton! But—Jolly—you don't mean to say that it crops out like this?"

"Do I mean to say that it crops out?" smiled Jolly. "There's a vein of it a quarter of a mile long lying in plain sight and as thick as the body of a man."

Philip closed his eyes and began to think quickly. Rock as thick as the body of a man, a quarter of a mile in length, of unknown depth, and running thousands of dollars to the ton—why, such wealth was simply incalculable! When he looked up again he saw that the circle had changed. The faces around it were pale, and the eyes glittered.

"Where, Jolly?" asked Rivers in a hard voice.

"That's the question," began Jolly sarcastically.

Then he changed, with an afterthought.

"All right, Doc. You'll know everything, along with the rest of us. My God, if we can't trust you and Phil, then there's no use trying to trust anyone in the world."

And Maizie rather astonished Philip by adding: "That's right, Jolly. That's true."

"Wait till I run up to my room and get that map on the wall," said Jolly. "I can point it out better, that way!"

He hurried from the room, and he left behind him a thick silence.

In the kitchen, they could hear the chink of the dishes and then the rattle of the pans, as the cook washed up after the meal. But in the dining room there was no conversation. They heard the footfalls of Jolly mount the stairs three at a time, heard his door crash, and after that silence began. It lasted for long minutes.

"What happened?" asked Maizie impatiently.

"He's looking for the map," said the father.

"Map? It's hanging right on the wall!" said Maizie.

They stared at one another with a vague surmise of

trouble. Still the silence lasted, and finally Doc Rivers stood up from his chair and grasped the shoulder of Philip.

"Look at that damn dog of yours!" he commanded.

CHAPTER XXIV

A HOUSE was a place of dread to the great wolf-dog. Usually he worked as much of his body as possible under the chair of his master and remained flattened on the floor, his ears pricked, his big amber eyes darting from side to side to follow every sound.

Now, however, he had come to his feet from his place of shelter and he was stalking towards the inner door of the dining room, his mane bristling and his eyes green with a dangerous light.

The people stood up.

"I never have seen him act that way before," admitted Phillip. Then he added: "Except the other day, when Harry Sheldon was coming around the corner of the house."

The wolf-dog, in the meantime, with consummate care stalked towards the door, and coming closer to it, he reached out his paw and strove with the upturned nails to draw it open.

"There's something outside!" said Maizie in a frightened whisper.

Old Delmar reached the door with a soft stride and flung it open. Philip could look straight down the hall from the place where he stood, but he could see nothing; yet Loafer showed the greatest signs of emotion. He first crouched low, and then with bristling mane, with bared teeth, he shrank back from the empty threshold as though from before some superior and very dangerous foe.

Doc Rivers drew a long and rattling breath.

"My God," he whispered, "there's—there's a ghost—

121

it must of walked into the room. Look at that dog!"

Loafer had regained the feet of his master and against Philip's legs he backed, trembling convulsively, and showing all the signs of an animal desperate with fear, and yet incapable of striking back. To the others it was uncanny; to Philip, who knew the iron nerve and the mighty heart of that dog, the thing was totally unbelievable.

Even his hand on the neck of Loafer did not compose that stiff mane; even his voice did not make the trembling cease.

"Something's in his head," said Philip. "I—I don't know what. I've never seen anything like this."

Then Maizie said hurriedly, "Has anything happened to Jolly? Why doesn't he come? Why doesn't Jolly come? Call him, Dad?"

Delmar called: "Jolly, Jolly!"

There was no answer. The sound went gently echoing through the hall and up the stairs, but not a voice came back to meet it.

Then Maizie leaped into the doorway.

"Jolly!" she screamed. "Jolly, Jolly! Where are you!"

She hung there, clutching the edge of the door; but still the dreadful silence welled heavily from the dimness of the hallway. Loafer began to growl—not a deep and rumbling sound but a shrill voice, like hysteria of fear.

"I'm—I'm going to go see," said Maizie.

With all his might Philip made the great effort, and finally something snapped in him. He was able to hurry to her and take her arm.

"You stay back here," he said. "I'll go to see Jolly."

He drew a long Colt as he spoke, not through braggadocio, but by instinct of self-defense, for it seemed to Philip, for some uncanny reason, that this was more terrible than any moment he yet had faced. Not the attack of the Chisholms in the barroom nor the wild ride through the pass that same evening had supplied a horror and a danger of such a magnitude as this.

He would have thought that it was all in his own mind, but plainly, from the dog to old Delmar, every living

122

creature in the room felt somewhat the same emotion that filled him.

He made one step into the hallway, and then he heard something more than an echo of his footfall above him.

He hesitated, and down the stairs, slowly, came the form of a man. It turned into the hall. It approached him. Behind him, before his own eyes could distinguish, he heard the girl murmur: "Thank God— it's dear Jolly!"

In an instant he himself could distinguish the son of the house and he drew back to let him pass. Jolly came on with the same unhurrying stride.

He seemed very unlike one who rushes down with some triumphant information.

"He couldn't find the place on the map and he's trying to spot it in his memory," said Philip to himself. "He's afraid that he'll forget!"

He thought, as Jolly drew into the light, that the face of the young fellow was oddly white and that his eyes were dead and dark, but he had hardly an instant to recognize these features. He heard a violent scratching on the floor; there was a cry of warning from Doc Rivers, and Loafer went past him like a bolt, a half-growl, half-screech issuing from his throat. Philip tackled the big beast with a cry, and struck it down with the weight of his lunge. But it was all he could do to hold Loafer. The dog writhed and struggled with all its might. It had something serpentine in the cunning and the fury and the slipperiness with which it struggled. Once, Philip had it only by one hind leg, and Loafer turned and put his teeth on the arm of his master so hard that the sharp points clove through the cloth and pricked the skin. Yet Loafer did not bite. And again he was mastered by his owner.

Sweating and panting, Philip could straighten at last, for Loafer had pressed himself against the wall and lay with eyes closed, his long tongue thrusting out as he gasped for breath.

All that he saw of Jolly was the back of that young man disappearing through the screen door on to the porch; and then he was aware that the other three who were in the room were looking more than wildly at one another.

123

"He didn't say a word, did he?" asked Doc Rivers, in a faint whisper.

"It was the dog," said Maizie in a frightened voice. "It was just that Loafer frightened him—a little—"

"He'll be back in a moment," added old Delmar.

But Philip knew well enough that they were talking only in the vain effort to keep up their courage. They were far from at ease. He himself went back from the doorway into the hall and closed the door after him; Loafer was pressing against him, skulking in the same mortal terror.

Once more the ugly silence began.

Doc Rivers, grown desperate, broke through it.

"We gotta do something," he said.

They all looked at him.

After all, what was there to do.

Again Doc Rivers spoke: "You seen that dog before. He liked Jolly as well as he liked anybody. What made him go at Jolly's throat? I ask you that?"

They all winced. Of course they all had had the same thought and it helped not a whit to have the thought put into words. What devil possessed Loafer?

It would have been pleasant to say that the dog was touched by a bit of madness; but there was an uncanny feeling in Philip that the change in the dog had been brought about by the change in the man. What could that change be? What had made Jolly stay so long upstairs? What had made him come down the stairs, at last, without the map? Why had he walked like a white-faced automaton through their midst?

"Something happened upstairs," said Philip at last. "I'm going up to see."

He resolutely opened the door again into the darkness of the hall; then Loafer came whining and shaking to his feet and seemed to beg him to go no farther. He went on, however, filled with a mortal terror, but forcing himself ahead.

Behind him, he heard the voice of Maizie: "Doc, you go with him. Skinny, if you're a man, don't let Phil go up there alone!"

But there was no answer from Doc Rivers, and certainly no companionable footfall sounded behind him.

He turned on to the stairs and drove himself remorselessly upwards. There was a lamp burning with a small flame at the first landing, and as he approached it, it seemed to him that the flame shrank and changed a bit from yellow to blue; so that he remembered having read of a superstition that flames change color in just this fashion when a spirit approaches them.

He tried to tell himself that this was the rankest folly; but though he could say over the words to his mind, the repetition carried not the slightest conviction.

What would he find there on the floor above?

He remembered suddenly that he did not even know where Jolly's room was, and at that moment he heard a shrill voice—Maizie's voice—calling from below: "Phil! Wait! Wait! I'm coming!"

Then the patter of her feet.

"Keep back!" he managed to say. But it was only a whisper. And then there she was beside him, holding his arm, pressing hard against him. Loafer, too, was trying to shove his muzzle between his legs, and it seemed to Philip that the world was collapsing about him. It had seemed to him that two creatures under the sky were without fear. One of them was Maizie; the other was the great dog; but now both of them were pressing on him in mortal agony of fear.

"I don't want you to go on," said Maizie. "Phil, I want you to come down again. You've done enough. Don't go! For God's sake don't go to Jolly's room!"

The greatness of her terror gave him strength. His voice came to him.

"You go back, Maizie," said he. "There's nothing bad. You go back to your father and Doc."

"Down that stairs—alone?" she shuddered. "I'll stay with you!"

And he turned down the hall with her.

A door gaped at the end of it and he knew, somehow, that that was the door to Jolly's room. The moon was up; a pale shaft of its light was falling through the window into the chamber. What would it show them when they gained the threshold?

He pushed on, gritting his teeth; nothing but a blind speed could carry him over that entrance, so he trusted to the force of motion which brought him a full stride within the chamber before he had to halt.

He looked wildly around him. Nothing was wrong. Nothing was out of place. There was no sign of confusion. There was only the pale moonshine lying in a pool on the floor and a continual fall of ghostly light dropping through the open window.

CHAPTER XXV

MAIZIE ran suddenly ahead of him. It took his breath to see her venture so. She went straight to the window, and there she leaned low over the floor.

"Look, Phil!" she whispered.

Instantly he was beside her.

There was not much—just a trace of mold or earth, but it was in the plain outline of a man's shoe.

The girl darted to a closet and came back with a shoe which she held above the print.

"You see?" she said in the same dreadful murmur. "It's smaller than Phil's foot. Someone's been here before him! Who was it? Who did Jolly meet here? A Purchass, Phil! But—what did they do him?"

They stood up and faced each other, staring helplessly, with wide dark eyes.

"We've lost him again," murmured the girl. "Oh, Phil, we've lost him again, and now he'll never come back! They've got him and they'll murder him!"

He would have tried to comfort her, but the same horrible thought was strong in his mind, and no comforting words would come to him. Only, staring at her with wonder, for the first time he felt that she was barely more than a child. She had seemed armed in a complete self-sufficiency; now she was a weak and helpless girl.

Then, most cheerful and matter of fact, they heard the crunching hoofs of a horse biting into the sand and gravel of the back yard and they looked down from the window in time to see Jolly himself mounted in the saddle and riding from the yard the same horse that he and Philip had taken from the Purchasses, and leading another behind him. Philip did not need a second glance to make sure that the led horse, also, had been taken in the same adventure. He recognized the small, well-placed, eager head of the thoroughbred.

"It's Jolly!" murmured Maizie.

She leaned far out from the window.

"Jolly! Jolly!" she called. "Where you goin', dear?"

Jolly did not look up.

It might have been the mere effect of the moonlight, but it seemed to Philip that the face of the youngster was white and set, as it had been when he walked down through the hall and into the dining room.

"Jolly!" screamed Maizie.

But Jolly rode on out of sight around the corner of the house and the horses, reaching the dusty trail, were heard no more.

"What was it? What happened? It *was* Jolly, wasn't it?" she asked Philip, clinging to him.

"It was—I think it was—I don't know," he stammered. "We'd better get back down below."

They came to the door of the room and there the nerve of Loafer gave way with a crash. He bolted ahead of them towards the lamplight that entered softly into the lower hallway. They heard the scratching of his frantic feet, saw his shadow shoot past them, and Maizie dropped helplessly over the arm of the boy.

In the curve of his left arm he carried her lightly, wondering at her little weight, and lifting her high so that her head would fall on his shoulder, supported there, her cheek against his cheek. In his right hand he carried his drawn revolver, and with a sidling step, to look up and down the stairs at the same moment, lest danger should rush down behind, or leap up in front, he bore her slowly to the lower floor and then into the dining room.

Old Delmar, with a groan, received her, but almost instantly she opened her eyes, calling wildly: "Jolly! Has he come back! Is he here?"

She saw Philip and reached a feeble hand for him.

"Was it a dream, Phil? Did you and I stand at the window upstairs and see him ride away?"

He nodded, and at that she fell back in the chair, her eyes closed.

Philip repeated hastily to Doc Rivers and to Delmar what they had seen—the footprint near the window, obviously much smaller than one made by the shoe of Jolly, and the strange spectacle of Jolly riding away through the moonlight with a white face, deaf to the voices which called to him from above.

"We'll follow him," said Rivers.

Delmar raised his hand.

"Let him be! Let him be!" he said. "I never forced a child of mine an inch. I'll not start now. Let Jolly go. It—it looks to me like he had something on his conscience. That footprint upstairs—tell me, was it small enough to be the footprint of a woman?"

Doc Rivers groaned with relief.

"That's all it is?" he exclaimed. "It's only some girl that's dropped in on old Jolly and reminded him of something. Something that he took to heart. Thank God—because I thought—I thought—"

He bit his lip.

"Here, Maizie," he said, "have a drink of water. You look all done up!"

She pushed the proffered glass away. She had recovered from this spell of weakness with wonderful suddenness and now she sat up straight and tall on the edge of the chair, looking feverishly from one of them to the other.

"Something took Jolly away," she said. "It's no good following. The thing that could take him away in spite of himself would take him away again. We all felt it—I felt it, I mean. Did the rest of you feel sort of winter in your backbone?"

One and all they blinked in acknowledgment of the justice of that comparison.

They all were silent, no one daring to meet the eye of the other. What Philip was thinking of was the cold outer world, windless, chained up with the white, eternal frost of the moon; and he could guess that the others had the same picture in their eyes, and poor Jolly drawn away through that icy wilderness he himself knew not where!

Loafer came suddenly to him from the corner and licked his hand. The dog was himself again. The mane had fallen and the green light had left his eyes, and at the same instant Doc Rivers began to roll a cigarette and old Delmar to drum on the table with his finger tips.

It was like the lifting of a spell, and Maizie seemed to feel the change, also.

"It's gone," she said in a calm and natural voice.

"Ay," nodded her father. "It's gone. And Jolly with it."

"What was it?"

"A ghost," said Doc Rivers with grim belief.

"Ghosts don't leave footmarks on the floor," declared the girl. "And—ghosts don't carry Jolly away from his home."

"Carry him away? He went by himself."

She shrugged her shoulders.

"I'm going to have another look at his room," she said.

They all went up in a crowd, Loafer preceding them and turning down the hall above in the correct direction as though he knew perfectly well where they intended to proceed. As they came into the doorway, Loafer already was at the footmark under the window, and sniffing at it, he growled savagely, as only a wolf, one would have said, can growl.

They brought two lamps and flooded the spot with light. There was only the single mark on the floor. Maizie tried her foot beside it, and then looked up significantly, for it was pronouncedly larger than her shoe.

"And I'm no Cinderella," said Maizie, to complete her unspoken thought.

It could well have been the mark of a man's foot, they decided. The stuff which outlined the impression was simply the greenish dust and mold from the shingled roof that sloped down outside the window. In fact, when they held a lamp outside they plainly distinguished three or four places where that same mold had been disturbed, and one was a long scrape, as though the foot of the visitor had slipped.

"If I'd been outside, only, with a gun on him!" groaned Doc Rivers.

But they talked no more about it. Conversation could do no good, and the important matter was: What communication had the stranger given to Jolly Delmar at that hour of the night, in order to make young Delmar leave his home like a stricken man going to his execution? All the manner of Jolly, now that they looked back upon it, had been that of a man going to his death.

Everything about it was strange. It was most unlike Jolly, for instance, to have made such a melodramatic exit, stalking through the dining room in silence while the others gaped at him. Most of all, it was unnatural for him to have made no answer to the voice of his sister when she called to him from his window.

All that was most remarkable. But certainly Jolly was not the one to play a foolish part or take advantage of a singular circumstance to shock his family. A real calamity had fallen upon him. Of that there was no doubt.

He who had made that footprint on the floor of the room was the person who had brought the shock upon him. That, also, seemed reasonable. But at that point all further conjecture ended.

"Get Sheldon!" said Delmar suddenly. "He's got an eye for a sign. Get him here and let him work out this here trail if he can. Maybe an expert can get something out of it!"

Doc Rivers went to call Sheldon, whose room was further down the hall, but he came back to report that Sheldon was not in his room. Furthermore, no blankets were spread upon his cot.

"Gone, by God!" exclaimed old Delmar.

"He's a small man!" broke in Philip. "He might have made that track!"

"He might!" admitted Delmar. "Though why over the roof when he might of gone down the hall?"

They stared hopelessly at one another.

"That runt," breathed Doc Rivers. "A skinny runt like that Sheldon! What could *he* know? What could *he* say?"

CHAPTER XXVI

JOLLY did not come back the next day and neither did he come the following morning, after which it was agreed in the house of his father that there was very little likelihood that the boy would ever come back. Moreover, no matter how improbable it might appear, every one of the silent and gloomy people in the Delmar house was convinced that he must have ridden straight off into the arms of the enemy. Otherwise, if he were back in the neighborhood, he would have attempted to send them some signal.

They were convinced of this, but they were also convinced that nothing they could do would be of the slightest avail. It would be frightfully dangerous to scout anywhere near the Purchass house, a gloomy old stronghold among the hills. In short, they needed help, and it was Doc Rivers who proposed what they should do and how they should go about it. They must hunt out the Colonel and have speech with him. The law they could not invite in. If it were used, it might open the Purchass house—at some cost to itself—but if the boy were found, he would be found dead. And if he were found alive, he would simply be transferred to a jail.

All of this they agreed upon, and Rivers simply suggested that he and Philip ride at once to the Colonel and beg him to give his assistance.

As for the Colonel's price, since he was an expensive tool to use, he might be convinced by the talk of the mine, and above all by showing him the specimen of ore which Jolly had shown to the family. That specimen they still retained; the father had it under lock and key.

The plan was simple enough. If the ore interested the Colonel—and it was reasonably sure to do so—they might then offer him a share in the mine in case he would secure the liberation of Jolly. If Jolly were dead, the matter ended there. As for the share, the Colonel was to be proffered ten per cent of the profits; if need be, Doc Rivers was to raise the offer to fifty per cent of the total! And they felt it was more apt to be near that figure, for the Colonel was known to drive a shrewd bargain.

Maizie and old Delmar accepted the plan with enthusiasm. They would give up every penny of hope from the mine if they could only secure Jolly again; but it was doubted if even the great power of the Colonel could persuade the Purchass clan to part from their prisoner.

So Philip and Doc took the road at once. Doc Rivers was to be the persuading agent: Philip was the guard in case of danger on the road, for it was highly probable that the Purchass agents would attempt to take bloody revenge for the two whom Philip had hurt, perhaps mortally, in the valley. So they looked to their weapons, and it was while Philip was cleaning his rifle on the rear veranda of the house that Maizie came out and leaned against a narrow wooden pillar beside him. Loafer, who of late distrusted all strangers, now strode from behind his master and lay down on guard between him and the girl.

Yet she did not speak, so that Philip grew more and more self-conscious. At length, with clumsy hands he let a piece of chamois fall. It fluttered over the edge of the veranda and slumped to the ground.

"Get it, boy!" commanded Philip, and Loafer slipped over the veranda edge and leaped back, the rag in his teeth. At the feet of his master he put down the chamois and then again resumed his watchful position, this time seated, with his great head canted a little to the side.

"He's useful," observed the girl. "How old is he?"

"Uncle Oliver brought him home four years ago when he was a little puppy."

"Hunt with him?"

"He's great at that."

"What?"

"Deer and things."

"Deer?"

"He spots 'em. Then if they're up a pass, say, you can send him around to drive them down to you."

"You gotta hit the deer on the run, then?"

"Oh, yes."

"Humph!" said the girl.

"I suppose you hunt a lot?"

"I get a shot now and then. I'm not very good."

"It takes a lot of practice," admitted Philip kindly.

His color was growing more normal; and he wondered what was in her mind, for it was not the habit of Maizie to talk to no purpose.

"I've had practice," said she. "There's one thing I've worked over."

She pointed to a tall pine which stood near the end of the barn.

"You see that squirrel out there among the needles?"

"I see it," said Philip.

"I've tried for him a hundred times with my rifle. I've had the fur out of him, but never the blood."

"He's quick, I guess?"

"He's lightnin'," she assured Philip. 'He knows a rifle, too. Don't bother till he sees you put it to your shoulder."

"You might try a revolver, then."

"At that distance?"

"Oh, yes!"

"Oh, nothing," said Maizie with some heat. "Don't you tell me that you can hit a squirrel that far off, with a Colt?"

"Not fanning the gun," corrected Philip. "But like this."

The Colt glided into his hand, swayed up to the level of his eyes, and exploded. The twig on which the squirrel stood was cut in two beneath his feet. He tumbled head over heels, struck the broad branch beneath, and scampered in towards the trunk of the tree, chattering with terror.

"I missed," said Philip, blushing deeply. "I—I'm a little out of practice, I'm afraid!"

The girl looked not at him. She was studying the tree with care.

"That's sixty yards," she said presently.

"It's only a little over fifty, I'm afraid," said Philip.

"Humph," said Maizie.

She turned back to him.

"If that was a man—it wouldn't have hit his head—it would have cut his throat in two!"

"Perhaps."

"Phil!"

"Yes?"

"Have you ever fired a shot at a man?"

"No, thank heaven!"

"Would you hate it?"

"Hate it!"

"But before you're a week older you'll have fired."

"I hope not."

"And the man will die," said Maizie sternly. "Maybe a couple of him will die!"

Philip closed his eyes to shut out the thought.

Maizie went on: "If you don't want to have that kind of trouble—blood on your hands, I mean—you quit this trail. You leave the valley, will you? Go away some other place. Folks will always be glad to have you."

"I don't know very much," confessed Philip.

"You're about the strongest man in the world, and pretty near the straightest shot. D'you know that?"

He shook his head.

"But you're going to ride into a terrible lot of trouble. I gotta tell you that. They're devils. I mean the Purchass lot. They'd kill you with poison, if guns didn't work."

He looked straight before him, seeing this thing in detail, but he would not surrender.

"Where are you traveling?"

"To find work," said Philip. "I must make a home for Uncle Oliver."

"How old is he?"

"He's a good deal more than sixty."

After this, Maizie folded her hands together at her breast and looked past Philip into sadness and thought, so that he dared to stare into her face, and she seemed to him of a more than mortal beauty.

"I'll find Jolly or die on the trail," he told her gravely, feeling the words as he spoke them. And as he spoke, he knew that the determination was turning to iron in him.

134

She looked suddenly down at him again; Loafer growled softly.

"If ever Jolly comes home," she said, and paused there, but something brilliant in her eyes went on speaking to Philip, and a happy mist rushed over his mind.

Through that mist he dimly heard Doc Rivers calling, and through it he saw the two horses led out from the barn.

Somehow he was mounted; automatically he thrust his rifle into the long holster that dangled down beneath his right leg. He picked up the reins.

"When in doubt, ride hard!" called old Delmar.

The dimness lifted; Philip saw the girl waving to them from the veranda; and he told himself that he would live up to his promise or pay the price which he had vowed to her. She had not finished speaking out the promise, but he felt that she knew and that he knew what had been meant.

Suddenly the trotting horse jerked him past a string of trees. The narrow trunks blurred the sight of the veranda, and the waving girl, and old Delmar standing beside her. And just before they disappeared Philip thought he saw her turn to her father, sagging like the weariest of all creatures, and so fall into his arms. But it was only a flash. Then he was on the open trail, and Doc Rivers was regarding him with a thin, withered, sardonic face.

"Good old Phil!" he said, half sneering. "You sure are the champion simp!"

Philip shrugged his shoulders. He did not understand. He did not want to understand.

"I'll tell you something," said Doc Rivers. "She's a lottery. That's all. You got ticket number seventeen thousand four hundred and ninety-three. That's all. Write it down in your head. I'm telling you straight! And now, for God's sake, get that dizzy look out of your face. We gotta have both of our pairs of eyes open on this trip."

CHAPTER XXVII

THEY dropped rapidly through the hills. Philip's eyes were wide open, indeed, for anger had roused him, and he had checked himself on the verge of making a threatening retort to his companion.

They were riding down a narrow valley, from tall hills to low, with the prospect opening before them to the east. To the west a high fog was gathering, so that the tops of the mountains floated above it blue and light, like queer-shaped ships floating upon the heavier sea. The forest, ruined in that mist, tangled together for a few hundred yards, and then went out altogether in a massive wall of gray. But to the east there was not a suspicion of moisture in the air. All was bright and crisp, and cool with the autumn chill.

Doc Rivers announced that he would be well pleased to leave the verge of the trees, but as he also said, they might as well accept a small danger in the beginning, since they were likely to have far greater perils before the end.

"But," said Philip, speaking suddenly out of the midst of his thoughts, "you tell me that the Purchass people are terribly strong?"

"Strong? Like iron!"

"Then how could one man like the Colonel do as he pleased with them?"

"I dunno that he can," replied Doc Rivers. "But the Colonel never has failed, people say!"

"Failed to do what?" asked Philip.

"He's never failed to make a stack of money every year of his life since he came out here; he's never failed to keep out of jail; and he's never failed to handle his job. That's a good deal to win out in!"

"It is!" admitted Philip gravely.

"The point about the big Colonel is that he never takes a crack at the law. He leaves it be. That's where he's got the sense."

"Then how does he make his money?"

"Out of the crooks. Suppose that you're a ranchman. You gotta pretty good ranch, a doggone fine layout of cows. But those cows begin to drift. Well, you send for the Colonel. He says ten thousand dollars. You pay. The cow stealing stops. There ain't a cow rustled on your place, ever after that!"

"Does he stay on the place and guard it?"

"He don't have to, no more. At first he had to do some things. The Yerkes boys and their gang, he run into them, first. They told him to go to hell. He wasn't even an officer of the law. Well, he run them right up into the hills. He killed three of 'em. He wounded five more. He captured four men, tied 'em together, and he drove 'em down from the mountains barefoot. One of 'em died afterwards. One of 'em lost a foot from walking through the snow. And the other two, there wasn't enough manhood left in 'em to make up a boy between the pair. That broke up the Yerkes gang. I mean, it wiped it out! After that, people took the Colonel pretty serious. Personal, I'd rather have a chunk of hell after me than him!"

"I understand," said Philip, his eyes gleaming. "It seems a very good thing to me. He's a sort of independent officer of the law."

"He ain't. He's hired hell-fire. That's what he is! Law? He don't give a damn for the law. It's trouble that he lives for the sake of. Oh, he's a man! Look at Thomason. He had this part of the country staked off for himself. Every year he worked one bank robbery. Then Grier comes in. He begins to raid the banks right and left. He robbed four in three months. Thomason went to the Colonel. The Colonel went out and brought Grier in, tied to his saddle like a dead deer, you might say. Grier just lived long enough to confess that he was a yegg. They say that Thomason paid the Colonel twenty thousand dollars for that job."

"But I should think that it would keep down crime a great deal," suggested Philip.

"You would think that, but you don't understand. The Colonel don't go ravin' after criminals. He gives out a sort of a charter. Suppose that you want to come into the county and work some jobs in a big way—selling stock in mines that ain't, boosting the stock of railroads that never get down to tracks. Well, if you want to do that, you go to the Colonel. You pay him. He lets you go. He puts a stamp on you, you might say. You're his man. The rest of his men will give you a hand. They'll help you out. Even out of jail. Well, that's worth something. You gotta pay a price and a damn big one. It's the big money that the Colonel is after. He don't mind the little things!"

"And if the criminal on a big scale doesn't pay?"

"The Colonel goes down and cleans him up."

"How can he do that without getting put in jail?"

"Because he always has all of the evidence. He knows all of the crook world and the crook ways. He can do anything that he wants. Get any information that he wants. I was standing on Main Street and Fourth Avenue, one day. A big gent in long gray whiskers was setting in a runabout jiggering the reins and talking to another gent that had his foot on the hub of the front wheel of the buggy. Up comes big Colonel. He takes the whiskered gent by the neck and lifts him out of the wagon. He takes him down the street and chucks him into the open door of the jail.

" 'Stay there till you've been sentenced and sent up,' says he.

"Well, that gent stayed there. He had to. It was worth his while to stay there, mind you, because if he'd come out, the Colonel would have gone for him with a gun."

"If he could lift a grown man like that—from a high seat—he must be very strong!" suggested Philip.

"He's only six feet six. But you'll see him for yourself. You'll admire to see him, kid!"

He began to laugh, a little savagely, and Philip bowed his head.

After all, bigness of body is not the only important feature to be considered. He was keen with interest. Other men had been like children. They had broken, their strength had melted away like wax under red hot pincers

138

when he gripped them. But the Colonel, apparently, would be something of a different order, and he was hungry to see the big man.

They were going rapidly towards the town, now; and when they had put a good twelve miles behind them, either at raking canter or rapid trot, they looked from a hilltop into a pleasant little dale where a small cottage stood; and beyond the farther crest, they could see the city lying in the plain, streaked over with wind-bent columns of smoke. The pulse of Philip raced as he looked towards it. Somehow he felt that all of his adventuring consisted of the merest skirmishing upon the borders of things, but the heart of the adventure was still to come, when he reached the town.

"That," said Doc Rivers, "is his place."

"That little house?" asked Philip, in amazement.

"That little house," said the other.

"But see!" said Philip. "There are trees walking up to it on three sides! Any man with enemies—they could slip up on him there!"

"They have," nodded Rivers. "Charlie Hass, he sneaked up by way of the red barn, there. You see? Charlie, he got past the barn. He's buried a little to the right of it, because the Colonel believes in planting where the seed falls. That's his way of putting it.

"He made the grave right there in his back yard. He even put up a headboard. What d'you think that he wrote on the board?"

"Well, of course I can't guess!"

" 'Here died Charlie Hass for want of a better thing to do.' That's the Colonel."

Philip listened in amazement. He could imagine killing in the heat of blood; he could imagine only too keenly a furious and savage joy in the conflict. But he could not imagine one who laughed as he struck.

"Turl McGinnis come up through the west grove, there. He got as far as that birch, you see it? You can just make out the white streak of it! Then the Colonel took him from behind and busted him over his knee."

"His knee?" echoed Philip.

139

"Busted his back, you see? The sheriff got out in time to see him die and take *his* confession. There you are! It kind of discouraged the boys from trying to sneak up on the Colonel until a terrible red-headed gent comes up from Arizona and swears that he'll get the Colonel, by God, if he has to die for it, because the Colonel had killed his best pal. And Arizona Red, he took to the woods, also, and come in there from the east, and there he's lying low with a fine grassy grave piled up over him, and on his headboard is written: 'Here lies Arizona far from home.' "

"But how does he do it?" asked simple Philip. "Does he have spies who tell him what's happening? Does he keep the woods filled with his men?"

"Kid," said Doc Rivers with a sort of pitying gravity, "don't you think that if I knew what the Colonel knows I wouldn't be nothin' but another Colonel? D'you think that I'm self-contented, maybe, bein' nothin' but bullied at home by Ma? No, kid, I dunno how the Colonel manages it. Nobody knows how the Colonel manages it. He's got just one gent to take care of him, and that gent is a Chink."

Philip, riding down the hills from the south towards this affluent abode, felt as though he were approaching the den of an ogre, and his eyes danced. It was the first touch of life which matched with what he had left behind him with his books on Pillar Mountain.

They crossed a meadow where several horses grazed, and each of them was a mighty creature of sixteen or seventeen hands, powerful as a draught horse across the quarters, but finished fine and hard at every point.

"They can't carry him uphill," said Doc Rivers, noticing the direction of Philip's glance. "He does the hills on foot. But they can scoot him down the slopes, and they can gallop him over the valleys. He don't ride no ways except the way the wind blows. What the country looks like is nothing to the Colonel!"

They came closer, breaking through a meagre grove of poplars, and then Philip saw a man lying in an invalid's chair, wrapped in a blanket and sleeping in the sun.

"Hush!" said Rivers. "That's him!"

140

HIS eyes were closed. He was turned well south so that the full might of the sun beat against him, and as Philip and Doc Rivers came closer, dismounting from their horses, they could see that this must have been an old practice with the great man, for his very eyelids were bronzed by the sunlight, and above his eyes the forehead, usually shaded by the wide sombrero, was nut-brown almost to the verge of the hair, where indeed a pale streak occurred.

This was only the first impression of the giant, but a closer inspection showed that he was a book that would take much reading. In every way he was massive. The hand which hung over the arm of the invalid chair looked like a mighty engine of destruction. His pointed beard and elegant mustache could not disguise for a moment the power of his jaw, and upon his brow as he slept was the frown of might.

The giant opened his eyes and regarded them in leisurely fashion and with bright, unwinking eyes which appeared of an almost unreal blue because of the blackness of his hair and beard.

"You're young Rivers, I think," said he. "Forgive me if I don't get up! Li!"

He called loudly, and the woods or the face of the house flung back the booming echo once and again. The servant did not need to be told what was wanted. He appeared now carrying two chairs, which he placed, with a bow for each guest.

"I'm Rivers," replied Doc as he took a seat, "and here's a friend of mine. Sit down, Phil!"

But Philip first acknowledged this introduction by advancing a step, very frightened, and taking the hand of the giant. It hung loose and cold and moist in his grasp; it did not return the pressure of his handshake, and he returned to his chair depressed and more overawed than before.

"You've come a distance?" asked the giant.

"From the Delmar house," said Rivers, and waited a little.

"That's twelve miles and a half," said the Colonel. "How is everything with the Delmars?"

He had a lazy, luxurious way of speaking. His lips were astonishingly red and looked as though they had been polished; they parted and remained open for a moment, always before a sound came. And at the end, they were still parted, as though something more were about to be uttered.

"The Delmars are well enough, what's left of them," answered Doc Rivers.

"One of them dead?" asked the Colonel.

"Gone," said Doc Rivers.

"The pretty girl has eloped at last?"

"She's still home."

"It's the boy, then. He's been due for trouble for a long time."

"He's been havin' it, too, sir."

It seemed to Philip that Rivers appeared like a child at school in front of the Colonel, so stiffly did he sit in his chair.

Li brought tea and fruit and placed it on a little bamboo table between them, but Philip would not eat. He was too enormously interested in this man out of a fairy tale.

The Colonel pressed them. He pointed out the dark red cheeks of the pears and the rich yellow of ripeness which set it off. He picked up an apple and began to set an example by eating it. He ate with small bites, with very white teeth that seemed, like his lips, to be polished; so did they flash in the sun. And his blue, unwinking eyes flashed above. The sky at clear midnight reminded Philip of those eyes; he could imagine that the sea lying level and windless under the morning sun might be like those eyes. As for the light in them, it was like that which might slip and glide along a fine sword blade exposed for sale and slowly turned.

The eyes of other men were mere windows out of which they peeped, now and again, and through which others might have a glimpse of all that was inside; but the eyes of the Colonel were very different. They were a portion of the bright, blue, terrible soul within him. When he glanced at Philip, it was like the impact of a heavy weight, and the boy was glad that Rivers was occupying most of the attention of the great man. It was very easy to understand how he could run two or three counties, each as big as a New England state. It was only wonderful that he did not make himself a king in whatever part of the world amused him most.

"Young Delmar has been having his trouble, then?" said the Colonel. "He was out of date; he thought that he lived in the Garden of Eden. What about him? Is that your errand to me?"

"Yes," nodded Rivers. "Jolly's gone. I dunno how. They switched him away after the kid and me brought him in through their lines!"

He said it with a little ring of pride. The Colonel, at this, allowed his great head to roll slowly to one side, so that his attention bore full upon the face of Philip.

"Are you the one who came through the pass and threw the Purchass men about?" he asked.

Philip blinked. This sudden attention raised a lump in his throat around which he could not speak, and Rivers had to say: "That's the man, sir!"

The Colonel began to laugh, softly. He let his eyes close, and his laughter boomed in him as in a cave. Loafer got up and looked the giant in the face and began to growl.

"Hush!" said Philip, and the wolf-dog sat down between his legs.

"Five broken ribs, a broken hip, a dislocated shoulder, and a bullet out of their own guns. That's what makes it beautiful. That's what makes it a lovely affair!"

He drew a breath slowly, as though retasting the pleasure of that sport.

"One only has a few perfect moments in a long life,"

143

he said to Philip. "Treasure this one. Print it deep in your mind. It is better than a volume of poems. Now, Rivers, tell me what you want."

"I want you," said Rivers.

The Colonel merely nodded.

"Jolly's gone; the Purchass people have him; well, we want you to get him back."

"My dear boy," answered the Colonel, "I love the trusting way in which you approach me! But the Purchass lot are the strongest group in the mountains. I'm only a single man, and they're at least thirty effective fighting men, and more if they want to send out for them."

"Yes, sir," said Rivers.

"You know that; but why do you come to me?"

"Because I got this idea—that you and Phil, together, could smash through walls of rocks and beat armies to a pulp."

"He flatters us, eh?" said the Colonel to Philip. "Give me your revolver."

Obediently, Philip laid it in the hand of the giant, and the latter went over it in detail, examining every small point.

"Yes," he said, handing back the gun, "you've learned to shoot very well. Why have I never heard of you before?"

"He's just come into these parts," explained Rivers.

The Colonel closed his eyes again, and Philip was glad of it, for while they were open, he was under a constant strain.

"I don't see what I could do for you, Rivers," he answered at last. "Admitting that Philip is a fighting man of the first water—of the very first water—still, it only takes two bullets to end two men, and the Purchass tribe have a great plenty of bullets."

"I wanted to talk it all over," said Rivers. "I wanted to offer you something worth while, sir."

"Don't tempt me," answered the Colonel.

He pointed suddenly at Loafer.

"That's a dog," he said.

"Thank you," said Philip.

"He would take off my hand at the wrist, I think."

"He would, sir."

144

"Will he watch over you at night?"

"He will, sir."

"And guard you?"

"I have to keep him tied up every night."

"Young man, what price have you for that dog?"

The blue eyes of Philip opened enormously wide.

"I don't understand," said he.

"You speak English, I hope?" asked the giant. "I say, will you sell that dog?"

"He wouldn't stay with you," declared Philip. "He'd run away."

"Nothing runs away from me," replied the Colonel severely. "He would stay if I cared to keep him. Now, my lad, what's your price?"

Philip shook his head. He reached out a sudden hand and at the touch of it Loafer turned his head a little, and closed his eyes with joy.

"I wouldn't sell him," said he.

"You think not," smiled the Colonel. "Nevertheless, I shall buy him. I'll offer you a hundred dollars, my boy."

"It would be selling part of myself. Loafer—he's a friend, you see."

"Five hundred dollars," said the Colonel.

"Sweet—sufferin'—mama!" said Doc Rivers.

"No, no!" said Philip.

"Think what you're saying," said the Colonel. "I'm offering you now a thousand dollars in hard cash. Enough to set you up in the world. A thousand dollars for a dog, young man!"

"Phil, don't you be a fool!" broke in Rivers, his eyes starting.

Philip folded his hands together and squeezed hard. He could hardly hear the words. He could only see the flashing blue eyes that seemed to threaten him with untold dangers. Yet he managed to stammer: "It's not exactly that he's a dog. But he's a friend, sir. I couldn't sell myself. I couldn't sell myself; I couldn't sell the dog!"

The Colonel lay back in his chair again and waved a great hand airily.

"There you are, Rivers. You come to me to buy me. Learn from your friend. I can't even buy his dog!"

CHAPTER XXIX

Doc Rivers was greatly excited. There was some flaw in this reasoning, but he could not put his finger on it. The Colonel was talking down to him from a height, but he could not prevent the condescension.

"It's not the same," he ventured.

The Colonel shrugged his massive shoulders.

"There's a dog; here's a man. No price for one, no price for the other!"

Suddenly Rivers snatched out the chunk of ore and laid it in the lap of the Colonel.

"Look at that," he said.

The Colonel looked at it. It seemed to Philip that there was no alteration in his demeanor or in his expression, except that perhaps his blue eyes grew a little more flashingly bright, a little grayer, a little more like steel in the sun.

"That's an expensive bit of ore," he admitted.

"That's what the trouble's about," said Rivers. "I would of thought that Jolly was just a dead man, by this time. But this won't let me think that. Jolly found this. Somehow the Purchase gang knows about it. They got him now. They're putting the pressure on him. Maybe they're offering him his life if he'll tell them about where this here gold is. You see? Now you know why we're here talkin' to you, sir."

The Colonel nodded. He weighed the rock on his forefinger.

"Somebody will be enormously rich out of this," he suggested.

"Richer'n Rockefeller!" said Rivers heartily. "And why shouldn't you be one?"

"I?" said the Colonel, and raised his brows, as though rather shocked by such a thought. "I! But my dear fellow, let me tell you that there's something else worth thinking about. My own attitude towards life. You see that I live here quietly. I detest disturbances. I like enough money to live on. In a modest way, I collect enough for my needs. And there you are! No desire for a vast fortune. None whatever! None whatever!"

He shook his head with violence, and while his eyes remained closed, Rivers shot at the boy a glance expressive of disgust and rage. Even Philip could see that there was a touch of hypocrisy about this fellow with his speeches about modest ambitions, small requirements of living. It was as though a pirate should pretend to the manner of a philosopher!

"I jus' want to point out," said Rivers gravely, "that this here ain't thousands. Maybe it's hundreds of thousands—maybe it's millions, Colonel!"

The Colonel raised a protesting hand. It was as smooth as stone, that hand, and the fingers were long and tapering.

"You can't tempt me," said he. "You really can't tempt me, my friend. To introduce the management of a large fortune into my quiet mode of life, to occupy my mind with investments and—I couldn't dream of it. I couldn't dream of it! It is like the crash and roar of war. Years steal upon me; I grow more quiet. I lie here in the sun. I think of nothing. You cannot tempt me!"

And with that he looked so mildly upon Rivers and shook his head in such earnestness that Philip was almost tempted to believe what he heard.

Rivers closed his eyes and set his teeth.

"We'll offer you one-quarter out of every bit of profit that comes from the mine!" said he.

"If I bring young Delmar away from the Purchasses?" asked the Colonel.

"You and Phil, here, and me. We'd work. I know I'm not much good. But Phil is. I've seen him go through them like a canoe through water. They can't hold him. You and him together—that's what I mean!"

"A quarter for me and a quarter for Philip?" suggested the giant.

"Phil, he ain't interested so much in the money end of things."

"A young philosopher?" asked the giant, and he smiled vaguely upon Philip.

"Anyway," sad Rivers, "I want you to give it a think. Twenty-five per cent. If you do the job, you never have to think about the thing afterwards. It's just in your hands!"

"A very large and handsome offer," said the Colonel, obviously thinking hard and fast. "But one never can tell. These promising veins pinch out."

"We might even trim up that percentage a little," suggested Rivers. "Say that we called it a third? One-third, Colonel. That's money, I guess!"

"One-third!" said the Colonel, and his blue eyes flashed. Suddenly he shook his head.

"Let's talk of other things," said the Colonel, in his deliberate manner. "We waste our time about the mine. Besides, the business would be much too difficult for me. You overestimate me. I'm only mortal, Mr. Rivers!"

Rivers jumped up from his chair.

"Colonel," he said, "I'll go right to the top. One-half of everything for you—and no work on your part. One-half! One-half of the clear profits!"

The Colonel suddenly writhed in his chair, and for a single instant all the avarice in his soul was shown in his face.

"It's no use!" he declared. "By this time the Purchass people have made an agreement with young Delmar. His life in exchange for the location of the mine!"

"He'd never give in!" said Rivers.

"Ah? Is he a Spartan?"

"You laugh," said Doc Rivers, with a heat that surprised Philip. "I tell you, Jolly's better than folks take him for. He's been a fool. He knows it. He's wrecked his family. He knows that, too. Well, he's found the mine and that's his chance to even everything up and make his folks happy, and he'll die ten times quicker'n he'll tell what he knows!"

"Ah?" said the Colonel again.

"However," he added slowly, "there are ways of persuading people to speak!"

"He'll never give in," said Rivers obstinately. "I know it. I know how he's feeling inside. He'll die, quicker."

The Colonel sat bolt upright: "Young man," he said, "take your horse and go away. I don't want to talk any longer! Go at once. I—I'm tired and wish to rest in the sun!"

Doc Rivers groaned. He did not protest, however, but as one who knows that the end has been reached, he made a gesture of surrender and beckoned to Philip. The latter rose, also. He could hardly believe that the interview had been ended, so suddenly. Something had told him that the pangs of temptation were entering the giant, and that soon he would quite melt under the influence of the bribes which were being offered.

Rivers moved off hastily with a single word of farewell, but Philip lingered an instant, until the giant, without opening his tightly shut eyes—as though he felt the mere shadow of the young man's presence—said: "You too, my young friend. I wish to be alone."

"The dog," said Philip suddenly; "I wanted to say about the dog—"

At that, the blue eyes opened. They blazed out at Philip in a sort of unearthly brightness of triumph.

"You've changed your mind, have you? You'll sell your pet dog, after all?"

"Sell him?" echoed Philip with a shudder. "No, no! But I'll give him away! I'll make an exchange, I mean to say."

"Go on, then. What will the exchange be?" asked the Colonel, most of the brilliance of victory—whatever could have inspired it—disappearing at once from his glance.

"You help us with Jolly Delmar," said Philip, "then I'll give you Loafer. I'll give you Loafer before, if you'll shake hands on the business!"

"You'll give your dog away for that?" asked the Colonel, a shadow falling quickly over his face. "But I hear that you have no share in the mine?"

"Oh, no," said Philip.

"Then why are you in it?"

"The Delmars are my friends."

"Friends?" cried the giant, and his voice fairly shook Philip with its thunder. "I know friends and friendships. I've never found them to wear. I've never found them to have any truth of substance. They don't last. Nothing in this living hell is given without pay. Nothing! What else do you want out of the Delmars? What can they give you? Tell me the truth!"

He reached out his hand, leaning from his chair, and caught the arm of Philip. He did not exert a great pressure, but Philip felt that he was hopelessly imprisoned, as though by the touch of unyielding iron.

"There's nothing else," said Philip, not quite honestly.

"There is—you lie to me," declared the Colonel.

The point seemed to him of the vastest importance. Then he sank back in the chair and nodded his head.

"It's the girl!" he exclaimed. And he nodded again. "Is that right?" he asked.

"I must not speak about it", said poor Philip.

"You must not? Speak about everything to me. I am a sea into which all secrets disappear. I am like conscience; I understand!"

Then he added: "You have her for wife if you bring back Jolly Delmar? She promised you that?"

"She gave me no promise," answered Philip.

The Colonel scowled blackly.

"I don't understand you," he said at last. "You had better go away. You annoy me. I don't understand. There's no promise made, and still you wish to throw your life away? I don't understand. Go away, young man. I wish to be alone!"

Poor Philip stroked the head of Loafer. It was a comfort that the great dog was to stay with him, but it was a thin comfort, after all. He said good-by in the faintest of voice, but as he was turning away the voice of the giant flooded about his ears once more.

"Come back!"

He returned and stood before the Colonel.

"Look at me," said the big man, and Philip looked fairly into those wild blue eyes.

CHAPTER XXX

SQUARELY met, they were not so difficult to withstand. Within them the blue, cold light was pouring up as in wave on wave and rushing out towards Philip. But he could stand against it. With every instant it was easier to stand before the other, and he felt that never again would such dreadful awe overcome him in the presence of this monster. It was as though he had been given a touch of rare understanding, a clue to a mystery; there was something about the Colonel which he had known all his life, though he could not give it a name!

"You can look at me," said the Colonel finally, "but are you honest? Are you honest?"

"I don't know," answered Philip, always simple.

"A girl smiles at you. You go out to conquer the world. Is that right?"

"Oh, no," said Philip. "I only want to help Jolly, if I can."

"She didn't give you a promise?"

"No."

"But you're pretty sure. Tell me that! You're pretty sure that if you bring Jolly home she'll fall into your arms?"

Philip looked far off, and Maizie came close home into his mind, hard and gentle, cold and warm, so close to him that he could conjure her very flesh out of the empty air, and so far removed that he knew her not at all.

"I'm sure of nothing," he admitted gloomily.

The Colonel looked suddenly down to the ground, and it was impossible to doubt that some strength had departed from him. He looked older, to Philip, and whereas before he had seemed scant forty, he appeared closer to fifty, now.

"Will you smoke?" he asked.

"No, thank you sir."

"You don't smoke?"

"No, sir. I haven't learned."

The Colonel rolled a cigarette with tobacco which he took from a silver-chased box.

"Children unlock the door we stand without!" he murmured finally. He lighted his cigarette, and let the smoke roll upwards from his bright red lips; he was faintly obscured behind the mist of bluish white.

"My boy," said he, "you observe that I am older than you."

"Yes," said Philip.

"Older in years. Older in life. I have crossed many oceans. Voyaged to unknown lands. Lands you will never touch. As yet you are honest. Therefore I wish to give you good advice. Will you listen?"

"Yes," said Philip, filled with wonder.

"Then, like a surgeon, I use a knife. There is no time for an anæsthetic. My boy, you never will take young Delmar from the Purchass clan. Shall I tell you why? Because I, also, have been retained by that clan!"

It struck Philip dumb. He could understand, now, why the big Colonel had writhed under the temptation of the offers which Rivers had made. They had been bargaining for that which was already sold and delivered.

"Did you hear?"

"I heard," said Philip.

"You have lost him; you never can have him. But there is still another matter, more important. You are young. You must have room to grow. You should be in a country where you can come to manhood without being overshadowed by fixed and firmly rooted trees. This is not such a country. You will have no room to expand. I, my boy, already am here! My advice to you is to go at once. Ride into another range. There you can grow into a man—into a great man; here you will not prosper. Here your life would not last a great length of time. Do you understand me?"

Philip was dumb again.

152

"Leave everything behind you, take nothing with you. Forget the girl. Then, if you wish, I will be happy to provide you with funds. You speak like a gentleman, though a young one. I will give you means to live like a gentleman—in another part of this little world of ours. But you must know from your books, that there is always trouble when two kings strive to rule in one land?"

So, gradually, Philip came at the meaning, and turned crimson. The film of tobacco smoke seemed parted before the face of the Colonel, and he looked straight into the cold, terrible eyes. That speech had been calmly spoken, but it had an utter finality about it that overwhelmed him.

"I shall not go," said Philip. "I cannot go. I would be leaving my promises behind me!"

The Colonel leaned back in his chair once more and closed his eyes. He allowed his cigarette to fall to the ground. He was in every respect as Philip had first seen him, dreaming in the sun.

A farewell, now, would have seemed ridiculously out of place, so the boy turned hastily away and rejoined Doc Rivers at the horses. There he mounted, gave Loafer a kind word that sent the dog running ahead, and swung his mount back on the trail by which they had come.

"Well, kid?" asked Doc eagerly.

The mind and the heart of Philip were so full that he could not speak, at once.

"You look kind of sick," said Doc. "What did the Colonel drop on you?"

Philip shook his head.

"The damn hypocrite!" snarled Rivers. "He ain't interested in money. He don't want it. It'd disturb him. Why, there ain't a devil in hell worse'n him, and he knows it—and he knew that I knew it—but he knew that I didn't dare to answer him back!"

He writhed at the memory of his impotence, and so they journeyed back up the hill and turned on to the winding trail. For a half hour they jogged along, and then Rivers pointed to a trail that left theirs and turned to the right, stretching towards the mountains.

"I thought that maybe there'd be three of us coming back, and that the Colonel would go along with us to the

153

Purchass place. But we're beat. Damn him, why wouldn't he listen? I was offerin' him God knows what!"

"Because he's with the Purchass people; they've retained him," said Philip.

"What!"

"He told me that."

"You don't mean it! He actually told you that?"

"And he told me to get out of this part of the country. He said that there wasn't room here for him and for me."

Doc Rivers whistled softly.

"Are you as big as that in his eyes?" murmured the little man.

Philip sighed bitterly.

"What can we do?" he asked. "But now, I think, is our time. The Colonel is behind us. We know that much. We can get to the Purchass place ahead of him, no doubt. Doc, suppose that we start for them now, and see what we can do?"

"Do you mean that?"

"I mean that. What's there better to do?"

Rivers rubbed his hands violently together, as though they had turned numb with cold in spite of the hot sun. Then he grasped the reins.

"If the Colonel talked like that, then you got a chance to do anything in the world. Kid, I'm ready to take my chance. Come along, and we'll look at the tigers even if we can't get one of their skins!"

They went hastily up the trail. It divided into two forks, and Rivers took the left one, declaring that the other was the main-traveled way. This which they followed would take them around behind the house.

Steadily they climbed, with the western sun in their faces. Once Rivers exclaimed softly, "I can't get warm. That devil of a man has put a chill all through my blood. I can't get warm, kid!"

Philip felt much the same. And besides, a brooding gloom had settled over him. He had not the slightest hope; he felt that he was riding forward merely because there was nothing left to do. It was a forlorn hope, and they two were going to scratch at the door of the castle filled with ogres.

In the meantime, constantly climbing, they topped the first broad-backed ridge, and saw a narrow valley behind them. Rivers looked back, then spurred his horse into a little thick of saplings, and Philip followed him.

"It's him! He's coming!" said Rivers.

A moment later, Philip heard the crashing hoofs of a heavy horse. He could peer out through the close ranks of the saplings, and through them he saw a mighty horseman on a lofty horse rush past. The brim of his sombrero was blown straight up by the speed of that hard gallop, and the rider wore a cloak which flared stiff out behind him.

So the Colonel rushed past, and there was a fleeting glimpse of his wide shoulders, disappearing instantly as he dropped down the slope.

They looked at one another, slient and grim.

"He never goes no slower than that," said Rivers at last. "That's the way he always rides. And what about it, kid?" chuckled Doc sardonically. "Are we gunna get there before him?"

He rode out from the trees and pointed the head of his horse back down the trail.

"Come along," he said. "We're beat to a frazzle."

Then, seeing Philip was moving in the opposite direction: "What you mean, kid?"

"I'm going on," said Philip. "Just to have a look!"

"Phil, are you crazy?"

"I don't know. Only, I know that I can't turn back!"

Suddenly Doc Rivers ranged alongside of him.

"I'd rather of lost ten thousand dollars than of met you!" said Doc sadly. "Doggone me if you ain't a curse!"

"Go back, Doc," said Philip without reproach in his voice. "I don't ask you to go ahead."

"Shut up," answered Rivers angrily. And he actually spurred his horse ahead.

Philip, vaguely wondering, followed.

They launched into the valley; they slowly climbed the steep slope beyond, passed into a grove of young pines, and came out on the other verge in sight of a wide and shallow valley, and in the midst of it a thick clump of lofty trees. There was no house visible, but Philip knew that it was the Purchass place. He knew it as though he had seen it before, in some dream of fear.

CHAPTER XXXI

DOWN came the evening, still and soft and warm, and the two remained on the verge of the woods, Doc Rivers pressing urgently for a return to their friends, so that they could recruit forces to attack the house of the enemy. But Philip would not stir.

Numbers, he knew, they could not raise; at least, they never could command sufficient forces to rush the house. Whatever they accomplished they must accomplish by stealth, and all the chances were strongly against them, for it seemed apparent that the Colonel knew they had headed towards the Purchass house; for no other reason would he have been apt to rush so fast to gain the place before them.

On that subject, even Doc Rivers grew eloquent.

"We threw a chill into the Colonel," he declared. "He went like hell, didn't he? We threw a scare into him. I tell you, kid, that since we busted through them and got Jolly to his home, they're all more or less afraid of us!"

Doc Rivers, after the passage of a few hours, could not help giving himself a little credit for events in which he had no share whatever. He confessed that he had no desire to approach the Purchass house more closely, but he would not leave Philip. While their horses grazed on a slope behind, they lay on a bed of pine needles and stared through the glasses at the trees, until it grew dusk. Then Philip insisted on moving, and mounting his mustang, he rode down across the ridge and cut away towards the trees.

"It's fine, kid," said the uneasy Rivers. "You've done a lot. But what are you gunna do now? Scratch some boards off of the wall of the house and go in and tear up the gang like a lot of playing cards? There ain't any use in being too wild, old son!"

He began to groan aloud, as Philip persisted silently in pressing on towards the trees, which rose more and more lofty before them. Philip himself had no plan; he was drawn forward much as the bird is drawn by the snake's eye. At least, he was in the presence of the enemy, and that was some comfort. He would have at least that to report to Maizie, when he saw her again, and her bright and critical eyes fell upon him.

Close to the forest which surrounded the Purchass place, at last he made a halt. Poor Doc Rivers pressed close beside him. Even when he whispered, his voice trembled.

"Kid," he said, "are you gunna turn back, now?"

"We've got to have a look at things," said Philip.

"Sweet—sufferin'—mama!" groaned Rivers. "Look? Why, we can smell those trees! And if we're spotted, kid, they got horses that would be sure to run us down. You hear?"

"I hear you," answered Philip. "You go in here, if you want. I'll circle around and come in from the other side. I'll work as close to the house as I dare. If I find out anything, I'll come back to this place, and I'll wait for you here, if you haven't come back."

"Go in among those trees? Go closer to the house?" exclaimed Doc Rivers. "Kid, you're crazy, that's all. Clean crazy! I'll never touch the game. I—"

"Good-by," said Philip. "I'll come back when I can. You stay here with the horses, then!"

He dismounted, tossed the reins into the hands of his companion, and in a few steps the silhouette of Rivers was lost behind him in the dark. It seemed to him as he crossed the gap between him and the edge of the trees, that enemies must be ranged there at wait for him, guns in hand, smiling as they watched him walking into the trap. Only when he actually stood beside the broad, rough trunk of a tree did he feel a bit of comfort. The honest smell of the evergreens, the silence, the gentle wind that touched the trees reassured Philip. He waited for some

157

moments until his eyes were more accustomed to the deep shadows beneath the trees, then he started slowly forward.

Loafer led the way, stalking as though he knew that game and dangerous game lay before them. They passed through a belt of ancient pines, lofty and huge of trunk; then they reached a roadway, and Philip turned aside from this, not caring to take the risk of making noise with his heels on the gravel of the drive. He had barely changed direction when the dog stopped and crouched. Philip, his heart in his throat, sank upon his knees, and then saw two forms looming out of the night, suddenly, as forms always come through thick darkness.

He kept a Colt ready; this would be a case of shooting to kill, he knew.

They seemed fairly on top of Philip when they paused. Reason told him to shoot before they poured in their fire upon him, but an instinct made him hold on for another moment.

"This here is blind-man's bluff," rumbled a deep voice.

"Sure it is, Bert," answered the second man.

"Besides," said Bert, "he's crazy, but he'd never be fool enough to tackle this place."

"Not up the road anyway. The Colonel's getting old."

"I gotta mind to go back and turn in."

"He'll wring your neck, if you do.'

The other cursed softly, for a moment; Philip remembered those voices well. He knew that Bert and Archie Chisholm were before him there in the night and the chill of fear grew colder.

"One of these days I'm gunna stand up to the Colonel," said Bert Chisholm. "He's getting old!"

"He's a mountain," answered Archie.

"Where is he now?"

"Up on the roof with old Purchass. They're hatching something."

"Maybe the kid will come in by the roof," chuckled Bert.

"It's the only place he can get in."

"Ain't Purchass and the Colonel enough to guard the roof?"

"They won't be looking for anything that way."

"It's gunna be a long night. Let's hunt through the far side of the woods, there, and find a place to sleep in, turn and turn about. We can kick together a bed of pine needles."

They swerved to the side. Instantly they were lost to view, but there was no sound. Noiselessly as they had loomed up before Philip, so now they disappeared again into the dark among the trees. But Philip remained crouched, his thoughts spinning.

He was inclined to believe what he had heard the two say—that entrance into the house would be impossible, for if Purchass and the Colonel had devised a watch so careful that even the precincts of the house were patrolled, within the place there must be a strict watch. The only way was by the roof, and there on the roof the Colonel and Purchass were "hatching something."

Then he worked straightforward until he came to the verge of the trees and looked across a narrow clearing at the long, lofty black mass of the house. There was not a trace of life about it for a time. Then, inside one of the black windows he saw a faint glow of light, instantly extinguished—such a glow as comes when a cigarette is lighted and the match put out at once.

From that he could guess that men waited and watched inside the silence of the house, and he drew a long breath of dread. For suppose that he had attempted an entrance through one of those apparently sleeping windows!

Slowly he worked his way towards the back of the place, constantly watching the roof line. There were places where he might be able to climb, to be sure. But nearly all of those places ran close to windows, where a guard on the inside would be sure to hear him at his work.

The back of the house seemed to present no more favorable opportunity. It was, in fact, flatter and more unpromising than the rest of the building. But there was at least a noise which might cover any sound he made in climbing. For a great windmill stood near by, its wheel, raised above the tops of the trees, spinning in a great solid disk of shadow high overhead, and the pump clanking softly and steadily while some unoiled part of the gears groaned gently, at regular intervals. Listening more carefully, he even could hear the whisper of the wheel, as it worked.

The tank was built into the roof of the house, and there was a pipe running from the tank to the mill itself. Down that, of course, the water ran into the reservoir. Sometimes those pipes were the flimsiest tin; sometimes they were stout iron, and if this were an iron pipe, Philip saw that his work was not so difficult.

He went straight to the windmill and there crouched, listening, straining his eyes. He saw nothing, he heard nothing from the labor of the pump, and the whishing of the water inside the casing. So he made up his mind.

First he whispered to Loafer to sit down, and as the great dog obeyed, he knew that nothing would take the animal from that post until his master returned. Then he began to climb the ladder which stretched up the gaunt side of the mill.

He went up slowly, pausing now and again to look down into the dim pit of darkness which formed beneath his feet, or to scan the windows of the house. The upper-story windows took the light of the stars like dim mirrors of black glass, but never was there sight or sound of a human being.

He reached the lofty platform of the mill, at last. From that point of vantage, lying flat, he could look beyond the great grove of trees and across the surrounding valley to the hills. He spotted the direction in which he had left poor Doc Rivers, and vaguely he wondered if Doc's failing nerves would permit him to remain at his post of watch until he, Philip, returned.

In the meantime, his own position was very bad. If he were spotted on the windmill, he was cut off from all possible help. He was ended!

So he made haste to swing down below the platform to the point where the pipe ran from the casing of mill to the roof. He tested that pipe with all his weight. He jerked heavily on it, and heard a faint tremor go down the long casing. But the pipe seemed very solid.

He did not hesitate after that to trust himself to it, and he swung by his hands, working like a monkey down the pipe until he reached the tank. It was perfectly simple to make a landing. There was a small ladder running up the face of the heavy tank, and by this he got on to the cover of the tank.

He lay there flat on his face, recovering his breath, and when he could breathe more easily, he heard the voices of men speaking in the near distance.

Crawling to the inward side of the tank, he found that it projected a scant seven feet above the level of a flat roof; and now the voices were plainly audible. He almost could hear the words which were spoken; and certainly he distinguished at once the speaking tones of the Colonel. The air quivered with his great voice, though now it was subdued.

Both the speakers were hidden behind some irregularities of the roof, and Philip, without more ado, lowered himself from the top of the tank and prepared to step forward in the adventure.

CHAPTER XXXII

It was a spotted night, with clouds like vast continents hanging from a glimmering sea of stars, and yet this starlight was enough to show Philip his way across the roof and so, slipping furtively from place to place, guided continually by the voices of the speakers, he came in due time to a big, wide-built chimney from behind which he could peer at the subjects of his quest—and he saw before him the giant Colonel and with him a long-bearded old man whose back was a bow with age.

They sat in a flattened portion of the roof—a sort of roof-garden, though there was not a trace of greenery—and the pair sat at a little table. A closely hooded light burned upon it, and the graniteware coffee pot gleamed under that light, and the two cups of the companions.

161

The old man of the beard had reached a point of high excitement.

"Thorough! Thorough!" said the old man, and stamped on the roof his cane, or rather staff, for it was rough and rugged as the bough of a tree. "We ain't gunna do nothing halfway. We're gunna be thorough!"

The Colonel leaned back in his chair until it creaked under the clumsy burden of his bulk.

"Very well, Purchass," said he. "Thorough you may be, but not thorough in the way you wish to be, if I'm to be a partner of this affair."

The old man was very angry. The impatience of age was upon him, and he freshened his grasp upon his stick. They were enormous hands; on a day that must have been a Herculean form.

"Tell me," he demanded, "am I a fool?"

"You are a wise man, Purchass," said the Colonel in his quiet voice which, no matter how lowered, still possessed a ringing quality; so that when he finished speaking it was always as though a great bell had been struck in the distance. "I've not been near when you were in your youth or your middle age. But I've seen your sons and your grandsons. You've multiplied one stem into a good-sized forest, and I honor you for it."

"You're sneerin' and talkin' down at me again," declared Purchass as bitterly as before. "Every one of 'em crooked, you'd mean to be saying?"

"Strength is what we want in this world," declared the Colonel, unshaken by this bitter anger and hostility. "Strength is what we want, and strength is undoubtedly what you have. I've never seen a Purchass who was a weakling. I never expect to see one. I'm not sneering at you, my friend. You and your big family of seven sons— and I don't know how many grandsons—"

"Twenty-two," said the other.

He was old enough to allow himself to be knocked from the original topic by this maneuver of the Colonel's.

"My boys was nine, and seven raised families. They had twenty-two sons, and ten of 'em still are alive. Ten of 'em still are alive."

162

"Only ten of twenty-two? That's hard luck," remarked the Colonel.

"A damned high percentage," said the old ruffian, stamping the roof with his stick again. "They been high-blooded racers all of their lives. And in the kind of races that they run, hell takes the hindermost. A damned high percentage," he continued, raising his roar of a voice, which broke with a tremor of years. "I'm contented. I ain't raised a crop of wheat. I've raised a crop of men!"

"You have," assented the Colonel. "And you've done it well. You've done the thing that you started out to do. That's what I call success."

Melancholy instantly took the place of old Purchass's exultation.

"Success? It's nothin' now to what it was," he admitted. "There was a time that you can remember yourself, Colonel, when I had this country by the throat. No man dared to move without askin' me first. I was the boss. They had to come to me. I was fair; but I was boss. And when a man questioned me, I busted him like a stick! Well, we're different, now. The law come in like a rain. And you come, Colonel, too; you gave folks something else to think about. How many of my boys have died under your guns and under your hands?"

"Only four, I believe," said the Colonel.

And, huge as he was, brave as Philip guessed him to be, yet he shuddered when he thought of any man making such an admission in the very house of the Purchass family, and to this grim and patriarchal tyrant.

However, to his surprise old Purchass showed no signs of anger. He merely wagged his head, apparently in content.

"Some would of tried to stamp you out," he explained. "Some would of tried to kill you. I could of had it done. Btu it would of cost four more lives among my sons, and we couldn't spare that many. So I stopped 'em short. I called the feud off. Did I?"

"You did, Purchass."

"When we could rule with the bare hand, we ruled with the bare hand," said Purchass. "But after that time passed, then I seen that it was time to try another line, and another

163

line I tried. Brains! I used brains! You can't bully ten thousand citizens. I didn't try. I slipped out of the sun. I got into a corner. I lay low. Them that valued me come to me. That's the way that I worked it, and every year we get fatter. We got money in the bank, Colonel. We got money in the bank!"

"You've done very wisely," replied the Colonel.

"And now," went on Purchass, "comes the time I've been waiting for. Once in a life a gent sits in at a million-dollar game. Now, there you are! We got the million—and you begin to raise hell!"

"I don't raise hell," responded the Colonel.

"You stop me dead in my tracks!" snarled the savage veteran.

"While I'm in the house—yes!" said the Colonel. "I won't have it go on while I'm in the house!"

Old Purchass seemed too angry to make any reply. His big, gnarled hands grasped the stick as though they would break it, but eventually he shrugged his shoulders. He settled in the chair, his head fallen low, and his eyes gleaming from under his bushy brows.

"A million—and you're in on it!" he snapped.

"I don't want money in that way," said the Colonel.

"Bah!" roared Purchass, losing all control.

At this, the Colonel also settled back in his chair, and he poured himself a second cup of coffee, and carefully flavored it.

"Are you ready to listen?" he asked.

There was only a growl from Purchass.

"I had a call from the others today," he said. "They offered me a half interest, Purchass!"

"What others?"

"The boy—and Rivers."

"You broke their necks!" exclaimed Purchass.

"Ambassadors have certain sacred rights," said the giant, smiling.

"Sacred hell!" cried Purchass. "You drive me mad."

"I'm sorry. I wanted you to see the other side of this thing."

"They offered you half?"

"Yes."

"If you could find out where the mine was?"

"Naturally."

"Ah, but how could you do that?"

"Would it have been hard for me to get the boy to talk?"

Purchass stared. He began to rub his chin.

"But," said the Colonel, "I stand by my word. I made my first bargain with you, that I'd never have anything to do with the opposite camp, and I've never broken my word!"

"No," admitted Purchass. "You're an honest man. You're an honest man!"

He repeated this, as though he had to convince himself by saying the words twice over.

"Where's the boy now?" he asked suddenly.

"I don't know. Somewhere near this house, I suppose."

"Hey?"

"Somewhere near the house, Purchass. He's on this trail!"

"Let him be on it. He's mad. Is he mad, Colonel?"

"A little, perhaps. Very, very dangerous, Purchass. The most dangerous—"

He paused, unwilling to commit himself.

"I'll send in another guard," said Purchass. "I'm gunna keep that Delmar sewed up tight. I'll send in another!"

He raised his voice.

"Joe!"

"Tell me," asked the Colonel curiously, "how any man in the world could be foolish enough to get into this house —alone! Can you tell me that?"

"I dunno," said the old man. "But I take no chances. I take no chances. It's a million-dollar game. And another touch of the screws will make Delmar yowl like a cat!"

He began to laugh, and it was like the laughter of a demon. Philip, lying behind the chimney, turned cold as he listened. He was beginning to feel, more and more, that the Colonel was right, and that no one other than a perfect fool would have ventured to this house and thrown himself, practically, into the hands of his enemies.

What were the screws, another turn of which would make Jolly Delmar "yowl like a cat?"

A man who looked the part of a brown-faced puncher from the range appeared in the door which opened from the roof to the house.

"Well, governor?" he asked.

"Where's Dorman?"

"He's asleep."

"Why in hell is he sleeping?"

"He's just come in from the trail."

"I said all hands up tonight, I meant just that! Get the hound up!"

"All right," said Joe, and shrugged his shoulders.

"Get him up, and tell him that I want him in that room with Delmar. You hear me?"

"I hear you," said the other.

"And if he closes an eye before the morning comes, I'll have his skin off; I'll peel him alive and let him burn in the sun. You hear?"

"I'll tell him."

"Now get out."

The puncher disappeared.

CHAPTER XXXIII

Now that a stronger guard had been established over young Delmar, old Purchass might have been expected to relax, but his nervousness persisted. Presently he started up and declared that he would begin a circuit of the house to make sure that his men were properly posted; the Colonel suggested that he, at least, remain to watch the roof.

At this the old man snapped: "Is this boy, this crazy boy, a bird? Can he fly, Colonel? How's he to get up to this roof, I ask you?"

Said the Colonel: "There is a wise rule in case of danger, Purchass: Always expect the impossible."

166

"Be damned to your rules!" said the brutal old man. "Come along with me, Colonel. We'll look the sleepers over."

And he stamped the roof with his stick again, as he turned away towards the door.

The Colonel followed him. He had to bow low to pass through the doorway. Down the narrow hallway that showed beyond, Philip watched them pass, and saw old Purchass suddenly thrust open a door and snarl: "Delmar, you young fool, are you gunna talk now?"

With a racing pulse Philip listened for an answering voice, but he heard none. There was only a pause, then with an oath Purchass thrust the door shut. It crashed, and the echo rang like a shot through the house, causing a distant stirring, here and there, as though men were rousing in alarm.

"Now hell is gunna open for that young fool!" declared old Purchass, and he walked on down the hall, followed by the enormous form of the Colonel.

Philip grew weak with excitement. He had located the very room of the captive. It was close enough, to be sure, but every foot of that lighted hall swarmed with terrors; there was in the chamber a guard, naturally armed to the teeth; that formidable ruffian, Joe Dorman, was coming to double the watch, and would arrive at any instant.

Yet now, if ever, was his time to try—before Dorman arrived! The fear that held Philip trembling was counterbalanced by a whirlwind sense of confusion, and in that confusion a determination to strike forward. Now that he had come so near, he would take the last chance, lead where it might!

With the resolution turning to iron in his soul, he started up from the chimney hiding place and ran crouching across the flat surface of the roof. He headed for the hall, but as he ran, he saw Joe Dorman turn into it from below.

He jerked up his revolver to fire; but then he remembered that though Dorman was clearly in view, he himself might not be in range of the vision of the outlaw, for he was in the outer dark. He leaped to the side, therefore, and since he had no time to go to any other hiding place, he

167

crouched in the corner, close to the angle which the parapet of the wall made the upper story of the house.

He held his breath. The heavy step of Dorman came up the hall with a jingle of spurs which, apparently, that inveterate horseman never removed from his heels. Over the hook of his arm, Philip had seen a sawed-off shotgun with the beautiful steel of its double barrels glistening in the lamplight. He knew something of sawed-off shotguns, and like all Westerners, he dreaded them at close action more than any other weapon.

The heels of Dorman stopped jingling. There was a crash as of a door kicked open. Then loud voices conversed.

"You, Mac, why'n hell ain't you enough to look after a sick man on top of a house? D'you have to have a whole damn army to help you do nothin' at all?"

The voice of Mac was pitched shrill in protest.

"I never asked for no help!" he said. "Damned if I ever asked for no help at all."

"You lie," said Dorman. "You was afraid that mealy mouthed kid would come and bust you in two. Nothin' would do for you except help. You had to have me."

"I'd be damned before I'd ask for you to help me in anything!" roared the tormented Mac.

"Look out how you're talkin'!" snarled Dorman.

"I know how I'm talkin'. Because you're Joe Dorman ain't a reason that you can wipe your boots on me, and be damned to you!"

"I'm gunna have this out with you!" said Dorman savagely.

"Have it out when you please. I'll go out on the roof and have it out with you now!

"You skunk!" Dorman cried. "You know that the old man won't stand for any fightin' in his house. That's why you talk up so big!"

"Come down with me to the ground, then."

"You talk like a fool. Besides, you're bluffin'. Go on outside and cool off for a minute; I'll watch Delmar while you take a breath. Go on, Mac, don't be a fool!"

The words of Dorman were rough enough, but the tone in which they were spoken was so gentle that Philip guessed "Mac" was formidable enough to make even the celebrated Dorman think twice before inviting a battle.

"I don't want no trouble with you," said Mac, appeased at once. "Only, you gotta treat me like a man, Joe. I ain't a dog. Not yet! I never took water in my life; I ain't gunna start now."

"Go on and get out, kid," advised Dorman. "Take a walk on the roof. I'll watch this gent for you. You been cramped up here for so long that you ain't nacheral in the head. You're lookin' for trouble!"

Mac's footfall was heard down the hall, and Philip glanced frantically around him. The parapet which outlined the space of the level roof also ran a few feet down the side of the wall, so that a man could hang by the hands and work his way for some distance, until he was close to the first window—and that, Philip felt, must be the window of the room in which the prisoner was guarded.

He laid a hand on the parapet, about to swing himself over, but the shadow of Mac that instant stepped through the doorway on to the roof.

"Hello," said Mac, "who's that?"

Now, once or twice before, cornered by Uncle Oliver after the commission of some sin, Philip had been prone to work out an excuse by a pretense of weariness and nonconcern. And in his desperation, now, he was able to think of nothing better to do than to lean his elbow on the parapet of the roof and with his hand cover his mouth while he yawned deliberately and noisily.

Only, from the corner of his eye, he was watching the other keenly, aiming his gun, so to speak, before he drew it. Mac, however, seemed unsuspicious.

"Is that you, Pete, you lazy hound?" he asked impolitely. "Say, you got those two bucks that you owe me, yet?"

And he turned and bore straight down upon Philip, driven on by an evil Fate.

Philip dared not speak. The first word from him doubtless would call out a gun into the hand of the stranger, and whether he failed or won, the noise of one explosion would fill that roof with armed men.

He thanked God for the darkness of that corner, and with a shrug of his shoulder, he dipped his left hand into his trousers' pocket.

Moreover, that gesture was an excuse to dip his head, and only under the very edge of the brim of his hat did he watch Mac approach.

That unlucky fellow came with hand outstretched.

"I've waited long enough," he said. "Quit fumbling, and fork over, you big lump a—"

He got no farther, for at that instant he stepped into range, and as he did so, the left foot of Philip stole forward, gripped the roof, and his right hand shot over.

It seemed for an instant as though he had hit the head off the shoulders of Mac, so far back did it bob. The strong body of the man remained strangely erect, and Philip was able to catch it in his arms and prevent a fall.

Loose and senseless Mac rested in the arms of the boy, until Philip began to look wildly around him, wondering what he could do next. At least he removed the weapons from his captive, and what an armory!

There were two full-sized Colts on the hips of this man. In one coat pocket there was a bulldog revolver. Inside his belt he carried a tiny little two-barreled pistol which hardly filled the palm of a man's hand; but at ten yards doubtless it would kill a man or knock him down. Perhaps it was intended for that very purpose, thought Philip— placed so that it could be secretly removed, and covered all the while by the very hand which was holding it ready to fire! In addition to the four guns, there was a massive bowie knife which looked heavy and sharp enough to whittle down a tree, and inside the bowie knife there was a second bit of steel, a deadly little Italian stiletto.

Certainly Mac was an accomplished warrior, if he knew how to manage this complicated array of weapons!

But what should Philip do with him?

If he left him behind and went forward, the stunned man might recover consciousness at any moment. If he gagged him and bound him—for that he had no rope, and even if he had, he did not know how to accomplish a gagging. He was more apt to choke the fellow!

170

So, with cold sweat running on his face, Philip wished himself in quite another part of the world at that moment. Mac was beginning to revive, mumbling rapidly, and Philip, bending his head, heard a jargon of which he understood nothing:

"I'll raise you five, sucker! You can add ten to that! I'll go you five more—Well, here's twenty more to sort of round things off. I'll call that. Lemme see what you got, and lemme see it quick! My God—where am I—my head!"

The last words were gasped out as poor Mac found his feet, swaying heavily against the hand of Philip. The latter held the cold nose of a revolver under the chin of Mac. The touch of the steel roused Mac almost at once.

"You're safe, I hope," said Philip. "I don't wish to do any real harm to you. I'm very sorry that I had to strike you."

"I'm shot through the head," groaned Mac. "I can feel where your fist tore out through my brains."

"Will you talk quietly, please?"

"Hell, kid, I'll talk like a ghost," said Mac, with earnestness.

CHAPTER XXXIV

HE stepped back against the wall and raised his arms voluntarily above his head.

"That's not necessary," said Philip at once.

"Of course it ain't," said Mac, lowering his hands instantly. "I'd as soon take a chance with a grizzly as with you. You're the kid, ain't you?"

"My name is Philip," he answered.

"Yeah, you're the one. My God—and I wouldn't believe when Bert told me. My head is cracked in two!"

There was a mixture of careless mockery of himself and the occasion, with real pain and dizziness in this speech.

"I don't know what to do! I don't know what to do!" sighed Philip.

A wind which had been lurking in the heavens drove with a sudden roar through the surrounding trees and sent a stinging volley into the face and the eyes of Philip. In a moment the water had cut through his clothes to the skin. He felt himself growing chilled, and he needed his warmest and most active strength for this labor.

"Of course you dunno what to do," said Mac. "Only—what you after?"

"I think you can guess," said Philip.

"You come for Delmar, didn't you?"

"Yes."

"Poor kid," said the outlaw. "I'm goddam sorry for him. But he ought to of yapped. That would of fixed things for him. He ought to of yapped, I tell you. They would of let off on him. Now it won't do you any good to get to him."

"Why not?"

"Because he couldn't walk, even if he had the chance."

"What have they done?" asked Philip, hardly able to make the words come.

"It was Old Man Purchass," said Mac. "Of course he's a devil."

That answer was rather oblique, but it meant enough to Philip to make him accept it without further question.

"Will you tell me something?" he asked.

"I'll tell you."

"Is there any other man than Dorman in that room?"

"There ain't. Ain't Joe enough?"

He chuckled, and then added: "You're beat, kid. You've done wonderful fine in getting this far. I wouldn't believe it. I wouldn't think it could be done. How'd you manage it?"

"I came up the windmill," said Philip absently.

"The—hell!" exclaimed the other.

"Will you please speak more softly?"

172

"Sure—sure, kid. I forgot. You blasted the noise out of me. Windmill? I understand! You come all alone?"

"Yes."

"I've heard of such things," said Mac thoughtfully.

He seemed interested in the whole adventure in rather a detached, impersonal manner, as though there were little between him and the present moment.

"What you gunna do?" asked Mac.

"I don't know," sighed Philip again.

"Beat it," said Mac. "I wanna tell you something; who d'you think's here?"

"Who?"

"The Colonel, kid!"

He said it in a sort of savage triumph. Philip heard the vibration of silent, triumphant laughter.

"I know that," answered Philip. "He was here on the roof. I listened to him talking."

"Lord love me! And you didn't cut and run?"

"I've got to go on," said Philip sadly. "I can't turn back."

"They'll feed you to the dogs," said Mac with earnestness. "Kid, they say you ain't the world's champion thinker. Lemme help you out. Lemme give you the tip. Turn and git! Even if you get to him, what can you do for him?"

"Thank you very much," said Philip. "But I've thought of something. Do you mind walking ahead of me down the hall?"

"Are you gunna go into the house, kid?"

"Yes. When you come to the door of the room where they're guarding Jolly Delmar, please call out Mr. Dorman."

"Listen!" said the excited Mac, but he broke off short and merely growled: "Well, it's gotta happen to you some day. Why not now?"

With that he turned on his heel and led the way down the hall. Their steps were carefully chosen, and yet Philip thought that the echoes of their tread was as heavy as the booming of cannon. Cautiously he put his feet down in time with his leader.

Mac paused.

"What'll I say, kid?" he asked.

Now, as he turned in the light, and the lamp shone with some brightness against his face, Philip saw a great crimson patch along the jaw of Mac. It was puffing rapidly. Already he had to talk from one side of his face, and in addition, so terrible had been the shock of that blow, a small trickle of blood stained the mouth and the chin of unlucky Mac. His good nature, however, was unfaltering.

"You're only a goddam kid, ain't you?" he whispered, looking Philip up and down.

"I suppose I am," said Philip, feeling how vastly he lacked the wisdom of these worldly men.

"Now what'll I say?"

"I don't know. Something, to get him out here."

"I want to see his face when you feed that gun into it. I wanna see it," sighed Mac with a yearning light in his eyes. "Lemme think."

He raised his voice: "Hey, Joe."

"Hey?" queried a drawling voice inside.

"C'mon out, will you?"

"Aw, why should I?"

"I wanna show you something."

"What?"

"I wanna show you."

"Gwan away, will ya? I'm gettin' asleep."

"You better wake up, Joe. You better come out here."

"Why can't you come in here?"

"Open the door, and you'll see why!"

Philip caught his breath. It seemed to him that this surely exposed the situation. However, there was a clump of feet dropping to the floor, a rattle of spurs, and the door dashed open with:

"Why don't you take the mush out of your mouth when you start to——"

He paused and gasped.

The damaged face of Mac was grinning at him in a lopsided fashion, and over Mac's shoulder glimmered the steady muzzle of a long, heavy Colt.

"Will you raise your hands over your head?" asked Philip gently.

Joe Dorman jerked his hands so high that they rapped against the upper jamb of the door.

"Back into the room please!"

Mr. Dorman retreated. His eyes were enormous. He kept repeating with loose lips: "It ain't possible. I don't believe it. It ain't possible!"

Mac came next, and Philip, in the rear, thrust the door gently to.

As he stepped into the room, from the corner of his eye he saw the half-dressed form of Jolly Delmar lying on the cot, a bloodstained cloth wrapped around his head and his face ten years older than it had been at their last meeting. Now Jolly thrust himself up on his arms, and they shook violently under his weight.

"It's the kid!" he said, his jaw sagging down. "It's the kid," he echoed himself, hollowly.

And then he sank back on the bed, and rolled his feverish eyes at the trio as though it were a picture, a portion of a useless dream.

"You see?" said Mac. "What could you do with him?"

"I don't know! I don't know!" said Philip, growing white with both fear and horror.

"Go on back," said the dull voice of Jolly. "It ain't any good to be here. I can't walk!"

"You've got to walk," said Philip desperately, but still keeping his gun on the pair before him.

"Look!" commanded Jolly.

He dragged back the cover which was spread over his legs, and Philip had one blurred glimpse of redstained bandages around those legs, from knees to ankles.

"That's all!" croaked Jolly, and his head dropped back once more, loosely, heavily.

Philip moistened his dry, white lips. He tried to think, but his brain refused to stir.

"You see," said Mac gently, "you're beat, kid. There ain't a thing that you can do. You couldn't carry him down the windmill, son, I reckon!"

And the brain of Philip began to act once more. He set his teeth; his thoughts were clear.

"Face the wall!" he ordered.

175

And when they had obeyed him mechanically, only Dorman still muttering, unnerved, he picked up some cords which lay over the foot of the bed—placed there for some hellish purpose, he could guess.

With those, he secured the hands, and next the feet of the pair behind them, and after that, working feverishly, he stuffed a bandanna into the mouth of each, and next tied them back to back on the floor. They made a writhing mass of useless humanity. Joe Dorman began to turn purple, and worked his jaws convulsively on the gag, but Philip would not loosen it.

Sweat of fear and horror and despair was streaming down his face as he turned to Jolly.

"Will you live if you stay here?" he asked.

"I'll die before I'll talk to 'em," said Jolly savagely. "But lean over, kid. They can't hear. I'll whisper you where the mine is. Tell Dad, I was glad to die, this way. I didn't care. Tell him God bless him, and old Maizie. Leave me lie here, and you take the news back to them that the mine is—"

"Hush!" said Philip gently. "I'll never leave you here. What's the mine? It's you that they want!"

CHAPTER XXXV

STRENGTH is not a matter of poundage, but now and again—to one man in fifty million—there is given a strange quality of muscle and nerve which sets him out beyond the touch of the fellows who surround him; and that gift was Philip's.

He lifted the broken body of Jolly, and the latter groaned softly with exquisite anguish of soul, and flesh.

"It's no good. I'm gunna die!" whispered Jolly. "The mine is—"

"Save your strength, save your strength!" urged Philip.

He gave a last glance at the purple face of Dorman—pray God the man would not be choked, but now there was no time. He noted the interested eye of Mac, watching him with care. Then he stepped for the door, with Jolly Delmar lying in his left arm as lightly as the shotgun, not many moments before, had lain in the arm of Dorman.

He glanced up and down the hall. It was empty. A draught of air was tossing the flame in the throat of the lamp which lighted it. Jolly laughed weakly.

"Up and down," he croaked. "Like bein' in a boat! Like goin' over the waves, kid."

"Hush, hush!" pleaded Philip, and carried his burden swiftly out on to the roof.

He looked up, half fearfully, dreading to see all overcast, but instead, he found that every star was crystal clear through the mountain air, and a broad arch of scattered lights powdered half the universe. The glimpse of them gave him strength. He even paused and whispered to Jolly: "Look! There's the stars. We're going to win through, I think!"

"I don't wanna look at 'em," breathed Jolly. "It—it makes my head spin!"

And he tightened the grip of his arms around the neck of the boy. At the same moment the voice of Mac, unstifled by gag or intervening wall, rang terribly clear through the house, and booming out upon the roof: "Help! Help! They've got through! Help! It's the kid! Help! He's got Delmar. Goddam you, help, help!"

And, in answer to that wild appeal, a tumult of voices roared in the lower portion of the house. Heavy footfalls began to thunder on stairs. A gun exploded; it sounded to Philip like the hoarse bark of a dog that would soon leap on his back and tear the life from his body.

"You see?" gasped Jolly, as the boy stumbled hastily on across the roof. "You see? You can't do anything. That Mac—he spit out the gag. Damn him! You should of cut their throats! Leave me be! Leave me lie here! I'll tell you—the mine's up in the—"

"Be still! Be still!" said Philip, trembling terribly as he felt temptation grip him. For, after all, how simple it would be to let this inert burden fall and to speed away, light as the wind! He had done enough to strike men with wonder, so it seemed, merely by that exploit of reaching the house and striking, or trying to strike, a single blow. He would not have to make excuses.

That bitter temptation weakened him, as liquor weakens the brain and makes it spin and slide into the easier ways.

But it was the loose feebleness of those arms around his neck that made him cling to his purpose and—far off—a thought of Maizie, like a fragrance that floated across the night.

He reached the tank. Jolly could stay himself against it, while Philip swung to the top of it and then drew Jolly up after him, poor young Delmar gritting his teeth to keep back the complaint.

Down the ladder, then, on the farther side, and so to the dreadful bridge which lay between him and some hope of escape. The pipe looked as thin as a thread—a thread of silk! But necessity swelled big in Philip, and drove him on.

"You can't do it!" gasped Jolly. "It won't hold. We'll —we'll drop—"

"Hold on as tight as you can, will you?" said Philip. "Hold hard around my neck!"

And as he spoke, he sank his teeth in the coat of Jolly, gripped him with his legs, and dropped all his weight and the weight of that helpless body with which he was burdened, upon his arms.

He began to go hand over hand along the pipe. He had to swing himself forward, a little, and with every change of grip, all the weight came on one hand. He could hear the breath of Jolly gulped at his ear, as though the wounded man were drinking in great swallows.

It had been so easy to come across, carrying his own weight, that he had not noticed that the pipe was wet, but loaded with their extra burden, that wetness made his fingers uncertain in his grip. Twice he felt his fingers slide a fatal bit, and each time his heart jumped into his throat and choked him with its mad hammering.

"I can't hold on," said Jolly suddenly. "God, Phil—I— I'm faintin'! The mine—"

His arms loosened and dragged down from the shoulders of the boy. Still, with his teeth fixed, like the teeth of a wolf, Philip held that weight, and with his twined legs he supported it.

At the same time, he heard the flood of noise which had been rushing through the house, roar into the topmost story. Out of the corridor it burst upon the roof like the blast of harsh music from a hunting horn.

And he was the prey they sought.

His bowed head, strained down by the limp weight of his burden, made him look into the dizzy shadows beneath and, far, far beneath, miles beneath him, he saw a flat, glimmering streak of water. There he would strike if he fell!

And then his hand touched wood—a crossbeam of the frame!

It was better than the touch of the hand of any friend, a yielding, soft thing, that wood, compared to the iron of the pipe! He fumbled with it. At least, he had both hands free, and the passage of the greater danger gave him a wilder burst of strength.

He swung around the crossbeam, reached the ladder, and clung against it for an instant, gasping deep breaths, snapping at the air, like a wolf at meat.

Jolly Delmar groaned.

"My God, we ain't dead!"

"You're going to get through it. The worst part's over. Try to hold around my neck for a minute, Jolly!"

"You got across!" mumbled Jolly. "You got across!"

And he struggled his arms into place. His head sagged down beside that of Philip, and the touch of his face was hot with fever.

Going down was easy—wonderfully easy. Only, it seemed impossible to move rapidly enough! All his movement seemed clogged and stupidly slow.

And above, the yelling voices, like the cry of a pack, broke at last from the hall of the upper story and rushed out bodily on to the roof. Feet stamped. There seemed a dozen men up there.

Still lowering away—but with a sense of the ground a bitter distance beneath his feet—Philip looked up, and there he saw forms looming high above the little parapet of the roof—all outlined with amazing clearness because of the stars which burned above them, or the radiance which poured faintly from the corridor. More than that, and best of all, someone had brought a lantern, and as he came running, the figures at the parapet seemed to swing back and forth, unstable, light as air.

"It's him!" shouted someone. "Look there! Mac was right! Look there! Down the ladder of the windmill. See him! He's got Delmar in his arms!"

The crash of three or four guns drowned any answer. One bullet sang at the ear of Philip; one smashed the cross bar he was holding, and he slipped down with a violent jerk.

He never could reach the ground without some respite. He jerked out a Colt, swung a little to one side, and out from the ladder, and setting his teeth, he fired at one of those dacing silhouettes.

He saw his man pitch back; every other form at the same instant ducked out of sight.

And as he cast the revolver away and resumed the descent, he heard a voice screaming:

"He's got me. Sam! He's got me! Sam, I ain't gunna die. Sam, don' you let me die. I dun wanna die, Sam! God! God! I'm gunna die!"

Other guns were barking at him, but he was farther away. The shadows were closing over him, and every bullet sang wide. Then his feet touched the ground, and he could turn with Loafer whining with joy before him, firm footing, a drawn revolver in his right hand, Jolly supported in the crook of his left arm.

He was ready for battle now!

And he ran forward, swinging Jolly lightly in the might of his arm, and plunging for the trees.

He broke across the clearing. He crashed through a line of brush. And now he was running down the side of the roadway.

Once and again, like a vast firefly, a gun flashed from a thick clump of brush just before him. He leaped to the side, firing in return, but he had no real target—only a sense of where the flashes had come from.

180

The gun spoke again. It was like a thin ray of red reaching at him, and this time he felt a slash of pain across the back of his shoulder.

It seemed that having passed through those colossal dangers he was to be beaten down at the last moment by a single enemy. He could have laughed like a madman at the thought, and then he turned to charge straight in at the enemy.

But there was one far fleeter of foot than himself to make that attack. He saw the body of Loafer drive through the brush and the scream of a man followed, sharp and high with horror, mixed with the horrible snarl of the wolf.

"Loafer! Back!" shouted Philip, half sick.

There was an instant noise of crashing through the brush, as that guard fled, cursing and groaning, and Loafer leaped back into the roadway, and Philip saw even by starlight the flash of his grin of happiness.

At last he had struck one blow for his master!

CHAPTER XXXVI

THERE is no burden so clumsy to carry as that of a helpless man. Had an equal weight in a sack of wheat, say, been loaded upon the shoulders of Philip, he could have sprinted away with little hindrance. But even his power of arm began to relax, and his breath came in great, whistling gasps. Behind him, he heard distant voices shouting, and then the squealing of horses.

They would be after him like a river in flood, and not only from behind—straight ahead he heard the beating of hoofs, and round the next bend in the driveway came two mustangs, running hard.

In his heat and weariness, he poised a revolver, half determined to shoot down these charging cavaliers rather than evade them in the woods, but then he heard a voice calling: "Phil! Phil!"

He stopped, amazed.

"Here, Doc!" he answered.

Rivers brought up the two horses with a groan of nervous joy.

"I got you, Phil. Now, thank God! I been riding in hell, coming up this here road between the trees. I started when I heard the shooting. What have you got there?"

He was on the ground instantly. Together they lifted the sick man to the back of Rivers' own horse. He would be better there, for Philip was so much heavier than either of his companions that he would have to have a horse to himself.

Not a word did Rivers speak. He was no hero, and Philip heard the gritting of his teeth as he mastered his fear sternly. He could begin to see that it had cost the spirit of Doc Rivers as much to bring the horses up the shadowy dangers of that driveway as it had cost Philip himself to actually invade the house of the enemy and bring away the captive.

In silence they secured Jolly Delmar, who sat with both hands wrapped in the mane of the horse and his head bowed. He, also, said not a word of protest, though Philip knew that he must be suffering agonies from the chafing of his legs against the horse.

Then they galloped the horses down the drive, and the rattling hoofs beat with less noise, at last, as they left the trees.

A shallow draw opened a hundred yards or so to the right and towards this Doc Rivers turned. Philip followed obediently. In such a time as this, he knew that Rivers was a far better general than he. If only they could reach the shelter of the draw in time!

The starlight which, a short moment before, had seemed so dim and useless, now appeared as brilliant as the light of a sun, and Philip rode with his head turned over his shoulder, watching the mouth of the driveway. He could hear the riders roaring down the road inside the trees of the Purchass place. No doubt they were driven on by the promise of mighty rewards, if they should succeed, and above all, they would ride and fight like madmen for the sheer game of the thing, and for the pleasure of hunting down the fugitives.

But still, miraculously, they did not issue from the grove into the open, and now the two horses dropped into the draw. When they sat erect, they could see the Purchass place clearly. When they leaned far over, the bank was high enough to cover them. Even that shelter would be of little use if the pursuers, halting to listen, should wait to hear the beat of the hoofs of the two horses.

The draw deepened. It was no longer possible to look back at the enemy, and all they could do was to hurry their horses forward. And every moment, Philip expected guns to open from the bank at their left, or to hear the rush of many horses behind them, coming straight up the draw.

However, the bottom of the draw was sandy, not too soft for running, and Rivers' mustang, in spite of his double burden, ran straightaway for two or three minutes like the wind, to a place where a grove of poplars dipped over the side of the gully. Into that, without hesitation, Rivers drove his horse, and when fairly into the screen of the trees, he drew rein a little.

"I'm going to jog on," he said. "Go back to the edge of the woods. Look out and see what's happening, if you can. Then come after me. I'm heading straight up towards those two high hills with the forest between them."

Philip swung back, obediently, to the verge of the trees. And as he reached it, he saw half a dozen riders catapult out of the draw. They drew rein, but the heavy breathing of their horses was audible to Philip. He wondered that they did not hear the panting of his own mount.

"Where away?" asked one.

"I dunno. Where's the chief?"

"He ain't with us."

"A couple of you beat up the woods, here. The rest of us'll—"

"Two of us go alone after that hyena? Are you nutty, Bud?"

"Come on, then, we'll all go after 'em. Ride like hell! He's got a wounded man on his hands. We ought to catch

183

him if he came this way. If we don't catch him, we never can go home. The old man will be ravin' crazy!"

And they drove their horses forward into the trees.

Philip, when he heard the crashing of that noise, edged his own mount to the edge of the woods. There he had open running, and he galloped hard along the verge of the woods, trusting to blind chance that no other roaming riders might spot him as he hurried in the open.

He had not gone half a mile when he saw a horse with two dim shadows on its back emerge from the trees—a moment later he was beside Doc Rivers.

To his astonishment, both Rivers and Jolly Delmar were in high spirits.

"They went by us through the trees like thunder," laughed Doc Rivers. "We're gunna give these birds the go-by, kid. We're gunna make fools of them."

"How are you, Jolly?" asked the boy.

"I'm doin' fine, kid. The gallop sort of waked my blood up. My legs give me hell; but anything's better than that hell-hole back yonder!"

"Can you ride by yourself?"

"I can, if we had a third horse."

"Take this one. I'll walk for a while."

"You stay put on that horse!" exclaimed Jolly and Doc in one voice, and Rivers added that they were doing very well under their present arrangement.

However, Philip insisted. He felt reasonably sure that the danger could not have been ended so quickly. The Colonel—to say nothing of all those famous riders of the Purchass clan—was not a man to be thrown off a trail quickly and easily. And, before long, he was apt to come back at them, when least expected. If that time arrived, then they would need fresh horses, assuredly. So he lifted Jolly Delmar on to the back of his own horse, and he himself jogged quietly forward. All his life he had been accustomed to strenuous marches through the mountains, always up sharp slopes or down steep pitches, picking his way among fallen trees, through brush, scattered stones, rolling pebbles, so that over such going as this he felt perfectly at home.

Easily and smoothly he kept on his way, and the horses had to jog steadily to keep up with him. His main point of concern was Jolly, and whether his strength would last. But in fact, every moment in the open seemed to raise the spirits of Jolly higher. He was forgetting his pain.

Now and again they paused. They were climbing out of the valley and getting among the hills, and they halted again and again so that they might try to hear what did not come to their eyes.

In one of those pauses, Doc Rivers pressed Jolly to say something about his experience in the Purchass house, but Jolly put him off, with a groan at the mere memory.

And then the moon rose into an unclouded sky, and robbed them of their sense of security. It was almost as bright as the sun, and as it rose higher and higher, they could find fewer shadows in which to ride.

They kept busily on the lookout, but still there was no sign of the enemy. They crossed a shallow valley among the hills, with willows growing in the flat of the hollow. The wet ground took something from their laboring mustangs, and Philip came out on the other side clogged and weighted with mud. From the next height, they looked down along a great, gradual slope, with groves of huge pines and magnificent spruce scattered across it.

"Once we get inside of those trees, the devil himself can't find us!" said Doc Rivers with confidence.

They rode on in haste, therefore, so much so that Philip fell a good deal behind, and at the verge of the trees he glanced back and saw the thing which he had been dreading.

Half a dozen shadowy forms were sweeping under the side of the mountain, driving straight down towards the fugitives. They came out into the shallower slope, and the moon flashing on their sweating horses made them look like metal monsters.

Philip ran on, shouting, and presently he came up with the fugitives. He caught the stirrup leather at the side of Jolly Delmar.

"They're right after us," he said. "Ride for it, boys. I'll hang on to the stirrup leather!"

185

They began a wild dash through the woods with Doc Rivers well in the lead, to show the way. Philip would have been inclined to dodge constantly from one side to the other, striving to twist away from their pursuers, but Rivers would not do that. He only made two turns, each time slipping into narrow gaps between the trees, then driving ahead.

Moreover, he stopped several times, letting the horses drift ahead. In the manner he could listen, and they heard the crash of the pursuit swinging here and there behind them.

Apparently the hunters were driving along quite wildly and at random, and the noise of their riding faded farther and farther behind.

So Philip, badly winded, his head a blur from his frantic dashes at the side of the galloping mustang which Jolly Delmar bestrode, found that they were crossing a wide clearing between forest and forest, and looking back as they entered a long, clear avenue on the farther side, he saw a horseman come out behind them from darkness to light, a giant horseman on a giant horse, charging swiftly forward.

Without a word, he leaped up behind Jolly. And without a word Jolly and Doc put their horses to full speed. The Colonel was after them at last!

CHAPTER XXXVIII

THEY had not gone far before Philip realized that there was no escape. The giant behind them came fast, for he was so mightily mounted that even his enormous bulk did not seem to check the speed of his horse. Doc Rivers' mount was a poor one, and the other nag was carrying double.

186

Meantime, they were riding through a very open wood with the trees silver-flashing under the breadth and the brightness of the moon, and the ground splashed with jet black shadows. They could not expect to keep away from the Colonel very long in such quarters as these, and they could not expect to dodge him.

But they were two to one!

He had no sooner said it to himself than a gun clanged behind them, and the horse of Rivers dropped on its head and turned completely over, shooting poor Doc far out in front, where he rolled like a top.

There were even odds, now. Worse than even, for here was Jolly on his hands!

Poor Jolly was in a frightful state of mind.

"We'd better pull up!" he kept repeating. "It's the Colonel, kid. It's the Colonel. There's no use fighting. Nobody could beat him. No ten men could beat him! He's a devil. He's ten devils!"

He drew rein as he spoke, and Philip looked anxiously back. They were twisting, for the moment, around a curve of that natural roadway through the woods, and the Colonel was shut from view. He looked to the front again —and behold, a great branch swayed down above him.

He did not stop for the second thought but followed the first, reaching high and grappling the limb. It sagged only a little under his weight, and as he was jerked high from the saddle he gasped: "Ride, Jolly! Ride!"

In an instant he was stretched along the bough and saw Loafer sitting beneath, his red tongue lolling.

"Go ahead, Loafer!" he called, and waved. Loafer instantly cantered on.

And now he could see the Colonel coming. He looked to Philip even more magnificent than he had seemed when dashing across the ridge of the mountain the day before. The same cloak fluttered back from his shoulders in long, sweeping lines. The brim of his hat was furled by the speed of his horse. And he sat tall and straight in the saddle, one hand for the reins, one hand balancing a revolver for a second shot.

That second shot must not be fired!

187

And snatching out a gun, Philip aimed through the twigs at the charging giant.

He could not fire. It was such a target as any child could have hit, but he would not, or could not release the hammer—and here was the Colonel sweeping closer, a scant stride away, the revolver tipping down for the shot—

There had been no forethought in Philip's mind. He merely had planned to rid the horse of the double burden and thus, perhaps, give poor Jolly a chance for his life. He had not hoped to give himself ambush to fire upon the Colonel. Certainly he had not planned on what he now did. But the thought exploded in his brain like the leap of an electric spark, and he hurled himself down from the branch.

Like a panther leaping, with more than a panther's weight he crashed against the Colonel and the speed of the horse knocked both men out of the saddle. Philip, blinded and stunned by the shock, prayed vaguely that he might be able to fall clear of the big man, and that prayer was more than answered. For the Colonel landed heavily on his side and Philip's impact on the ground was broken by the body of the Colonel himself.

Philip, reeling, gasping, hardly able to realize what he had done, dragged himself to his knees and hands and saw the Colonel lying flattened against the ground, his enormous arms thrown out crosswise.

That sight inspired him. It cleared his mind and set a fierce light of joy in his eyes, so that he leaped up at once and ran lightly to the fallen man. One revolver lay far away, gleaming in the moonshine. The second one was even now in the hand of the monster—so instinctively had he acted even in that instant of crisis!

That gun Philip, stooping, snatched away, fumbled at the body of the big man to find another weapon, if possible —and instantly was taken by the throat!

It was as though vast levers had caught him. Crimson flames shot through his head, and he struck half blindly for the face of the Colonel—

His fist struck something—the hand relaxed from his throat—and Philip stumbled back to his feet, still dizzy from the paralyzing effect of that grasp. Through the shadows of his half-stunned mind, he saw the monster lurch upwards.

Like a tree the Colonel loomed before him, and then rushed in, with arms extended, eager, with the certainty of a rushing avalanche. There was no hope in Philip, but the vast energy which despair gives. He could not flee; the rush of the Colonel was as inescapable as the swooping of a bird—or so it seemed. So Philip slid suddenly forward, dipped his head, and then smote upwards at the beard of the giant—smote with all the sway of his body, and the lift of his muscles, and the speed and power of hand and shoulder behind that blow.

There was a shock, as though he had smitten a crag of stone. All his arm went numb, and electric pangs raced up and down from wrist to shoulder; but the Colonel's rush had ended.

Ay, incredible though it seemed, the whole vast bulk of the man rocked back upon his heels, and his arms fell helplessly to his sides. He had been knocked out of his stride—knocked almost flat on the ground, and by a single blow!

A shadow came skimming like a bird, a great dark bird, along the ground.

"Keep back, Loafer!" called the boy. "Keep back, Loafer! I—I don't need you!"

And he leaped in headlong at the mighty form, for he felt that the giant was effectually stunned, and that another blow might send him down. Eagerness nearly ended the life of Philip in that instant. Something as huge as a beam, weighty as a log, swift as a striking cat, darted out at him. He threw up his guard. It beat down his arm, and struck through on his breast with such an impact that Philip was literally picked up and hurled back.

He fell on his hands and one knee, vaguely saw the monster lunge towards him, and then gained miraculous strength to spring up and to the side.

Almost he was clear of that sweeping danger, but not quite. The next instant, as a man is caught by a whirlpool, so Philip was clutched by the giant, and they stood breast to breast. The great arms went around him; instinctively

189

he clasped a barrel as vast and as hard as the trunk of a tree, and put forth his might.

As he had lifted at the black rock, so he strained now, desperately. He had labored, on that day, for the life of a dog, and next for the pride of his heart. Now he had the added might of terror.

Around him were cast arms which contracted with the power of steel bands, red hot and shrinking into place. The flesh was ground against his bones. The same red flames of agony leaped into his brain, but even in that misery it seemed to him that the huge body of the Colonel was not so rigid, that it gave a little—ay, it undoubtedly yielded, and he heard the half gasp, half groan of exhaled breath.

The crushing grip of the Colonel was abandoned. He swayed up a hand like the head of a sixteen-pound sledge and Philip saw that danger swayed darkly above him. He pressed his face into the shoulder of the monster; the blow glanced from his head, and heaving then with all his might, he lifted the massive bulk to a tottering uncertainty, and then tipped it—swayed again, and pitched it to the ground, himself drawn down in the fall.

He could hold the monster down no more than he could control a struggling bear. They stood on their feet again, a little distance between them. The breath of Philip came and went rapidly, but he heard a hoarse gasping from the Colonel, and it seemed to Philip the sweetest music that ever had sounded in his ear.

"Boy," said the Colonel, "I love courage when I find it. You are young. You will grow into a man worthy of the name. On this one night I let you escape from me. You may go! But if we meet again—"

"This is the first time and the last," said Philip, peering at that contorted face. "I've met you fairly, hand to hand, and I've mastered you. And I'll take you back and show you to my friends like a tame dog on a rope."

He sprang in. Those huge arms rose to strike but there was a glory of confidence in the heart of Philip, now. It made him light as a feather to whirl between those driving blows and strike again, and again.

The Colonel went reeling back under the shadow of the nearest tree, and as Philip followed with tigerish haste, he heard the rending of wood.

There was a small limb that thrust out from the trunk of the tree. It had failed to mature like an honest bough. Stunted, half dead, leafless and twigless, it stuck out like a spur from the body of the tree, and this the Colonel had grasped and torn away with desperate strength.

Philip saw the danger and strove to dodge it, but the blow beat down his arm and fell on his head; and an explosion of blackness covered his brain as he reeled away. He found himself staggering helplessly, as though he walked in deep mud, and there was a deadly weakness behind his knees, threatening to make him fall.

He heard the sudden clangor of a gun, a voice shouting that seemed the voice of Doc Rivers, and then he could see.

It was Doc Rivers indeed, running forward, and still calling out, but the monster form of the Colonel no longer was before him. Instead, there was a sharp whistle from somewhere in the brush, and then Philip saw the horse of the giant gallop into the woods in answer to the signal of its master.

CHAPTER XXXVIII

HE was bewildered both physically and mentally by the disappearance of the monster and by that crushing blow which had fallen on his head. A foul blow, it first seemed to Philip. For surely, after he himself had failed to take advantage of a helplessly prostrate foe, it seemed that the latter might at least have fought out the battle fairly, hand to hand. As it was, Doc Rivers undoubtedly had saved his life, for the giant, rushing in, might have shattered his skull like an eggshell at the next stroke. The whistling bullets which Doc fired had put the Colonel to flight.

And suddenly it seemed that their work was done. With the Colonel removed from the fight, beaten, even all the myrmidons of the Purchass clan seemed a mere nothing.

Doc Rivers fairly embraced Philip.

Then he stood back, dancing grotesquely in the moonlight. Doc himself had been badly mauled in the fall of his horse. Blood was caked with dust down one side of his face, his coat was rent from shoulder to waist, and he limped as he danced. Nevertheless his thought was not for himself.

"I seen you knocking him before you. It was the Colonel, kid! It was the Colonel! There ain't anybody else as big as that in the whole world!"

"It was the Colonel," repeated Philip slowly, for he himself hardly could realize the miracle of his own strength as it had been revealed on this night. The glory of the lifting of the Black Rock was drowned and lost in this blaze of triumph. So he repeated slowly: "It was the Colonel!"

"Sweet—sufferin'—mama!" gasped Doc Rivers.

He added: "Your hands, kid? You was only usin' your hands?"

"I was only using my hands," answered Philip. And then a wave of savage anger and exultation, commingled, passed over him. "And when I meet him again," he said, "I'm going to tie him up and lead him home like a tame dog, to show to the people!"

He remembered, he had told the Colonel that. He would tell him again, when they next encountered. But they never would fight hand to hand again, he could guess. Not if the Colonel could leave the decision to weapons!

But even with weapons, Philip no longer feared the giant. He had tested him and found him wanting; now with rifle or revolver he would take his chance with the Colonel day or night, sun or shadow!

Now it seemed to Philip as though that dreadful encounter in the moonlight at last had cleared a cloud from his brain. There was a great cut on his head; from it blood trickled down, and the salt taste of it was in his mouth as he spoke.

"We've got to find Jolly," he said. "Can he last out the trip home?"

"Unless they've blocked him off," answered Doc Rivers. "He'll sure last it out unless they've blocked him away on the road home. It ain't so far off, now!"

"Hurry!" said Philip. "We've got to run!"

And run he did, swinging steadily forward through the woodland ways until Doc Rivers staggered and stopped. He leaned a hand against a sapling and gasped for breath.

"I can't run another step," he declared.

Impatient anger flared in Philip. He made a step closer.

"You have to," he said. "You have to run on, Doc!"

Doc Rivers mopped his brow.

"Don't threaten me, kid," he said. "I've done my best. I ain't an iron man, like you. I'm human, thank God. Let's walk. Even running, we couldn't catch up with a horse!"

No doubt there was some sense in this, and Philip walked impatiently on through the woods. Even then he set a pace which Rivers hardly could follow, though the latter broke repeatedly into a dogtrot, and then begged his companion to slow down and go more easily. But Philip was relentless and they pushed on at an even, heart-breaking pace.

They left the woods, at last; they turned on to the highway, and a voice called suddenly to them from the shadows—Jolly Delmar rode out into the moonlight to them.

"What happened?" he cried. "I came on and waited here. I couldn't go any farther. I should have turned back quicker and tried to help—but boys, I didn't dare to. I was more scared of being taken back to the Purchass place than I'm scared of hell-fire. Kid, you forgive me? But it wasn't the Colonel, after all?"

"Jolly," answered Doc Rivers, solemnly, "it was the Colonel, and the Colonel is busted."

Jolly gaped.

"He ain't so much as a major or even a captain. He's only a doggone private!"

'How come?" asked Jolly, in a voice that shook with excitement.

"Me, with my own eyes," said Doc Rivers, "I seen the kid back the Colonel into a tree. You could hear the thudding of his fists clear over here, if you'd cocked an ear to listen. He was dodging the Colonel's fists and whanging him—it was somethin' to see. You wouldn't believe it, otherwise. Then the Colonel peeled a branch off of the tree—"

"Hold on!" said Jolly.

"I seen it, you fool! With that branch he hammered the kid over the head and stunned him. God brought me along, just then, and I turned loose with a gun, and the Colonel turned and run. He was beat. He was fair beat. I seen it. I'll swear to it!"

"I know what I know, too," replied Jolly, "and I believe it. And now, Phil, we got 'em spread out and helpless. The Colonel and the whole damn Purchass gang is beat hollow. After this, we begin to collect. We begin to get fat!"

And he laughed like a boy.

There might have been ten thousand enemies lurking in the woods; but they would not have cared. They went on talking loudly. Jolly, forgetful of pain and weakness, even began to sing, and so they topped the last hill and saw in the hollow beneath them the well-remembered outline of the Delmar place.

Doc Rivers halted and leaned wearily on the massive shoulder of Philip.

"When was it that we started out, kid?" said he. "Was it about fifty years ago, maybe? Was it about that time that we went over and seen the Colonel?"

He sighed.

"You've made an old man of me, kid," said he. "Damned if you ain't piled a stack of years onto my shoulders!"

And they went happily down the slope towards the house. They entered the yard. They turned to the back, and the broad, thin shaft of light from the kitchen window poured out.

"It's Dad," guessed Jolly. "Won't have slept much since I left! Sneak up soft, and we'll see!"

They assisted Jolly from the horse. He could sit the saddle well enough, but he could walk hardly a step, and Philip picked him up and carried him to the window. Looking through it, they saw old Delmar bowed over the kitchen table, his head in his folded arms.

They were able to open the door and half cross the floor before he started up, and Philip never would forget how those long, lean arms were thrown out to welcome his son.

He carried Jolly through the dining room amid a rain of questions, hasty anwers. Everyone was talking at once.

In the hall a small white cyclone descended—Maizie in a white dressing gown, with flying hair, and so they completed the progress to Jolly's room. There, while Maizie hastily prepared food, the three men undressed Jolly and removed the wrappings from his legs. What they saw made them turn white.

Tenderly they bathed that bruised and torn flesh, and Doc Rivers, who knew about such things, laid on the bandages.

"Hell!" said old Delmar suddenly. "That's where they'll all go; that's where they've all come from!"

At last they had Jolly settled in the bed as Maizie rattled in with a tray covered with edibles. Jolly, exhausted but joyous, lay back, propped high with pillows.

"I'm not gunna talk. I'm not gunna tell you anything tonight," he said. "I'm just gunna be happy and enjoy lookin' at you. Only, before I'm a minute older, I'm gunna tell you where the vein is."

Philip, instinctively, stepped to the window, and stood there with a hand on the butt of his revolver, for it seemed to him that the word which had been so many times on the verge of being told was now sure to be interrupted, and interrupted with dangerous force.

There was nothing but the naked moonlight in the back yard beneath him; though it seemed to Philip that a ghost of Jolly and the two horses once more passed beneath and disappeared down the roadway.

He heard Jolly's voice telling the tale briefly. Just what the details were, Philip could not understand, but the names of creeks and hills and mountains were all familiar to the other listeners.

After that, Jolly's supper proceeded merrily. Maizie and his father remained to feed him and take care of him. Philip and Doc Rivers, starved with their long fast, went down to the kitchen to cook their own supper.

They had fried ham and eggs and laid out the platter with steaming coffee and chunks of hard bread. They had washed grime and blood from their faces as well as they could, and they were about to sit down to the table when Maizie came in to them. She went up to Philip with a face as pale as her dressing gown.

"Jolly's told us," she said. "Jolly's told us everything. I'm trying to believe it. But my head swims! I—I saw the shoulder of his coat—where your teeth had cut through the cloth."

"Doc," said Philip, "you step outside for a minute."

Doc Rivers silently vanished from the room, and Philip stood above the girl. She was no longer a dreadfully mysterious creature to him; she was only a pale and slender child.

"When I left," he said, "we had a sort of agreement, Maizie."

Her eyes half closed.

"I know. I'd never go back on it, Phil."

He found that his words were snapping out, sharp and hard.

"D'you say that because you care a lot for me, Maizie, or because you're afraid of me?"

Her eyes closed altogether, at that; she grew whiter than before, and when she looked up at him again, he could see the naked terror in her soul.

"I don't know," said Maizie.

But Philip knew, and all the joy and the glory of that night was snatched away from him like a robe of gold, and he was left clothed in tatters.

"We go back to the beginning," said Philip, then, "as if we'd never said a word to one another. Is that better?"

"Are you angry? Are you hating me?" asked Maizie.

196

When he saw her grip the back of a chair and sway back a little, a touch of pity came to Philip for her, but he was hard and cold in his heart of hearts.

"Let's talk facts," said he. "I'm beginning to see facts. The other day I was still a young fool. Well, Maizie, I've grown up. You know the story about Midas and the touch of gold. There's the touch of steel, too. I think that I've had that touch on me. At any rate, I can look through a good deal. When you first found me, Maizie, you saw that I was quite young and quite a fool. Is that right?"

Her lips stirred, as though she were trying to answer, but no answer came; and her eyes wavered on his face, as though she were reading a large and crowded page.

"I'm sorry that I put it as a question," said Philip. "It's simply a fact. Of course I was ridiculous, but you thought that I might be useful. That night among the trees you were drawing me on. You saw that I'd lost my head about you, and you wanted to make sure of me. Am I right?"

"Phil," she began.

He waited, but she could not speak.

"You had your job for me. It was to bring back Jolly. Well, I've brought him back twice. You'd thrown out a sort of bait for me. Not in words. We were too delicate for that. Only a hint between us—I would have you, if you had back Jolly. Is that right?"

She drew a long breath; he felt that she was fighting hard, merely to face him, merely to stand before him.

"As a matter of fact, there's some other fellow, of course. You picked me up because you needed me. Don't look so scared, Maizie. I'll never harm you. And the truth —you ought to be able to stand that. You see that I come down to a simple thing, in the end. I let you off the bargain, Maizie. And here's my hand on it!"

He held forth his hand. Her own dropped limply into it, and suddenly her lip trembled and tears poured into her eyes.

Philip half turned from her.

"I don't want to see you cry, Maizie," said he. "I think I'd really despise you, if I did!"

And, when he looked again, she was gone without a sound—only a whisper was in the hall and then, on the

197

stairs, a faint murmur of a stifled sob. The lip of Philip curled, and stepping to the back door, he threw it open, and called Doc Rivers in. The latter came, shivering from the cold.

"Damn it, kid," said he, "you've kept us so long, the steam's off the coffee! What's the matter? You and Maizie have a falling out?"

"On the contrary," said Philip. "We've just had an understanding!"

"Oh," murmured Doc Rivers, and suddenly busied himself with his food.

And it seemed to Philip that, like Maizie, Doc Rivers was overcome with fear. Every movement, indeed, was furtive.

CHAPTER XXXIX

EARLY the next morning they removed to town, with Jolly lying on a mattress in the bottom of the buckboard. Philip sat beside him, partly to care for him, but chiefly as his guard. They felt that once they were safely ensconced in the town, they could shrug their shoulders at the Purchass clan. The sheriff and the law would receive them, and as for Jolly's danger from the law, that was something no longer to be feared. With the money from the mine they could hire such lawyers as would maintain his innocence successfully. So thought the Delmars, and in the gray of the dawn they hurried towards the town, old Delmar riding in the rear, and Doc Rivers in the van, riding most dauntlessly and gallantly, while Maizie sat on the driver's seat and put the horses to good speed.

The roads were black and wet with dew, and the fields were glistening gray, for the pale gold had been fading rapidly, as harvest fields will do. There was a good, cheerful feeling in the air, a chill that heartened one and brought color into the face.

Philip marked down these details without emotion, as one jots down notes on a pad of paper. He felt detached. He was a mere observer. Jolly, Maizie, they both lived in this world. So did old Delmar. So did even Doc Rivers. What the difference was, Philip began to guess. They had families. They came out of a known past. They were rooted in facts. But he was a plant that had grown in the air, so to speak. It had no relation to society and therefore society would have nothing to do with him. He was held off at arm's length.

The light freshened to pink and bright rose. Maizie was talking from time to time, and when the sun rose, Jolly had the pillows heaped higher under his head. He wanted to look that sun in the face, he declared, for he had felt, the night before, that he never would see the warm, kind, honest, cheerful sun again.

So Philip propped him higher, and then Jolly began to talk about the mystery of his disappearance from the house. He had gone up to the map and was removing the thumb tacks with which it was pressed into the wall; they had rusted in their places, and he had to pry them out, carefully, with his knife blade. He had three of them out, he remembered, when he felt something behind him; like a chill striking in from the window, Jolly said it was.

Finally he turned around, and he was amazed and oddly shocked to see Sheldon standing inside the window, looking steadily at him. He asked Sheldon what he wanted, and Sheldon said that he had come to speak about leaving.

"Leave if you want to," said Jolly impatiently. "I'm busy with something else. You talk over your wages with Dad!"

"You'd better talk to me," said Sheldon in a queer voice, and Jolly looked at him carefully, in some alarm and in some curiosity.

Sheldon had always been the quietest sort of a man, but now there was a touch of danger in him. Jolly said that it was hard to define. Certainly the eyes of the little man were fascinating. They had changed. They had grown very dark, and they looked flat and black—

199

"Like black velvet?" put in Philip.

"Just exactly like that," exclaimed Jolly. "How did you guess that?"

He went on to say that Sheldon had repeated several times: "I want to talk about leaving the house. You'd better talk with me about it. You'd better talk about leaving it, yourself. Do you hear? You'd better talk about leaving it yourself!"

This he repeated over and over in a monotonous voice and all the time Jolly was staring into the face of the puncher until all at once he felt himself growing rather dizzy. Thereafter he was not sure of exactly what had happened, except that Sheldon began to speak about the horses, too. And that he kept saying: "It would be a good thing, when you leave, to ride those horses back to the Purchass place. They'd be glad to see you, there! You'd better ride the horses over. Over to the Purchass place. Do you hear? You're going to ride them over to the Purchass place."

This thought had filled Jolly with horror. But he felt himself impelled by resistless power, and after that, his mind was completely a blank except for two moments.

One was when he walked through the dining room and wanted with all his might to call out for help, and to beg the people to catch him and keep him from going; but he found that his lips were locked. The next moment was when he heard the voice from the window of his own room calling to him. It had not seemed like another person speaking. It had seemed like his own ghost standing up there above him, and calling to him to come back. But again he dared not answer. And a strange wonder came to him. Was it really he who sat on the Purchass horse? Or was it his ghost, while the real Jolly Delmar remained in the house? Then he remembered nothing, except that the senses which had been stolen from him returned, and he found himself in the Purchass house itself, with armed men all around him, and the devilish face of old Purchass himself before him.

He was lying on a cot, the same cot where Philip finally had found him, and little Sheldon was leaning over him, with the same eyes of black velvet.

He had wakened totally in the hands of his enemy, and Purchass, inside the first minute, had placed his proposal before Jolly.

He would give that youth his life and forget about the death of the young Purchass whose loss had caused the feud. In return, Jolly was to hand over information about the location of the mine. How the Purchass outfit had learned about it, Jolly never knew. At any rate, he told them gravely that he would far rather die. Then old Purchass had the others tie Jolly down on the bed and he himself remained alone with him.

"To bring him to reason," as he said.

There followed a torture so dreadful that Jolly confessed he had screamed like a woman, and the old satyr had laughed in his face and told him that he would tear him to shreds unless the secret were revealed.

Shortly afterwards, Jolly fainted, and that saved him further agony for some hours. But again and again he was put under pressure. Until, the day before, when he was on the verge of surrendering beneath this mortal agony, the enormous form of the Colonel had burst into the room.

He had taken old Purchass by the back of the neck as one might lift a terrier and told him that he would throw him through the window unless this hellishness ceased at once. Old Purchass had snarled an answer, but he had submitted and allowed himself to be taken from the room.

The last of that argument, Philip himself had overheard on the roof of the house.

Now when Jolly had made an end of his story, they came out of the woods, made a sharp turn, and the town was before them, in the full brightness of the midmorning sun.

CHAPTER XL

PHILIP became all eyes.

This was at last the great goal of his ambition; this was the seat of those lovely stars which he had seen from the height of Pillar Mountain on clear nights. But what he found revealed to him had not a shred of glory attached. It was simply a shambling, widespread, broken-down mountain town, so cheaply constructed that every building was old before it reached its third year. He felt that he could have blown down the general merchandise store with a huff and a puff. And as for the widespreading hotel, he was sure that he could have kicked his way through its flimsy walls.

There was little paint; there was much dust; there was in every vacant lot a jumble of junk, rusted wire, barrel bands, broken wheels; chickens scratched up the front yards and dusted themselves in holes which they had scratched in the grass-plots. Dogs ran out and barked furiously at the riders and the buckboard. Slatternly women came and leaned in doorways, arms akimbo, and looked after the little procession. And far and near Philip heard the rising of a voice which he never had heard before and, once heard, he never could shake out of his consciousness: and it was composed of the crowing of roosters in the distance and the cackling of hens on their nests, the clanging of a hammer on a forge, the rattling of kitchen pans, the banging of doors, and the braying laughter of a man somewhere far off, together with other sounds of human voices. Into this jargoning the creaking of stirrup leathers, and the groan of the ill-greased wheels of the buckboard, and the rattling of its loose boards and spokes melted perfectly. It was all a harmony. In spite of its many parts, it was not overloud. Certainly it was not deafening. It was indeed rather a weight upon the spirit than a burden upon the ears.

But Philip did not need to be told what it was. It was the voice of man, which the poet calls "the still, sad music of humanity, nor harsh nor grating."

He remembered that phrase, and he laughed loudly and bitterly. Maizie turned on the driver's seat and glanced sharply back at him, in wonder. It was the first time she had met his eyes that morning, and when he looked boldly back at her, she flashed her glance away to a spotted dog trying to jump a high front fence to come and bark at them.

They reached the hotel and there they put up. Philip carried Jolly into the building and he was shown by the fat proprietor where to take the invalid up the stairs. Old Delmar followed, and said abruptly to the owner: "You send the sheriff word, will you? I got my boy in town, and we want the sheriff to take charge of him. He's got a charge agin Jolly, you know!"

By the time the sheriff came, Maizie and Philip had made Jolly comfortable in his bed, piled pillows around him, lighted his cigarette. He had a hand on one arm of each of them.

"Lemme have a chance to look you over," he said. "You rest my mind, to look at you. I don't give a damn about anything else. Except Dad. You look to me like you was made of gold and set off with about a million diamonds. You, Maizie—you always was a trump. But Phil, here, that was willin' to die—oh, I know that it wasn't for me! I know that it was for you, Maizie! Why d'you blush so much? Look, Phil, she's all red and embarrassed!"

Philip looked, coldly and curiously. He thought that Maizie was a thousand times more beautiful than she ever had been before, but he took a perverse pleasure in keeping his glance cold and level and direct. He was filled with an enormous power. Nothing could daunt or disturb him. He could cut his heart out of his own breast and hold it in his hand. He could smile or laugh while he hung in flames!

Certainly no one ever should know that this girl had hurt him.

The sheriff came in. He wanted to have the room to

himself, Mr. Delmar, and Jolly, while they examined the wounds and talked about how they had been received. Therefore Maizie and Philip went outside. She started to hurry away, but he called her back.

"I want to say a few things," said Philip. "You're embarrassed about me, of course. Jolly and your father and even Doc Rivers seem to think that we're—er—practically engaged. Shall I tell them that we're not?"

"I don't know," said the girl.

She stepped back until she was pressed against the wall, with her hands flat against it on either side; she was pale and big of eye.

"I wish you wouldn't act that way," said Philip bitterly. "I know that you're not afraid of me. Why do you act that way, Maizie?"

"I don't know," said the girl.

He grew hot with anger. After all, she had seen that she could twist him around her finger, and this affection of simplicity and muteness was a sham that made him rage.

"It won't do," said Philip. "I'm not so simple as this, Maizie. You understand that I don't want to bother you. Just tell me what you want me to do to make things easier for you, and I'll do it."

"Yes," said Maizie.

"But," said Philip, "please let's be open and frank with one another. That's all that I'll ask of you."

To this she said nothing. She had not altered her position. She looked as if she expected him to strike her, and Philip turned on his heel and walked away, angrier than ever.

He went out on the veranda of the hotel and stood with the sun beating against his face. It helped him to confront its burning brightness, for pain kills pain, and the sun for all its power could not reach to the bitter coldness of his heart of hearts.

He wanted to despise Maizie for her wile, her cunning, her clever acting of a part; but instead, he knew that he loved her more than ever. He despised himself, therefore.

Someone lurched from the hotel door with laughter and banged against Philip's back. He had to catch the nearest pillar of the porch to keep from being pitched into the street on his face. He turned and found a huge, red-faced cowpuncher who had been indulging in some horseplay with a pair of companions.

"Don't stand in front of the door, kid, if you want to keep out of trouble," said the big man roughly.

The eye of Philip grew small with a wicked joy. He took the big man by the elbow and the shoulder and flung him across his hip and spinning to the roadway, where he landed flat on his back and the dust spurted out on either side of him like water. He lay still for a moment, then pitched to his feet with a roar and a gun in his hand.

Philip watched him calmly.

"Put up that gun," said he, "or I'll kill you."

The cowpuncher stopped a roar in its midst.

"My God!" he murmured, and dropped the gun back into its holster. Then he disappeared around the corner of the hotel.

Philip, turning, saw that half a dozen had looked on at this byplay. They regarded him now with strained attention, but though they looked at him, not one of them looked into his eyes.

He noted that, and he felt contempt for their weakness. As he approached the door, they split away silently on either side and he walked slowly through and back up the stairs; behind him he heard a hushed voice say: "Well, that's that!"

He hardly knew what was meant by the speaker; he certainly did not care.

In the upper hall, he was met by old Delmar, who drew him into Jolly's room, saying: "The sheriff's boiling! He says that he'll run the Purchass gang out of the mountains, now. He says that this here outrage is enough to get the people together. And he says that there'll never even be a trial for the shooting of young Purchass. Phil, we're out of the woods! We're out of the woods! The sheriff is going to give us an escort of ten men to get up to the mine and locate it proper! And the game is in our hands!"

Philip found the sheriff in the act of rising from his chair. He came to Philip and shook hands. He, at least, was strong enough to look one in the eye.

"I've met you before," said the sheriff. "I remember. I thought you'd given Dorman a hand. I was wrong. And now, young feller, I've been hearing a lot of amazin' things about you. And I want to tell you a couple of things from my point of view. You keep your ears in and your guns in your clothes and you're gunna be a fine citizen. But if you start runnin' away with yourself, you'll hang before you're much older. I guess that's all. Mind you, I'm your friend, as long as you'll let me be your friend!"

After this rather odd speech, he left the room abruptly, only pausing in the doorway to say:

"I suppose that you feel safe enough here, so long as you got the kid with you?"

"Safer than if I had an army around me," said Jolly happily. "You been damn square with me today, sheriff. I'm never gunna forget it!"

"All right," said the sheriff. "You pay me back by keepin' your strong man under his hat." And he disappeared.

"He didn't seem to like me," said Philip.

"Don't you be scared," said Jolly, reassuringly.

"I'm not," answered Philip.

"But you've been through the mill," said Jolly, "and it's made you like milled steel—a little mite hard, partner. You foller me?"

Philip did not, but he settled down in a chair beside the window and looked across the woods and the rolling of the dark hills towards the heights of Pillar Mountain in the distance. He felt as though twenty years lay between him and his life on Pillar Mountain.

Jolly began to speak again.

"I'll explain about the sheriff," he said. "Of course, the Colonel has been the biggest man in the range for years. Everybody's been afraid of him. And when the sheriff heard that you'd mastered the Colonel, it sort of scared him. Made him afraid that you'd start in where the Colonel had left off. That's why he talked kind of mean to you. But he don't mean no harm."

Philip made no answer. He was beginning to wonder if the sheriff's suspicion might not be correct.

CHAPTER XLI

THINGS moved fast during the rest of that day. Report came in that the Purchass gang had fled from their house; then came word that they intended a covert attack on Jolly and Philip in the town itself.

In the meantime, the sheriff had taken matters into his hands. Philip was left with Jolly; the sheriff with Doc Rivers, old Delmar, and a posse of no fewer than fifteen picked men, rode out to the Purchass house, found it completely deserted except for two youngsters taking care of the horses which remained in the stables, and then the party rode on to locate the vein which Jolly had discovered. It was found, measured, staked by old Delmar, and he and the sheriff returned to the town alone. Every other member of the posse remained on the spot to prospect for other outcroppings of that monstrously rich ore!

Even Doc Rivers, quite out of his head with excitement, disregarding the promise of old Delmar that because of his work in the rescue of Jolly he should have a substantial share in the mine, refused to return. When the sheriff came back to the town that evening, the report went out in all directions; and before morning, half the men of the community had packed their kits and rushed for the mine.

The town was mad with gold-fever. Every event had been exciting recently. The Purchasses finally had been driven to the bush because of the outrages they had practiced upon Jolly Delmar. And the great Colonel himself had been met, matched, and beaten by an unknown youth who, a little later, had picked up a strong man and thrown him from the veranda of the hotel as another would shy an orange into the street. Such things, together with news of gold, were enough to bring the town up to fever point.

And, twenty-four hours later, the flood returned from the hills with the news that Jolly Delmar's outcrop was the only vein that had been discovered. Old Delmar himself now was on the ground with a force of trained miners, breaking rock. But the rest of the townsmen returned.

They returned, but not to settle down. They were keyed up to a high pitch, as the sheriff very quickly discovered, for three gun fights and an infinite number of promises of more encounters disturbed the citizens. Women began to keep their children indoors, and no man ventured on the streets unless he was loaded with guns. The sheriff in vain tried to bring everyone back to his senses. He interviewed leading men. He organized a standing force of deputies. But still the air was filled with an electric promise of danger. Some great event was expected, and it was to Philip that the particular promise of it came.

He had become a great man overnight. The tale of his adventures had gone abroad from the lips of Doc Rivers. Doc never had had the name of an enthusiastic friend, but his worship of Philip amounted to idolatry. From his mouth came the story in detail of the crushing of the two Chisholms, and the break through the Purchase lines to get to the Delmar house. From him came, above all, the expedition against the Purchase house. Of part, Rivers was an eyewitness; part he had heard from Philip; part came from Jolly Delmar, and that the most wonderful part of all. There were plenty of temptations for Doc Rivers to talk. Men were willing to set up drinks for the whole house so long as Rivers would narrate the great adventures. Whatever he said was believed, and when whisky colored his vocabulary a little, still he was believed. Above all, men wanted to know again and again how Philip had carried Jolly Delmar from the Purchase place; and again, they listened hushed and keen of eye when they heard of the terrific struggle with the gigantic Colonel. Not one of them but knew that monster, few of them who had not seen some exhibition of his strength, but at last the impossible had happened, and he had been matched and overthrown!

A small bit of evidence they accepted willingly as proof of a great thing. The doubters were reminded how Philip had tossed a grown man and a strong man from the hotel veranda into the street. Indeed, that story was repeated by the victim himself. He was Church Harmon, a puncher out of work, and the disgrace of his fall ceased to have a sting when he learned that his conquerer was a sort of mystical hero, and that drinks would be provided when he told about his overthrow. So he told it many times over. He improved on his first versions. He became no more than a feather in the enormous grasp of Philip, in his final form of the story.

And so the whole excited town accepted Philip of fact and Philip of fable at one and the same time; and the boy found himself converted in spite of himself into a mere legend.

He did not like it. He did not like the way men lowered their voices when he came near. He did not like the manner in which they made way for him. He was troubled by the silences that went before his face and the whispers that stirred behind his back.

People did not smile at him; they merely stared. Only the children were gay and made free of him and his presence whenever he dared to put foot in the street. He no sooner appeared than a shouting procession formed before and behind and around him. They caught at his hands; they tugged at his coat; they shouted and cheered at him.

The town had found a hero, but a hero a little too terrible to take to their hearts. Everyone watched him in the expectation of some immense event.

He himself tried to stop the talk and the excitement. He called on the sheriff and took him to one side.

"I'm very sorry," said Philip, "that people seem to be talking about me."

"Sure you are," said the ironical sheriff.

"I want to tell you—and you can tell others—that the fight with the Colonel was *not* easy—"

He opened his shirt and showed his throat, bruised brown and black where that terrible grip had fallen.

"I'm bruised all over," confessed Philip. "Every breath is still painful! Just tell them that I'm like everybody else. I'm not a giant!"

"Thanks," said the sheriff, "but I'll let them use their eyes for themselves!" And he nodded wisely.

Philip went back to the hotel more nervous than ever, and more irritated as the children swooped down upon him in a drove. But on the way the great news came to him, with Doc Rivers bearing it, and a crowd around him to witness the truth of the tale, which, simply, was that Doc Rivers had been in Grogan's saloon relating the adventures of Philip to an admiring crowd, when the two Chisholms boldly walked into the place and stood one on each side of Doc. It was Bert who spoke, his back to the bar and his hands on his hips, so that he could keep everyone under due surveillance while he talked.

He bore a message from the Colonel to the effect that the latter had learned of certain false stories now being circulated in the town to the effect that he had been fairly beaten by Philip. He branded all such tales as open lies. To prove his point, a week from that date he would ride in person into the town and there encounter Philip before the eyes of men, whoever cared to stay and watch. He would come between the noon hour and one o'clock, so that his arrival would not keep anyone from his work.

Having delivered this message, the Chisholms lingered for one drink—Bert drinking while Archie watched the crowd, and Archie drinking while Bert kept guard. Then they backed along the bar to the rear door, leaped through it, and were gone at once, unpursued. In fact, there was no specific charge against them, except the general charges against all the Purchass clan and their agents.

No one cared to play the hand of justice in this case, and the pair went off scot-free. So Philip received his message and went on to the hotel with Rivers to discuss the meaning of it. Rivers loudly declared that it was sheer bluff. If the Colonel intended to right himself and recover his lost ground, he surely would have come straight in, without sending a message before his arrival.

There was something else to talk of when they reached the hotel. For the first mule-loads of ore had been carried into town and assayed. They turned out less rich than had been expected. Also, the vein was discovered to be pinching out rapidly; but even so a large fortune was assured from it. Old Delmar had come in with the mules; and that night there was high festivity through all the hotel. There was only one spot of gloom, and that was the face of Philip himself.

CHAPTER XLII

WE live according to a definite scale of values. The old scale for Philip had been composed there on the heights of Pillar Mountain, looking down on a world represented, so far as men were concerned, by the starry twinkling of distant lights. He had come down out of a dream which possessed him so thoroughly that he refused to see the facts until Maizie had wakened him. And, since that awakening, no other set of values was given to him.

He hung now in a sort of limbo, unsure of himself, unsure of everything around him. He was haunted by a constant yearning for the girl, and he was cursed with a constant denial of her. She had seemed to him at first a bright and beautiful angel, somewhat given to slang. She seemed to him now a beautiful spirit of evil, treacherous and dangerous and filled with wiles.

The day after the arrival of the news of the Colonel's threat, Jolly Delmar tried to open a difficult subject.

"Look here, Phil," said he, "I want to talk to you a minute about Maizie. It seems that you and her have sort of fallen out, and from what I can gather——"

"Why should you and I talk about it?" interrupted Phillip. "Maizie and I are both happy?"

"Are *you* happy?" asked Jolly.

"Of course," lied Philip.

"Then let it go," said Jolly, and closed his eyes, with a frown of trouble.

In the meantime, Maizie avoided him sedulously. Twice, passing him in the hall, she had lowered her head and gone

211

by swiftly, silently. There was a sort of slinking guilt in her manner, he told himself. So he made himself hold his head high, and smiled upon her with a bland indifference.

But time hung heavily on the hands of Philip. He would above all things have preferred to leave the town simply because Maizie was in it. He wanted to flee to a great distance, in the hope that perhaps intervening leagues would make her memory less sweet. He wanted to commit himself to some new course of action, but he could not think to what he could turn himself. In the meantime, a mortal hardness was growing in his heart. The awe, the reverence, the fear which attended all his goings and comings meant little or nothing. He shrugged his shoulders at even the danger of the Colonel's coming.

Sometimes, in the mornings, he would walk out to the edge of the town and use his guns on any convenient targets. Otherwise he gave no heed to the famous Colonel. For, after all, he had met and beaten the Colonel once with his bare hands, and he had no fear as to what would happen when their hands were filled with weapons. In some manner, he felt that the first encounter had established not so much a physical as a spiritual superiority over the Colonel, and he was perfectly willing to wait for the appointed day. Indeed, it was the one touch of actual interest in his life at that moment.

He was sitting alone in his room in the hotel, with the Colonel's coming a day and a half away, when he heard Loafer begin to howl and bark in the street, and the sound passed on into the hotel and up the stairs until it stopped with a mighty clamoring at his door.

He opened it, and Loafer leaped in on him.

"This gent says he's a friend of yours," said the proprietor.

He stepped back, and Philip saw before him the gray head and the bright eyes of Oliver Aytoun.

It was a mighty shock to him. In the turmoil of these last few days, he almost had forgotten the man of the mountain. Now he drew Uncle Oliver into the chamber and placed him in the chair by the window, and brought a lamp and placed it on the little table near by him, so that he could see Aytoun's face.

"Have you had supper?" he asked.

"No," said Oliver Aytoun.

"Come with me and I'll get you something to eat."

"I've walked down here to talk to you, Philip," said Aytoun. "I'm not thinking of food."

"Has something happened to you?"

"No, not to me; to you!"

"I don't know what you mean!" said Philip.

"You've grown up, in these few days since you left me."

"Has it been only a few days?"

"A handful."

Philip was silent, thinking back.

"It hasn't been long—in time," he admitted.

Loafer was going joyously from one of them to the other, as though he wished to draw them still closer together, and Aytoun smiled on the dog.

"Philip," he said suddenly. "You're not happy."

"I?"

"Tell me."

"No, I'm not happy."

"And it's because of the Colonel?"

"How do you know about him?" asked Philip curiously.

"All the mountains are ringing with the news that you are to fight the Colonel here the day after tomorrow."

"Even Pillar Mountain?"

"I went down to take some wolf pelts and skins. They told me at the trading store. I decided that I'd better come here."

"It's nothing," answered Philip. "I've already met him once."

"Never with guns, I believe?"

"Never, but it will be the same thing."

"You're not afraid?"

"No."

"Nevertheless," said Aytoun, "you must not meet him."

Philip waited. "Will you tell me why?" he asked, when there was no immediate continuation of the talk.

Oliver Aytoun paused to fill his pipe, packing it carefully and solidly, just as Philip always remembered him doing. And that small act, for some unknown reason, brought tears into Philip's eyes.

He waited while the pipe was lighted and the smoke was drifting upwards in a thin mist.

"I've been trying to think of ways about," said Oliver Aytoun. "I would go to the Colonel, but I don't know where to find him. And I've had to come to you."

"Yes," said Philip.

"I've come to ask you not to meet the Colonel, Philip."

Philip was silent, astonished. He did not need to ask for a reason, but almost immediately Aytoun added: "Because he's a friend of mine. Is that enough?"

Philip tried to speak. He hardly had thought that there was a thing in the world which could excite him; but now he had found reason enough. It fairly stopped his heart.

"Uncle Oliver!" he cried out.

"Yes, my boy."

"Do you know what it means?"

"Will you tell me, Philip?"

"It would mean sneaking away. After I've told everyone that I'm not afraid of the Colonel. And I want to tell you about him—"

He paused.

"Go on."

"No, because I haven't many good things to say—and he's your friend."

"Do you think he's a bad man?"

"Do I think? He—he's a man, Uncle Oliver, who hires himself out to the highest bidder."

"He's not a coward, Philip?"

"No, he's not that."

"Does he keep his word?"

"Apparently he does."

"Is he cruel?"

"No, he wouldn't let them torture Jolly Delmar. I suppose that you know about that?"

"I know about nothing, except that you're not to meet the Colonel."

Philip was silent.

"Will you promise me, boy?"

"No," said Philip, "I'm sorry that I can't promise."

Oliver Aytoun got up from his chair; his face was

ghastly behind the thin veil of smoke. Still he kept his voice wonderfully quiet.

"I think I have a right to ask a good deal from you, Philip."

"God knows you have!" cried Philip suddenly. "Ten lives, if I had that many. You have a right to ask anything except my honor, Uncle Oliver!"

"So—so—so!" murmured Aytoun in a voice that was hardly more than a whisper. "I should have guessed that it would be on that plane."

He added aloud: "Then I shall have to pay an enormous price, Philip, to keep you from this meeting."

"You pay a price, Uncle Oliver?"

"I shall have to pay the price. Hush! Did I hear something under the window?"

He leaned out and looked down.

"There's a veranda there, Philip," he said.

"It opens on to the room of a girl who never would listen to voices in my room," answered Philip. "She wouldn't care what was said up here. But you said that you would have to pay the price?"

"The price of your affection and your faith," said the old man. "I am going to show you that I have been a scoundrel, Philip. I go back to the old story of how the rider brought you to my house. You remember, of course?"

"I remember, of course."

"I told you that he never came back. That was not true. Five years later he returned. He wanted you. At that moment you were playing high up the hillside with a tame rabbit. I told him that you were no longer with me. I told him that you were dead. It seemed a hard blow to him. I watched his face, and if he heard your voice coming back towards the shack, I told myself that I would kill him, Philip, and never let you know what had happened. I wanted you for myself! Have you ever heard of a worse thing done by any man?"

Philip was silent.

"And always I was afraid to come down into the world, because you might be taken away from me. But at last

215

I've had to let you go, and now I have to tell you everything. Because God himself would call out from Heaven if you met the Colonel, Philip. He's your father."

CHAPTER XLIII

PICTURES began to flash across the mind of Philip, almost blinding him. He saw the street of the town thronged with watchers in the white, hot hour of noon; he even saw the heat waves rising from the roofs, and the whirlpools of dust racing here and there like little tornadoes; and a huge man on a huge horse, with a cape flung back over his shoulders coming slowly down, a rifle balanced across the pommel of his saddle.

He saw that same form dashing through the woods of the mountainside and reaching the shack with a child in his arms. He saw the same monstrous form stretched in the invalid's chair, facing the sun. He saw him stagger back into the shadow of a tree, stunned and beaten.

At last he said: "I should have guessed. I could not have got such strength in my hands from any other man."

He had no answer to this, and looking around him he saw that he was alone. Loafer was lying across his feet. Even the wisps of the pipe smoke had been drawn away out the window, though the fragrance of the tobacco was still in the room. At that, he ran hastily down the stairs and inquired on the veranda, but the oddly dressed old stranger had not gone out that way.

Philip turned back in despair. Aytoun, of course, had taken the long silence of the boy as a heartless condemnation. So he had slipped away, and now he was working quietly back toward the lonely shack on Pillar Mountain. Well, what did the world and its opinion matter, compared with one moment of pain in such a soul as that of Oliver Aytoun?

He went straight back through the hotel to the stable, saddled the mustang which had been given for his use by old Delmar, and swung on to the back of the horse. He would have liked to say farewell to Rivers and Delmar, but their faces would have been hard to confront. No, it was much better to go off quietly, like this. Let them think their own thoughts about him!

Only one thing was of importance. When Uncle Oliver reached his shack the next morning, he must find smoke curling from the chimney to welcome him home. After that—well, let time take care of itself!

He found a rear way from the hotel corral behind the stable, and then turned across the open fields. He had to cross two stretches of stubble, before he gained the trail among the pines, and as he turned on to it, he heard a horse whinny behind him, but he paid no attention to that noise.

It was very late. A cold wind made him aware that he had gone out without a coat or a slicker. The clouds blew across the stars. Rain fell in sheets, icy cold, and drenched him to the skin, but he was aware of his misery only now and again. Then the blanket of his wretched thoughts closed over him again and the flesh was forgotten.

The moon went up, at last, unseen after the first streaks of ghostly light in the east, but yielding a faint glow even behind the clouds. He could see them, mountain-big, driven before the wind, sometimes with their edges turned to translucent pearl by the moon behind, but more often obscure outlines, guessed at rather than seen. The wind was out in high force. He heard it marching through the woods, or screaming far off, then leaping suddenly upon him and deafening him with its whistling; he heard the groaning of the boughs against one another; and twice, at least, the frightful crash as some giant was toppled and fell crushing and crushed.

But Philip rode on, keeping the horse grimly to the trail which now was more easily visible as the moon stood at the height, and made the runlets of rain water gleam like dull silver. For still the rain came down intermittently, now crashing on his face and stinging his body even through his shirt, and now a tender mist.

217

Through such a mist, at last, he saw the form of a rider in the trail before him, and as he came nearer, he called out. He had a faint hope that it might be Uncle Oliver, but Aytoun on one of his mules was not likely to have covered so much ground as this. No, he was back in the forest, struggling slowly along.

He called more loudly. The rain fell in a dark torrent. It cleared again, and the wild wind in the heavens tore the clouds apart.

His horse stopped of its own volition and touched the nose of the other which was in its way, while Philip found himself looking down on the wet face of Maizie Delmar.

"You!" cried Philip huskily. "What are you doing here? What made you follow me?"

"I found your slicker," said Maizie. "I had an idea maybe you'd want it, a night like this."

She held it out to him; he let it fall into the mud. And then the wind hurled the clouds together in such dense masses that little enough light came down to the gloomy world and that little was further dimmed by a blinding downpour of the rain. When the thunder of it eased a little, Philip could hear the hissing of the runlets, as they shot down the face of the trail, scouring the ground away.

He brought his horse a little nearer, and reaching out, his hand found the cold, wet surface of a rubber slicker.

"What made you follow me?" he repeated.

"I dunno," said Maizie. "I sort of needed the air, I guess."

"Maizie, Maizie, are you going to make a joke of me still? Am I always a fool, in your eyes?"

"A fool?" said Maizie. "I'd never let a fool break my heart!" And she added, with a sudden tremor of her voice: "And you've busted mine to bits, Phil."

He drew still closer. The steam of her sweating horse came up to him. He drew still closer. The fragrance of the girl was in his face.

"You were on that veranda!" he said.

"I was," said Maizie. Then she added: "I ain't a fine, clean-minded, honorable person like you, Phil. I'm just a hard-headed girl that don't miss a trick if she can help it.

218

I listened under your window. I heard every word that was said, I think. Poor old man!"

"Ah, yes," said Philip. "Poor Uncle Oliver."

"And you?" said Maizie.

"I?"

"You wouldn't waste any pity on yourself, I guess."

"I'm a grown man, and a young man," said Philip. "It doesn't matter about me."

"*I'll* cry for you, then," said Maizie. "I can't help crying. You baby!"

"Maizie," he said, finding her arm and pressing it. "I wish that you'd stop crying."

"I would if I could," said Maizie. "I don't want to."

"It makes me dizzy and a little ill," said Philip. "I—I never knew that you cried—except when there was something to gain by it."

"And there's nothing to gain now, I guess?" said Maizie through her sobs.

"Ah, no," answered he. "I'm a disgraced and ruined man. I'll never dare to look the world in the face again. I've brought shame to my few friends. But what are you going to do?"

"I don't know," said Maizie. "What will *you* do?"

"I'm going on to Pillar Mountain."

"I'm going on to Pillar Mountain too," said Maizie.

"There's only a shack there. It's quicker and easier for you to turn back."

"Phil!" cried the girl, in a suddenly changed and terrible voice.

"Yes, Maizie," he answered, shocked and abashed.

"Phil, come closer to me!"

He drew still closer. Her hands caught his and shook them savagely.

"Phil, d'you hear me?"

"Yes, yes! Are you ill, Maizie?"

"Ill? I'm dyin'! Phil, don't you see that I'm wild in love with you? Won't you tell me if you care the least mite? If you don't love me, I'll come along anyway and cook for you and the poor old man, if you'll let me."

There are thunderbolts of joy as well as of sorrow. Philip sat transfixed.

"Are you gunna tell me that I'm only play-actin' now?" cried Maizie. "Will you speak one word to me, Phil? Will you just say yes or no?"

"Hush!" said Philip.

He took her within one great arm, gently, and the kind moon broke through enough to let him see her face.

"O God in Heaven!" said Philip. "O glorious God!"

There was no rain, there was no wind for them, there was no darkness. The golden beauty of autumn and the green, sweet face of spring crowded about them all that night, and a sun of joy smoothed the path before them. They laughed, while the thunder beat, and they waited for the lightning flashes, to see each other with eyes filled with love.

So the sun rose and found them. The wind, changing, brushed the sky clear above them, and they were winding slowly up the side of Pillar Mountain.

"Will you tell me a thing?" said Philip.

"There's nothing left to tell," said Maizie.

"Ah, but there is."

"Well, then?"

"I want to know when you really first thought you cared a bit for me, Maizie."

"I'm ashamed, Phil."

"I want to know."

"Well, it was when you held me up and talked to me like I was a man and told me that you saw through me. I began to love you then. It went through me—sort of like a cramp, Phil."

He laughed, and still they laughed joyously together; at one another, at the world, at the tall, proud trees, at the glorious sun which God had hung for them in the sky, at the flashing creek—

"Look!" cried Philip. "He's beaten us after all!"

For they had come in view of the shack, and smoke curled slowly from its chimney and blew away, snatched by the wind.

THE END